# A Mile above the Rim

Also by Charles Rosen

HAVE JUMP SHOT WILL TRAVEL

# A MILE ABOVE THE RIM

### A NOVEL BY

## Charles Rosen

**ARBOR HOUSE**

*New York*

## ROSTER OF THE 1980–81 NEW YORK STARS

### Coach - Wayne Smalley

| NO | POS | NAME | HGT | WGT | PRO EXP | COLLEGE |
|----|-----|------|-----|-----|---------|---------|
| 25 | F | Ardell Bartholomew | 6-11 | 235 | 7 | Mississippi Southern |
| 8 | G | Dave Brooks | 6-6 | 215 | 3 | Michigan |
| 10 | G | Quinton Brown | 6-5 | 210 | 12 | Southwestern State |
| 12 | G | Reed Carson | 6-3 | 205 | 4 | Houston |
| 34 | F | Larry Graham | 6-9 | 220 | 1 | Colorado |
| 17 | C | Kevin Harmon | 6-9 | 245 | 0 | St. Bonaventure |
| 14 | C | Jeremy Johnson | 7-0 | 211 | 3 | Detroit |
| 20 | C-F | Jack Mathias | 6-10 | 228 | 0 | USC |
| 7 | F | Sylvester Sims | 6-7½ | 205 | 1 | Savannah State |
| 16 | G | Tyrone White | 6-4 | 185 | 10 | UCLA |

### Trainer - Buddy Patella

# A Mile Above the Rim

# CHAPTER ONE

SILKY SIMS caught a glimpse of Spencer Lavelle's eyes and was chilled by the arrogance he saw there. But Silky had good defensive position: He was overplaying the base line left, and the heel of his right hand was banging into Lavelle's hip.

Whenever a ball game was on the line, most of the teams in the league came straight at Silky with a confusing barrage of picks and screens. Silky didn't even mind it so much. It seemed almost like a private affair, with Silky's embarrassment showing up only on the game films. But the Seattle SuperSonics were not a very sophisticated team. They simply cleared out a side and let Lavelle come after Silky one-on-one on Broadway.

Lavelle's eyes told Silky he didn't have a chance. But Silky was puffed up like a cobra.

Spencer Lavelle hid his dribble and turned his back to Silky. And each one of Lavelle's 240 pounds began to twitch with a schoolyard disco-boogie beat. Silky rammed a forearm into the small of Lavelle's back and bumped the bigger man with his hip. Silky quicked himself a half-step away and danced and leaned, trying to destroy Lavelle's syncopation.

A roaring hysteria began to gather inside Silky's head and he suddenly had trouble concentrating. There were millions of people memorizing Silky's every move. Silky had to be cool.

Lavelle snatched up the ball and flashed his sinister eyes at the basket. Silky crouched and strained to keep his feet on the ground. Silky wondered where his help was. . . . he wondered how good he was looking. . . .

Lavelle's first head fake released Silky high into the air, where he swatted a spindly right arm at the ghost of a jump shot. But the time Silky landed, Lavelle was at the top of his own leap. The dice in Lavelle's wrist clicked as the ball was launched. Silky turned his head to watch the shot descend . . . for an instant he thought the ball would hit the front rim and fall short. The ball hit nothing but hole.

"BASKET BY SPENCER LAVELLE! SEATTLE LEADS ONE HUNDRED FOUR TO ONE HUNDRED THREE!"

Some confusion on the court, an official blew a whistle . . .

"TIME OUT, NEW YORK."

Silky was the last player to reach the Stars' bench. A towel was tossed into his face and he slumped into a chair. He could feel the fans' shock buzzing against the back of his neck. He sank his face in the towel and prayed that Wayne would leave him alone.

But Wayne Smalley was paying very little attention to Silky Sims. The Stars' coach was leaning over the edge of the court and raging at one of the officials.

"Hatcher!" Wayne shouted. "It was a fucken charge!

4

He leaned right into him! You fucken asshole! You blew the call! You choke bastard!"

Nick Hatcher stood unmoved on the opposite side of the floor. The veteran official wiped his face with a slow handkerchief and chatted with the writers over the press table.

Wayne started to give Hatcher the finger but remembered in time where he was. "Ahh, shit!" Wayne agonized, then turned to join his team and show them how to win the ball game.

There was a space reserved for Wayne in front of the bench. Jack Mathias and Kevin Harmon, the team's only rookies, closed in behind him. For just a moment Wayne glowered silently over the bench. The players tensed.

"Okay, superstar," Wayne snapped. "You left your feet. We're gonna have to tie your jock around your balls so you won't lose it."

Silky slung his head forward and tried to think of nothing but the drops of perspiration that fell from his face onto his sneakers.

"Goddamn, Silky," Wayne said, and a whine bent his words into a question. "Gimme a fucken break . . . okay?"

Silky dug his folded arms into his stomach. He couldn't help thinking of razor blades, can openers, lead pipes, rubber hoses.

Wayne grabbed a petulant towel from a ball boy, briskly rubbed it across his swollen face, slammed the towel to the floor and loudly clapped his hands. "It's okay. Everything's okay." Wayne showed his team his most magnanimous smile. "We still got nine big seconds left to pull it out. Okay! Here we go. . . . We get the ball at midcourt so let's run a 24S2. . . . No, no! Forget it! That's one of their plays. Here! Let's run this . . ."

Wayne knelt on one knee and a snap of his fingers produced another ball boy bearing a miniature basketball court. Wayne grabbed it and began shuffling the tiny magnetic X's and O's. "Tyrone," Wayne said without looking up. "You're inbounding the ball right here. But remember . . . this is our last time out so something's got to go no matter what. Jack. You're setting a pick up here . . . right up here, for Silky. Maybe you're overplayed, Silky, so then you go back door. Right? Dell. You're picking for Brooks here and then you go hard to the boards. Let's make Brooks the first option. Look for your shot, Dave. But remember you got Silky on the weak side if you get in trouble. That's the second option. The third . . ."

The buzzer detonated and swayed the players away from the huddle. "Don't force it!" Wayne shouted after them. "We've still got plenty of time! Think! Don't guess!"

The official was about to flip the ball to Tyrone when the sound of the buzzer once again came searing through the craziness of the crowd.

"SEATTLE SUBSTITUTION, MEL WILSON FOR FRED BROWN."

The New York fans prided themselves on being the most knowledgeable in the league. They all read Murray Klurman's columns in the *Dispatch* so they knew that Wilson was a stumblebum. Wilson wore his long hair in a ponytail and made no bones about his dislike of everything that most Americans held sacred. As soon as Wilson stepped on the court, the hostile crowd saturated Madison Square Garden with boos and obscenities.

At seven feet one and a half, Wilson was more than nine inches taller than Tyrone White.

Tyrone watched the big man pull at his jock and clumsily attempt to dance his legs loose. Then Tyrone heard Wayne's frantic voice pitched high above the crowd. "Think out there! Don't guess!"

Tyrone blocked out all of the noise when he accepted the basketball from the official. Then the reflexes conditioned by a ten year career moved Tyrone to slam one side of the ball and yell "go!" It was also Wilson's signal to start bouncing around and wave his hands. Tyrone couldn't find Dave Brooks. But just as the official was cocking his arm for the fifth and last count, Tyrone saw a white uniform spring clear of the pack. Tyrone sent the ball whizzing expertly past Wilson's left ear and hoped for the best.

Silky Sims outleaped two Seattle players, hauled in the pass with a flourish of slashing elbows, and spun to seize the basket. He was only mildly surprised when he saw the rim blinking like a neon light.

He faked right, took one swift dribble to his left. He stopped only when Seattle's seven foot four center Tom Burleson jumped out at him near the top of the key. But Silky's head felt sharp, clean and easy. Before he could think of what he was doing Silky pulled up and jumped straight to the moon.

Silky's right wrist jerked out a madly spinning shot that tangled the net on the rim as it sliced through the hoop.

There were still two seconds showing on the game clock, but the lights in the building flickered and the buzzer exploded.

"NEW YORK BASKET BY SILKY SIMS!! THE STARS WIN, ONE HUNDRED FIVE TO ONE HUNDRED FOUR!! AND THE STARS WIN THE PLAY-OFF SERIES FOUR GAMES TO ONE!! THANK

7

YOU FOR COMING. DRIVE CAREFULLY, CROSS AT
THE GREEN AND ARRIVE HOME SAFELY!!"

Near the Stars' bench, several of Silky's teammates
pounded his back and congratulated his hands.

"Mr. Silks does it good!" Quinton Brown shouted.

After prancing about for a few moments the players
turned and ran into the dressing room. A sudden swarm
of jubilant fans threatened to spill over a corpulent ring
of security police. The crowd clutched and picked at the
players as they ran by. Silky was the only one who
lingered. He stood motionless at the lip of the ramp;
turned to gold by the frenetic chant that the crowd
roared down on him.

"SILL-KEE!! SILL-KEE!!"

Silky was instantly blown out. He had never heard
anything like it. Not even back at Savannah State.

"SILL-KEE!! SILL-KEE!!"

The cadence raised a wild pulse in Silky's soul. Silky
tentatively lifted his right hand, and twenty thousand
voices jumped into another roar.

"SILL-KEE! SILL-KEE!! SILL-KEE!!!"

Silky waved once more, then ran down the guarded
ramp, frisking like a junkie lamb in a meadowland of
springtime poppies.

Wayne Smalley stood in a corner of the locker room,
sucking at a sour cigarette, his eyes red with anxiety as he
watched his buoyant players milling about.

"Where's the champagne at?" yelled Quinton Brown.

Within the privacy of the dressing room the ballplayers were free to maul one another and yell with delight. Palms slid off palms with neat little slaps, but their
enthusiasm fell heavily on Wayne's ears. Wayne was a

street-corner huckster with a Basketball Jones and he didn't really trust any of his players. He also knew they all hated the air he breathed. Hatred, fear, respect . . . all the same as far as Wayne was concerned. He was convinced that the ball club's passion brought them together in a common cause, melded them into a team with a chance to win the title. But Wayne wasn't quite ferocious enough looking to fit entirely into the Vince Lombardi mold. Wayne didn't want to fight anybody.

"Okay!" Wayne yelled at large. "Great! Great! Now for the Utes! Bring on the Utes!"

"Fuck them chumps!" Quinton screamed. "We'll stomp them motherfuckers too. Bring on the Lakers!"

Wayne winced.

In the Walter Brown Division, the Lakers had swept through the Boston Celtics in their initial play-off series. Los Angeles had never played better, while the Stars had been sloppy and erratic against Seattle. The Lakers and the Stars were still one series away from a championship confrontation. L.A. already had the DC Darts down two games to none in the second round. The Stars' semi-final opponents were the Salt Lake City Utes, a dangerous ball club. . . .

"Forget about Jabbar," Wayne shouted. "Let's concentrate on the Utes first. Okay?"

Wayne's warning put an immediate damper on the locker room festivities, and it wasn't long before the ballplayers quietly returned to their routine post-game involvements:

Ardell Bartholomew was on his knees offering thanks to his Savior. Ardell's heart was filled with joy and yearning for grace. He knew for sure that the New York

9

Stars were going to be the champions of the National Basketball Association. He knew for sure that Jesus loved him. . . .

Along the wall to Ardell's right, Jack Mathias bounced exuberantly on the balls of his feet. Jack inhaled a long can of beer. He felt nothing but a slight dampness in his throat, so he swallowed another one.

"Way to go, big team!" Jack shouted to no one in particular. "Way to DO IT!" . . .

In the adjacent space, Kevin Harmon looked up from his fingernails. "Yeah, guys," Kevin yelped. "Way to go!" Then Kevin returned his attention to his cuticles. He couldn't wait until the season was over. . . .

Tyrone White leaned over and carefully cut the adhesive tape from his ankles. He wondered if the official scorer gave him an assist for his pass to Silky. . . .

Reed Carson bent over and spit into a paper cup. He sneered at Ardell praying in the corner, then accidentally spit on one of his own sneakers. "Fucken shit," Reed said loud enough for Ardell to hear. . . .

Larry Graham and Jeremy Johnson stood near the entrance to the shower room. They were head to head and bubbling with conspiratorial giggles. Larry and JJ were the Stars' primary pussyhounds, and neither could wait until the ball club reached Salt Lake City. . . .

Quinton Brown was stretched out on a large wooden table set in the middle of the room. Quinton's eyes were closed as he puffed on a cigarette. A short bald white man hunched over Quinton's knee and poked it with an ice bag. Neither man spoke to the other. Quinton lay peacefully on his back concocting silent schemes and blowing perfect smoke rings. . . .

Dave Brooks sat on the floor up against the far wall. He sipped at a cup filled with crushed ice and organic apple juice. Dave was physically exhausted but his restless eyes swept the room. Dave wondered how much longer Wayne would wait for Silky. . . .

When Wayne noticed Silky's absence he angrily mashed his cigarette out with his shoe. Silky Sims was a goddamned ingrate, but the last thing Wayne wanted was a showdown. Not right now, anyway.

Wayne's anger cooled long enough for him to brush an ash from his khaki safari suit. Abruptly his melon face split into a ripe grin. Silky had certainly bailed him out. And on national television at that. And then his smile collapsed in a hurry. He had forgotten all about the gangling, distracting limbs of Mel Wilson. Russell had almost out-coached him. Almost. Tyrone had spotted Wayne's mistake for sure. So had Brooks and Quinton.

Wayne coughed and lit another cigarette. He realized with a twinge of thanksgiving that he had to pee. If Silky wasn't there by the time he came back out, then goddamn it, he'd fine the black bastard.

# CHAPTER Two

WAYNE SMALLEY addressed himself to a spotless, sweet-smelling urinal. He noted with a smile that the gurgling of the drain swallowed the babble from inside. A luxuriant burst of laughter came flying through his fleshy lips. The NBA rules allowed a coach to keep the dressing room locked for ten minutes after a game. And Wayne knew that the world didn't mind waiting for a winner.

Wayne twisted his head slightly so he could see his reflection in a full-length mirror on the far wall. Wayne admired the way his dark blond hair hung in lacquered hammocks across his forehead. He also liked the way his custom-made clothing made him radiant with style and well-being.

"Not bad for a thirty-seven-year-old dude from Bridgeport," he told himself.

Then Wayne's mind stepped in quicksand:

Wayne used to love golf. . . . The endless search for the perfect, static stroke. Throughout high school, Wayne earned his pocket money caddying on weekends and wound up at Eastern Connecticut State University on a golf scholarship. Wayne shot in the low eighties when he entered college and left four years later without having taken a single stroke off his game. To settle an argument with a fraternity brother he also tried out for the basketball team in his sophomore year. Wayne was a decent athlete who had never taken basketball too seriously but did manage to hustle his way onto the squad and eventually learn to play tenacious defense and carry the coach's spear. Throughout his varsity career he never took a bad shot. He finished with a field goal efficiency of thirty-four per cent. By his senior year he was a starter and was appointed team captain.

Wayne was a physical education major . . . Joan was a dance student and a cheerleader. They lived together off-campus. Wayne and Joan.

In Wayne's senior year he threw a golfing match to the superintendent of the Brian Township public schools. The coaching job at the high school was offered to him in a matter of days. Wayne and Joan were married a week after graduation.

Wayne's teams at Brian Township High School played below .500 for three years. Then the county was gerrymandered and a slice of black ghetto fell into BTHS's new territory. Wayne suddenly found himself enjoying the talents of a six foot five center named Delray Northington. The reinvigorated ball club reached the finals of the state championships for two years running, and came away a loser both times. Delray Northington graduated and went on to an undistinguished career at Valhalla College in upstate New York.

Wayne Smalley landed a new job at Savannah State University, where he took to wearing turtleneck sweaters and Robert Hall blazers and rapidly gained a local reputation for being an unusually "innovative" coach. SSU's meager athletic budget made it difficult to recruit blue-chip players but they were all very well-dressed in Wayne's brilliant strategies. His teams ran gimmick zones and stack offenses. He got all the credit when the team won, and none of the blame when it lost. He enjoyed security, prestige and even an opportunity for some low-key political maneuvering.

Wayne was especially fond of the solitary hours he would spend attempting to fathom the beating heart of the game. On brittle autumn nights he would stay late after practice, dissecting game films until his eyes burned. With a touch of a switch, he could make the ballplayers run forward, run backward, speed up, slow down, even stand still. It was all so sweet, so pure, so satisfying. It was the stuff of his "innovative" moves.

And then one afternoon in July of 1976, while visiting his in-laws in Trenton, New Jersey, the future laid itself open before Wayne's unbelieving eyes.

He'd been sent to the A & P to fetch some more beer and was stretching his errand by watching a game of playground basketball. It was there that Wayne came upon Silky Sims, and the knot of their lives, for better or worse, was tied.

Silky answered to "Sylvester" in those days. He was a scrawny, six foot six street urchin who lived in a three-room apartment with his mother, two sisters, one younger brother and a series of visiting "uncles." Sylvester was nineteen years old and had dropped out of high school when he was kicked off the basketball team in the middle of his junior year. The coach had freaked out when he'd caught his daughter blowing Sylvester in the back of the team bus. Sylvester had haunted the playgrounds ever since, hustling up dollar bets on spot-shooting matches and games of one-on-one. During shooting slumps or bad weather Sylvester augmented his income by running numbers for a local bookie. With his pockets bulging with money and incriminating slips of paper, Sylvester would dribble a basketball from stop to stop through the ghettos of Trenton. It was the perfect cover, but he always wore a razor strapped to the inside of his leg. He also was bright enough to be increasingly bitter and dissatisfied with the way he lived, understanding very well that street people sooner or later wound up doing nigger time in jail or behind a rack in New York's garment district.

In that fateful nothing game in the Trenton playground, Sylvester was pitted against a player who outweighed him by at least forty pounds. But the mismatch didn't stop Sylvester from hurling vicious taunts at his opponent throughout the game. . . .

"Dumb country nigger! You ain't worth dog shit in the street. . . ."

And Sylvester had scurried about the court like a mad scientist trying to catch light in a bottle. At the end of most of Sylvester's ravenous scamperings came a weirdly spinning jump shot that invariably rattled the chain nets. His unorthodox form frightened Wayne, but the shot was deadly from every conceivable angle and distance. And every so often Sylvester would further astound Wayne by going without the ball when his man turned his head. It was pure, unsoiled basketball instinct.

During the course of that magic game Wayne Smalley also became very dissatisfied with his life.

The young man was sullen and suspicious when Wayne approached him after the game. Sylvester was dressed in tattered corduroy pants, a torn undershirt and a pair of red Space Hoppers secured to his feet with

15

adhesive tape. There were a few awkward hairs sprouting from his defiant chin, but his face was cold and insolent. His lips were full and quivering, and his darting brown eyes were hooded under a prominent forehead. Sylvester's skin was as black as empty space and pressing up from underneath was a stringy network of wiry muscles. He reminded Wayne of some kind of aboriginal tailless lizard.

As Sylvester stood there sweating, fondling a basketball and listening to Wayne's sweet talk, his eyes became glassy in spite of himself. He couldn't believe what the man was saying. . . . Basketball scholarship? Room? Board? Who was this fool trying to bullshit? Savannah who? Finally it dawned on Sylvester that if this fast-talking white man wasn't jiving him, he had found a way out of his life. Going to college was a goofy idea, but it certainly beat hustling. Savannah State University!?

Wayne laughed when Sylvester asked about a cash bonus for signing. Sylvester didn't like that, but he was already nodding his head. "Sure, Mr. Smalley," he said. "You get me graduated from high school and into your college and I'll do whatever you say."

Wayne subsequently dropped the word on a certain politico-alumnus and presto chango . . . Sylvester passed a privately administered high school equivalency examination and was duly admitted as a student in good standing at SSU, where he proceeded to enjoy his stay: sleeping until three o'clock every afternoon, finding an occasional envelope stuffed with money in his locker, and managing to fuck all the white cheerleaders before the season started. And every night for the next two years Sylvester got an additional education at dinner with Wayne and Joan. Over hamburgers and tuna casseroles the Smalleys made sure that the boy knew just exactly who was responsible for his sudden good fortune.

In addition to being a master propagandist Wayne was also an accomplished basketball technician. So it was no trick for him to turn Sylvester into an atomic scoring machine. Wayne also recruited a matched set of illiterate, six foot ten, 250-pound twins who loved to make other people's bodies go crunch. Wayne taught them both how to pick, rebound and commit sanctioned atrocities. His guards were two nifty ball handlers from a shady community college in Florida. Sylvester scored 34 points a game during his freshman year, the team averaged 103 points and SSU zipped through the frightened local competition with a record of 29 and 5. Sylvester was named to several small college All-American teams.

"Mr. Smalley," Sylvester said every time he saw his picture in the newspaper, "I think I owe you my life."

"Don't think," was Wayne's constant rejoinder. "Just keep shooting."

In his sophomore year, Sylvester upped his average to 38.6 and the team went 28 and 4. All of these numbers were impressive enough to bring Savannah State a bid to play in the National Invitational Tournament in New York City. The NIT was the founding father of all post-season collegiate tournaments, but in the eyes of many experts it had long since been reduced to a gimmicky affair featuring only local colleges and outlaw schools with freaky records.

SSU squeezed through the field, beating Long Island University in the final. Sylvester was thoroughly sensational. He scored just over forty points a game and was unanimously acclaimed as the tournament's Most Valuable Player. Sylvester's shooting and jitterbug speed thrilled the imagination of the city's sportswriters. They hadn't, they said, seen anything like Sylvester Sims since the legendary days before the great Julius Erving came down with bad knees.

Sylvester was ecstatic about his reception. For ten days he held New York by the tail. The famous Murray Klurman even wrote a feature article about Sylvester, wherein he christened him "Silky." Sylvester was still grateful to Wayne, but also began to entertain the notion that just maybe he could make it by himself from here on in. This viewpoint was reinforced four weeks later when the New York Stars selected Sylvester in the NBA's hardship draft. Sylvester signed a four-year, no-cut pact worth a half million dollars and he said goodbye and good riddance to the Smalleys.

In his very first game with the Stars Silky was matched against the dean of the league's forwards—thirty-six-year-old Rick Barry. Silky hit his initial shot, a twenty-footer from the shadow of the base line.

"You can't stop me, old man," Silky snorted. "I'm Super Rookie!"

"Sure you are, kid," Barry said just before cracking Silky's ribs with an elbow and scoring ten straight points. Silky learned to keep his mouth shut after that but his stifled street ego trembled with rage and frustration whenever anyone made him look bad . . . just as he would soar into blissful highs when he played well. Silky averaged 16.3 points a game in his rookie season. He also finished the year with twenty-nine technical fouls, $3700 in fines and two paternity suits.

The venerable Red Holzman coached and inspired the Stars into the championship series against Los

Angeles, but Kareem Abdul-Jabbar was unstoppable and the Lakers won in five games. In a move that surprised no one, Holzman announced his retirement the day after the season ended.

Back in Savannah Wayne Smalley coached his squad to an unsatisfying 19 and 11 season, and waited for his telephone to ring. . . .

Wayne's reveries were jolted by the naked form of Dave Brooks shuffling through the bathroom on his way to the showers. Brooks was wearing a pair of clogs and carrying two towels in his right hand. Wayne quickly stepped back from the urinal and zipped up his fly.

"Is Sims in there?" he blurted.

"Yeah," Brooks said evenly. "He came in a couple of minutes ago. They're all waiting on you."

Wayne stared blankly at the fresh bruise under Brooks' right eye and his mouth hung open in expectant silence. Wayne never knew what to say or how to act in front of Brooks. He never could come up with an appropriate wisecrack.

"I got to shower up," Brooks finally said. "I played forty-seven minutes, I'm beat." He lurched past Wayne and vanished into a shower.

"I'll deal with you later," Wayne shouted above the rushing water, then hurried back into the dressing room.

All of the dressing alcoves were structurally identical. Each wire-mesh unit featured three shelves, innumerable clothing hooks and a footlocker built into the bottom. Despite this general uniformity several stalls did have their individualizing characteristics. Quinton Brown's trunk, for example, was a constant source of amusement. It was an infamous repository of moldy socks, festering jocks and half-eaten tuna fish sandwiches. The wall above

Quinton's stall was bare, and a worn copy of New York's schedule was taped to the front edge of a shelf.

In the place next to Brown's, Silky Sims' trunk was always open, loaded to the brim with neat stacks of fan mail and piles of newspapers and magazines. A gift from a fan hung suspended on Silky's allotment of wall space: against a background sheen of black satin the name SILKY was hand-embroidered in gold thread.

"You're beautiful!" Wayne exclaimed as he walked over and gave Silky a one-armed hug. "You're absolutely incredible!" He stood back and chuckled. "You know? I was thinking that maybe I should cuss you out more often!"

The two men exchanged an automatic titter and Wayne sneaked a look at Dave Brooks' locker. Dave hadn't come back yet, but Wayne turned to Silky with a confident grin and Silky stared into the aching capillaries that laced Wayne's eyes. They locked glances for a moment and then Silky turned away. Wayne clutched at Silky's shoulder once more.

"I could tell it was good from the second it left your hand," Wayne said. "The play worked out all right, didn't it? I mean everything turned out fine anyway, right . . . ? Okay!"

"Okay, yourself!" Tyrone White piped from where he sat, still picking at his ankles. "Let's get shakin', Wayno."

At that moment someone out in the corridor began banging on the front door. The ten minutes were almost up, the sportswriters were panicking, getting ornery. Wayne made an urgent signal for Buddy Patella to go outside and soothe them for another few moments, then lit his last cigarette and seated himself on the trainer's table.

"Okay," he announced, "there's not too much I want to say. It was a beautiful game and you handled the pressure well. It's the Utes next and I know what you're all thinking . . . we beat them four out of four during the regular season so all we have to do is show up and they'll lie down. That's a very dangerous attitude. And we shouldn't have been played so tough by Seattle either. So before we leave tomorrow I'm adding an extra practice. We have to be perfect to beat Jab— the Lakers. I think we need some more work to iron the bugs out—"

"Fuck it, man," Quinton Brown interrupted. "The only bugs in our game is crabs, man. We're tired, Wayne."

"I know you're tired, Quinton," Wayne said with whatever scraps of compassion he could muster. "I'm tired too . . . everybody's tired . . . but we can all get all the rest we want once the season's over. . . . If we want the title there's nothing for it but to keep on busting our ass. We can't afford any mistakes against the Lakers. . . ."

Buddy Patella popped in through the front door to give Wayne the high sign. The writers were still smiling at Buddy's funny stories and scribbling the punch lines. But Buddy's act was over.

Wayne stood up. "Oh, yeah!" he said. "Now that I think about it, I wasn't too thrilled about the way that last play was run. The execution was very sloppy. But I must admit that I did like the result . . . the *net* result!"

Kevin Harmon and a couple of clubhouse boys broke into subdued laughter. Wayne would have to remember to lay the line on Murray Klurman. "Okay! We got a short practice tomorrow at ten. You'll need to get taped. Then we'll look at some films. The bus leaves . . ." Wayne turned his head to Buddy.

"The bus leaves at two o'clock sharp," the trainer

chimed. "And the flight to Salt Lake City is at three-fifteen. It's all there on your ittitterary."

Wayne slapped his hands together. "Okay. That's it." Then he nodded to one of the ball boys and, with Murray Klurman in the lead, the gentlemen of the press came into the room.

It was early April and there was still a slush of gray snow littering the streets of New York, but Murray Klurman's suntan was going strong. Klurman looked natty in his burgundy double-knit pants with a plaid jacket to match, a Bill Blass navy Qiana shirt and a pair of navy patent-leather loafers. He was in his middle forties, but lean and sprightly from spending two afternoons a week at his tennis club. All the writers on the NBA tour loved to see Murray coming. He knew a million stories and told them in grand melodramatic style. Murray could also hold his booze, and when encouraged could talk all night about the sports column as art form. True, Murray was a bit compulsive about his writing but he was always good for a laugh once his nightly stories were called in. Murray had been covering sports for seventeen years and the New York Stars for fifteen. His salary was paid by the *Dispatch*, the city's only surviving afternoon paper, but the Stars' front office always picked up his tab on the road. Murray Klurman was an institution.

The demands of turf and seniority insisted that Murray ask the first questions. Every so often, one of the writers from the *News* or the *Times* would interject a query they thought Murray had overlooked. But they usually contained themselves until he was through. It saved them a lot of time and trouble. The other writers were also aware that Silky Sims could sometimes be a very touchy interview.

Two dozen media people pressed thickly around the three New York reporters without touching any one of them. The network tv man and several writers wandered over to Wayne and were neatly ushered into his private office.

"Nice game, kid," Murray said to Silky. "How did you feel when Lavelle hit that shot over you with nine seconds left?"

Silky laughed. He was feeling loosey-goosey. "Spence is a great ballplayer. One of the all-time greats. Spence been around here for a long time and he gets paid good money to light up cats like me." Silky was righteous with sincerity.

"What do you mean, cats like you?"

"You know . . . inexperienced cats is what I mean." Silky loved talking to the writers when his game was going good. "This is only my second year in the league and I'm still runnin' a little confused out there. I'm still gettin' myself orientated, you know? There's just somethin' cookin' all the time . . ."

"What's cooking?" Murray asked with a straight face. Everybody laughed but Silky.

"What I mean," Silky said gravely, "is like there's somethin' happenin' on one side to set up somethin' on the other side. It's really deep, man. You got to concentrate just to keep up."

"Yeah, kid. Tell me how the last play of the game was designed."

Silky coughed and spat into a towel. "Sure 'nuff," he said, then sipped at his cup of grape soda. Got to act cool to be cool, he told himself. "The last play was designed to score a basket," Silky said with a sly grin. "And it worked."

"Yeah, I see. All right, kid." Murray was already getting impatient. He needed some quotes for his story and Silky's answers were straight-faced stuff. Murray ached to be inside the coach's office, milking funny lines out of Wayne. "Why don't you describe your winning shot?"

"Well . . ."—Silky gathered himself together and took another drink of soda—"I beat Spence up top and then Tyrone threw me a perfect pass. I started going into my thing, but Burleson cut me off past the key. He was leanin' a little forward, lookin' to bump me or somethin'. So I just took off and shot the ball. It went in. The shot wasn't nothin' special."

"Did you have any doubts when you took the shot?"

"You know, man"—Silky winked—"it's tough to think and shoot at the same time. I was just worried about getting it off with that big dude blocking off the sky."

"What do you think of your chances of going all the way? Do you think anybody can beat the Lakers the way Jabbar's been going?"

"Can't say, man. That's too far ahead. I'm too busy worryin' about beating Utah to think about anything else."

"Thanks, kid," Murray said, then dashed across the room to have at Wayne.

Another sportswriter whom Silky didn't know pushed into Klurman's place ahead of the *Times* man. He was smoking a noxious cigar and puffing the smoke directly into Silky's face. Silky plucked the cigar from the man's mouth and gently dunked it into his cup of soda. Everybody laughed, including the offended reporter.

Silky was having fun now that Klurman was gone. He could do whatever he wanted to the rest of these suckers. He was a superstar.

John Burrows, the *Times* man, asked the next question: "What about the rumor that you're looking to renegotiate your contract because you're having such a good year?"

"Well, I got this here agreement with my agent, you dig? He don't do my thing and I don't do his. I'm interested right now with bringing a title back to New York. The high finance can wait till later."

There was still a group of ten or eleven people pushing in on Silky and someone he couldn't see shouted out another question. "Would you say that tonight's winning bucket was your greatest thrill in sports?"

Silky laughed and shook his head but didn't answer.

"You had twenty-five points tonight," Burrows said. "And your average is up around twenty-two now. What's the main reason for your improvement over last year?"

"A lot of things, man. A lot of things." Silky laid back again and allowed the corners of his mouth to droop with humility. "I can't just pick only one out. . . . There's the trade they made just before training camp. . . . Walt Frazier for Ardell Bartholomew. I mean, let's face it, man. Everybody knew that Clyde was losin' a step, you know? The deal made us stronger off of both boards so we could run a lot more too. Another thing, I been around for another whole year. I mean, like I have a year's experience now. That's probably the most important thing. Then when Wayne took over, he changed our offense some. We more forward orientated now so I'm handlin' the ball some more. And Tyrone is havin' the best year of his career."

The *Times* man ducked back and the knot of

sportswriters shuffled and regrouped. A microphone was shoved in front of Silky's mouth. "Here we are, live from the Stars dressing room. And here's Silky Sims, the hero of New York's play-off-clinching win over Seattle. Silky, in all your career have you ever had a bigger thrill than winning tonight's key game with your dramatic basket at the buzzer?"

"Yes," Silky deadpanned, then pushed his way past the announcer and headed into the shower room.

# CHAPTER THREE

DAVE DIDN'T want to awaken Nancy, so he forced his eyes open just an instant before the clock-radio was set to go off. It was no trick at all because the night had been a rough one for both of them. Nancy was well into her eighth month and the baby was sitting on her spine and her bladder. Dave had stirred when he heard Nancy's little gasps of pain.

He shook the dew from his head. There was something else too: a pair of red-veined flickering eyes that tracked him through every fragment of dream. Wayne Smalley's? Dave shook his head again and climbed softly out of bed.

"Dave?" Nancy was awake anyway. "Should I fix you some breakfast?"

"No, honey. I'll pick up something downtown. Just stay put."

It took Dave only ten minutes to rush through his early morning routine, then tiptoe back into the bedroom, climb into a clean pair of blue jeans and hoist a red flannel shirt over his broad shoulders. Then, sitting lightly on the edge of the bed, he pulled on a pair of sweat socks sticky with the residue of adhesive tape and pushed his feet into a pair of hand-tooled leather boots—one of his few indulgences.

When he was fully dressed Dave ducked back into the bathroom to brush his hair and wash down a handful of vitamins. He grabbed his goose-down parka from the hall closet and carried it with him back into the bedroom. He knew that Quinton and Silky would make sure to tease him about the plump red jacket, but it was cold in Salt Lake City. Whenever the Stars visited Buffalo, Denver or Milwaukee during the winter months Dave's teammates also ribbed him about his thermal underwear. But Dave Brooks was the only ballplayer who hadn't missed a game all year. Only fifth in team scoring, he led everybody in minutes played.

When Dave leaned over to kiss Nancy's cheek, she opened her eyes and smiled.

"I'm up," Nancy said. She smelled warm and fecund.

"I've got to go soon, honey. How do you feel?"

"I didn't sleep too well. Did you hear me?"

"A little." Dave brushed an imaginary hair from her forehead. "You know, it's really strange," he said. "In a crazy way your discomfort makes me feel good . . . I mean, it's healthy . . ."

"I know, honey," Nancy said, and craned her neck to kiss him. Her long black hair had been carefully knotted into a pair of thick braids but the rubber bands had worked themselves loose overnight and the ends were unravelling. Her cheeks were a bit pale but her bright brown eyes made her face blossom. Finally, with a mighty effort, she propped herself up into a sitting position.

"Dave? You're not worried about me, are you? Mom's coming over later and—"

"No, no, honey. I know you'll be . . . all right." A slight flush lit up the corners of his thin mouth. "I'm just a little tired, is all."

"It's Smalley, isn't it? You didn't sleep well either."

"I guess," he said, and then let his rawboned, calloused hands melt into Nancy's cheek. "I don't know. He's great figuring things from game films, mechanics, but then in the game he just makes so many mistakes. It's a miracle that we won the game last night. There's so much talent on the ball club that we win in spite of him. It's crazy. I can't figure him out. I don't understand the things he does. There's no flow, there's no trust. . . . It's all so complicated. I wish I could just go out every night and play basketball. I wish it was that simple."

"Why don't you sit down and have a talk with him? Tell him what you think. Let him know how you feel."

"Maybe I should. But it's so hard for me to talk to him. He nods his head and says yes, but he doesn't listen. And we're so close to the end. I think we have a shot at beating the Lakers and I don't want to ruin anything. I really think we can beat them—"

The doorman was buzzing up three times now from the lobby, and Dave was suddenly thankful that the building had a twenty-four-hour security force. They were trained to handle all kinds of emergencies and it would help ease his mind while he was away. He reminded himself to speak to Max before he left.

"Reed's here," Dave said reluctantly. "I've got to go. Call me if anything . . . you know. I'll speak to you tonight."

They held one another in a parting embrace.

"I love you, babe."

"I love you too, Dave."

And a lingering moment later Dave got up, grabbed

his jacket and Adidas bag and walked slowly out to the elevator. . . .

Dave Brooks was born and reared on a small dairy farm near Winona, Michigan. He was the youngest of three brothers and two sisters and his childhood was crammed full of hard work and energetic play. His father's 120-acre spread was set on the northwest ridge of the state. It had a swimming hole and a huge red barn with an adjoining aluminum silo. Hanging from the maple tree that stood between the house and a single lane asphalt road was a swing that Dave's father had fashioned out of an old tire. The farm also lay exposed to a bone-stabbing winter wind that drove down through Canada and honed its edges along Lake Superior.

Old John Brooks was a spry sixty-three years old nowadays, and he remained a force to be reckoned with. Along with his eldest son and his daughter-in-law John still made the farm run. In addition to loving his land, the brusque old man also prided himself on his children. Old John had taught his children well. They were all married and fruitful and they all knew their Bible. He taught them how to survive the ruthlessness of both the weather and their fellow men. John's wife had died when their youngest child Dave was only eighteen months old. According to the old man's light, love and compassion were as necessary to survival as was food and air. . . . "You can't never throw people away," John always told his children. "No matter how much you think you hate them."

Dave had often heard his sisters talking about their mother's death. They said she had gone into labor during the most severe snowstorm in anyone's memory. The only help that had made it through to the farm was an

Indian midwife from the nearby Ontonagon reservation. John always saved some goat's milk for her and she had come to "borrow" a pitcher for her grandson. But none of the old woman's skills could save the baby or stop the hemorrhaging. John Brooks wept close and private tears for almost two days before he could relinquish his wife's soul into the care of his God. After that John took special pains to make sure that all of his children grew up ready to assume full responsibility for their deeds. He didn't want them using their mother's untimely death as a crutch, and so like the rest of his brothers and sisters Dave had learned very young to shut out self-pity and abhor self-indulgence.

Dave turned out to be an exceptional athlete, at first favoring baseball over any other sport. Actually it wasn't until he was fourteen and a junior high school student that he was turned-on to basketball. It happened at a free basketball clinic that Phil Jackson annually conducted on the Ontonagon reservation. Dave was the only white youngster the Indians invited to the program and at first he felt a little strange. Under Jackson's easy tutelage, though, it wasn't long before Dave became thoroughly engrossed in having a wonderful time. It seemed to him that Jackson was enjoying himself even more than his pupils were, and he couldn't imagine a similar situation in baseball. As a result of the clinic he tried out for his high school team the following year, made the team as a freshman and wound up its leading scorer during the last third of the season.

Eventually he set all kinds of records at Winona High, but it was a Class C school so nobody ever made much of a fuss. Dave was offered basketball scholarships to only four colleges: Western Michigan, Illinois Central, Saginaw College, and the University of Michigan. The last one, of course, was a shocker. It seemed that the Wolverines had spent most of their basketball budget in recruiting the fabulous Hazle Brimley and were now in dire need of a solid, low-key performer who could work the offense around Brimley. They also required someone who could be recruited as cheaply as possible. So for four years Dave Brooks was the perfect second banana. He averaged four points and eleven assists a game and finished with an academic index of 3.8, majoring in dairy engineering with minors in sociology and psychology. He was astounded when the Stars made him a fourth round draft selection. He was even more surprised when he made the team.

Red Holzman spoon-fed Dave's confidence and carefully regulated his playing time, so that going into the 1980–81 season Dave had a pro career mark of only 2.8 points per game. When Wayne Smalley took over the ball club Reed Carson was a big-shot matinee idol and Dave was just another one of Holzman's hunches. In the first few training camp scrimmages Wayne followed form and started Reed alongside Tyrone White. But it didn't take Wayne long to see that something was breaking down. The starting five's offense was continually jammed up and the scrubs always wound up getting much better shots. Then Wayne began filming all their practice sessions and discovered what was happening—Dave Brooks was making Reed bleed every time he tried to move. Sometimes Dave overplayed Reed and denied him the ball. Other times Dave played him loosely and suckered him into charges and turnovers. In his confusion Reed trailed the ball around the court and clogged up the patterns. According to Wayne's charts Reed shot a measly thirty-six per cent in head-to-head competition with Dave Brooks.

The films also showed that Dave played both ends of the court, was forever on the move, never forced a shot, got everybody into the offense and rarely made a mistake. Dave Brooks was the perfect catalyst. Before the exhibition schedule was over Dave had quietly slipped into Walt Frazier's slot in the Stars backcourt. . . .

The panelled elevator doors slid open and revealed a portly figure in a gaudy maroon uniform. A script emblem on the man's breast pocket announced that he belonged to "The Belvedere Arms." A gold braid dangled smartly from Max Muhlman's left shoulder; Max—senior member of the building's elevator corps.

When he saw Dave, Max's professional grimace of good cheer turned into a hearty smile that tightened the creases across his cheekbones. "Mr. Brooks! What a terrific game last night! Me and the missus want to thank you again for the tickets. We really had a terrific time for ourselves."

"That's great, Max, I'm glad you enjoyed it."

Dave stepped into the carpeted elevator and assumed a position behind the engineer. Dave loved to watch Max work the old-fashioned crank-screw brake, steer the elevator compartment as carefully as if he were piloting it across the Atlantic.

"You know who was sitting right behind us, Mr. Brooks? You'll never guess in a million years . . . Woody Allen! That's right! Wearing a big floppy hat that covered his head so no one could tell it was him. But the missus is such a movie fan . . . when she spotted him she couldn't stop laughing the rest of the night. He's a real funny man, Mr. Brooks. A talent like that is a gift."

"I know," Dave said, and smiled. It certainly wasn't one of his.

Dave enjoyed Max, but also felt uncomfortable whenever an older person called him "Mr. Brooks." He'd once asked Max to call him "Dave," but the old man had stiffened with dignity.

"Oh, no, Mr. Brooks, we can't do that, we're not allowed to refer to our clients on a first name basis, it's the rules, Mr. Brooks, and I go by the rules, play life strictly on the up and up, the only way.... Say, Mr. Brooks, what are you doing up and out so early? You got a morning flight to Salt Lake or something?"

"No, Max. Just a practice. Flight's this afternoon."

"That Mr. Smalley, he don't even give you guys a day off to celebrate, hunh? Must be a hard man . . ."

Dave answered with a neutral grunt.

"I know what you mean, Mr. Brooks. But, you know, it must be hard getting up for a series with a team like the Utes. I'll bet you're all really looking forward to the Lakers? That Kareem is really something."

"He sure is, Max. Kareem's the most dominant player in the game."

Dave flexed his shoulders slightly and reset his feet. He rubbed at a tight spot on his neck. "Say, Max? Do you think you could do me a favor?"

"Sure, Mr. Brooks. Anything. Just you name it."

"I'd really appreciate it if you could keep all the neighbors' kids away from Nancy while I'm gone. Sometimes they come around and bother her for pictures and stuff. It's not that she minds—"

"Say no more, Mr. Brooks," Max said with a wave of his hand. "A woman in Mrs. Brooks' delicate condition needs all the peace and quiet she can get. You just put it out of your mind and leave everything else to me. I'll pass the word along to the rest of the staff."

"Thanks, Max, I'm much obliged."

Max reached up and pulled at the lever that opened the elevator doors. Dave hadn't even realized they'd come to a stop, that the elevator car was on a dead level with the polished marble floor of the lobby. He could barely trace out the seam.

"Here we are, Mr. Brooks," Max announced. "And there's Mr. Carson's car right out there in front waiting for you. Right on time like always. It sure is a rotten shame about his ankle though, hunh, Mr. Brooks? It still doesn't look right."

"You're right," Dave said as he sidled toward the front door. "Still hurts him, and cuts down on his movement. . . . Well, take it easy, Max."

"Have a nice trip, Mr. Brooks. And don't you worry about those kids."

As Dave made his way out onto the street Max steered his machine down into the basement, put the controls on automatic, hurried into the employee's dressing room and over to a telephone. He called his bookie and bet twenty-five dollars on the upcoming Salt Lake-New York game. He took the Utes with seven and a half points.

Reed Carson's spanking new Mercedes-Benz was conspicuously double-parked in the drive. But when Reed spotted Dave he honked the horn anyway. Reed didn't much like to be kept waiting. His triangular face was rippling now with annoyance, his sharp features were turned into knives, and his irritation brought color to his lean waxy cheeks. His famous teeth sparkled in the gray morning as his mouth framed a shout: "C'mon, Dave, move your ass, buddy!"

Reed's eyes were a nervous frigid blue buttressed by neat little folds of flesh. He was considered good-looking, in a tight sort of way, and led the ball club in commercials. He'd made another toothpaste commercial after practice just last week. This time Quinton had teased Reed about the narrow cleft that bit so deeply into his chin. "Let's see that million-dollar smile, Hollywood," Quinton had said. "When you're finished selling your teeth, you can rent out your chin for toilet paper commercials."

Dave was smiling as he curled into the front seat. Quinton sure had a way of puncturing people.

"What are you smiling about, chump?" Reed asked with an insistent grin.

"That toothpaste commercial," Dave said.

"Yeah," Reed snorted. "It was sure enough funny. It was so damn funny that I made myself ten thousand dollars for an hour and a half of doing nothing."

They drove through the heavy morning traffic in an easy silence.

"You see a paper yet?" Dave finally asked. "Do the Lakers and the Darts play tonight? I forgot."

"Naw. I didn't see nothing. I don't want to talk about basketball. Okay? It's been a nice day so far and I don't want to ruin it."

"Your ankle still bad?"

"Shit!" Reed said. "You ain't hurting nowhere? Don't tell me. It's April, man. Everybody's hurting."

Dave watched Reed pick at the skin on his neck. He could never figure out what made a Reed Carson tick. They'd been roommates for two years and he still didn't know him. When Reed joined the Stars in 1978 his bad reputation came along with him, but Dave took his father's advice and asked Reed to be his roommate. As that first season unfolded Dave was amazed at how closed Reed's head was. He couldn't believe how life-and-death important it was for Reed to be a stick-out professional athlete. Reed was snotty, overbearing and demanded the spotlight forever shine and shine on him. Except for talking about basketball and places to eat, Dave and Reed found little common ground for even casual conversation. It took Nancy to put Reed into a much simpler perspective: "He's got the worst vibes I've ever seen." . . .

Reed Carson had been an authentic pheenom in high school. As a senior his angular face had already been spread over the cover of *Sports Illustrated*. He went on to lead the country in scoring at the University of Houston and was subsequently drafted by the financially delicate Houston Rockets franchise. The Rockets signed Reed to a major five year contract worth almost four million and there was much ballyhoo from the media. Reed was to be the latest in a long line of white hopes and franchise saviors. There were even rumors that the NBA office, backed by New York and Los Angeles money, had underwritten the deal.

The league's officials watched over Reed like guardian angels, so he averaged 27.3 points his rookie year. The Rockets finished in last place in their division for the third year in a row but their home attendance was up by twenty per cent. Nobody was much surprised when Reed's natural arrogance began to run out of control. If Reed took thirty shots in a game he was pissed because nobody got him the ball when he was open for number thirty-one. He ranted at his teammates, and there were fights. His average climbed to 30.3 the following season but none of it could keep the Rockets out of the cellar. The Rockets fans' enthusiasm wore thin, and attendance returned to normal by the end of the year. Reed responded by freaking out at every opportunity—he blamed the press, he continued patronizing his teammates and he battled both the coach and the front office. There was even a famous incident in which Reed went into the stands after a peanut vendor he thought was coming-on to his wife.

Two stormy years of Reed Carson were enough for Houston. He and his gargantuan contract were peddled off to save the Cleveland franchise. In return for Reed the Cavaliers gave up two top draft choices they couldn't afford to sign away. Cleveland had finished the previous season with only one white ballplayer on the roster and their fans were about to revolt. Once again, it was said that the league office underwrote Reed's annual salary.

Reed led the NBA in scoring the following season, but the Cavaliers supplanted the Rockets as the division's doormat. There were predictions that unless somebody took Reed off their hands the Cleveland franchise would finally go down the drain. None of this fuss modified either Reed's exalted sense of himself or his appetite for taking an enormous number of shots. And then, two years ago in 1978, the New York Stars had shocked the known basketball universe by buying Reed from Cleveland for $250,000 in cash and a second-round draft choice.

Walt Frazier and Tyrone White were New York's starting backcourt then. At first Red Holzman tried to con Reed into believing that becoming the Stars third guard would be the turning point of his career. Reed wasn't buying. He pointed out his 29.1 lifetime scoring average and told Holzman he doubted his career really needed a turning point at all. Holzman smiled and told Reed his name would be placed on the waiver list if he didn't shape up. Reed laughed in Holzman's face and stormed out of the coach's office. The following morning Reed Carson's name topped the waiver list. For ten thousand dollars any club in the league could claim him and the still healthy remains of his contract. The NBA also issued a private message to all the owners stating that they were *not* prepared to support Reed's contract any longer. After three days Reed came back to Holzman and begged for another chance.

Reed was used whenever the Stars offense needed what Holzman called "a kick in the ass." He was launched into the game at strategic moments with a license to shoot whenever the spirit moved him. But if Reed missed four shots in a row Holzman would yank him and wait to try him again in the second half. Murray Klurman nicknamed Reed "Instant Points." The New York fans were suckers for flawed, erratic heroes. They loved "Points" like a wayward son returned to the fold, and they forgave him all his excesses.

Then Walt Frazier was dealt to Chicago after Holzman retired and only the thought of Points' inheriting Clyde's starting slot could soothe the fans' bereavement. They subsequently were very unhappy when Dave Brooks had supplanted Reed during training camp. Brooks had never made a television commercial. The Stars finished the 1980–81 season with the second best winning percentage in the NBA, but Dave Brooks was still considered an interloper. . . .

A mottled Volkswagen swerved into their lane and Reed had to tromp on the brake. His eyes lit up when he saw a woman behind the wheel of the VW.

"Damn bitch," Reed snapped as he whipped the Mercedes past her. "Did you see that?"

"Yeah," Dave said, and suddenly wished he had gotten up a half hour earlier and taken the train into the city.

# CHAPTER FOUR

THE STRAIN of the unfamiliar morning hour was easy to read on Quinton Brown's face. His eyes, a gooey yellow, looked like they might drop out and roll around the locker room floor. The bald spot on the top of his head was wet with perspiration and his garland of oily hair was a jumble of tangles. He may have been a twelve-year veteran but Quinton partied like a rookie—he'd spent the past night bedded down with three stewardesses.

Quinton always reported for a practice much earlier than any of his teammates, simply because he needed the extra time to prepare himself. First there would be a thirty minute session in the sauna to get his heart beating again. Then his bad knee would need fifteen minutes in the whirlpool bath. And just before he was due on the court Quinton would duck under a quick cold shower. Now, though, all of Quinton's resuscitation was still ahead of him as he grunted with the effort of hoisting his garment bag onto a hook.

Quinton was a mess and he felt even worse. This state of affairs was actually a very considerable achievement. Even when Quinton was well rested, his appearance was unsightly. His nose was the worst offender. Broken several times, it squatted in the middle of his face like a misplaced mashed thumb. Quinton's other features were similarly squat and unappealing. His slightly pocked amber cheeks were only partially covered by a scraggly beard. Although Quinton was oblivious to the honor, he was a member of the NBA's all-time All-Ugly team. But had one of his peers broken the taboo and informed him of his selection, Quinton would scarcely have believed the news. For Quinton knew that the ladies loved him.

Quinton collapsed now on his stool and motioned for one of the nameless ball boys. The one in the classy white Adidas came over.

"Go and fetch me a Alka-Seltzer and a container of black coffee," Quinton said. "And make it a extra large."

"Which one?" White Adidas asked.

"Botha them, you dummy."

Quinton waved the boy off and slowly went about his pre-practice ritual. He was already in the sauna when Kent Solomon and J. B. McGrath—New York's two-man taxi squad—entered.

Ever since 1979 NBA clubs were only allowed to have ten players on their active roster, and the ten-man roster was the lastest burning issue between the club owners and the NBA Players Association. The abbreviating of team rosters, as well as the establishing of taxi squads, were direct results of the Supreme Court's ruling in the Oscar Robertson suit, by which the Court struck down the NBA's reserve clause, a mechanism which formerly tied a player to a team for one year after his contract expired. The landmark ruling made players in this situation free agents, allowing them to sell their services to the highest bidder. Within a year of the ruling the average player's salary shot up to $175,000 a year. Long-term contracts were now deemed desirable by both the clubs and the players, five and six year pacts becoming commonplace. They were considered the only means of insuring the stability and integrity of a ball club's roster. The additional expenditures caused the owners to rise up as one and scream bloody murder. They filled the news-papers and airwaves with complaints of "rising operating costs" and "the economy." Then, in the summer of 1978, when nobody was looking, the owners snuck the ten man roster into the NBA rule book. The players bitched, they argued, but nothing was to be done. The NBA's board of directors had sole jurisdiction over the rules that gov-erned the game.

According to the Players' Agreement the minimum annual salary for any "active" NBA player was $35,000. But taxi squad members were paid by the week and only during the run of the season. Kent Solomon was getting $400 and J. B. Smith $450. And the owners smiled.

If taxi squads and reduced rosters were unforeseen results of the Supreme Court's decision, there was one other effect some onlookers had anticipated. The court had also ruled that the team holding a player's original contract could retain the player by matching any offer made by any other team. The "match-or-lose" rule took effect in 1979, and many players deliberately arranged for their contracts to terminate at that time. It was soon discovered that very few ball clubs could equal the dollar signs dangled by the NBA's two wealthiest franchises, the New York Stars and the Los Angeles Lakers, who im-mediately began to corner the market on quality ballplayers.

The Lakers' plan was simply to sign up as many available all-stars as possible. Their current starting lineup included Kareem Abdul-Jabbar, George McGinnis, John Drew, Doug Collins and Phil Chenier. Guided by Red Holzman's last-ditch demands, New York went more for balance and character, picking up Larry Graham when his one-year contract with the Bullets lapsed, and signing Jeremy Covington from Phoenix. . . .

The next ballplayer to push his way into the Stars dressing room was the star Silky Sims. A triumphal entrance. Silky was resplendent in a formfitting, pinstriped, doublebreasted suit. On his head was a matching pinstriped fedora, and a black mink cape was casually draped over his shoulders. Silky's size fourteen feet were stuffed into a pair of Gucci shoes with four-inch stacked heels. He paused majestically at the door to nod a greeting in the general direction of Solomon and McGrath, then glided over to his stall and carelessly tossed a copy of the *New York Times* to the floor. The two remaining ball boys were quick to pick up the cue as they dropped what they were doing and came bouncing over.

"Silky!"

"How ya doin', Silky?"

Once more Silky bobbed his head at his subjects, then poked the newspaper with his shoe.

"Hey, Silky," a flashy pair of gold Pumas said, "what'd the *Times* guy write about the game?"

"You mean Burrows?" Silky asked with lifted eyebrows. "Sheyit. I never pay that sucker no mind."

"Lemme see," a pair of white utilitarian Cons shouted. "Lemme see it!"

"Yeah," Silky said. His face took on a playful, jaunty sneer. "You read that bullshit if you want to. I don't care *what* that chump got to say."

The newspaper was already well-creased, and as the ball boy riffled the pages it opened itself to Burrows' article. White Cons cleared his throat and began to read: "In a game played at Madison Square Garden last night, the New York Stars won the first round of the Trans-Continental Division play-offs by edging the Seattle SuperSonics, 105-104, on a clutch shot at the buzzer by Sylvester 'Silky' Sims, the Stars exciting second-year player whose spine-tingling variety of shots are rapidly becoming a trademark all around the league. . . ."

While White Cons paused to catch his breath, Gold Pumas was quick to interrupt. "Silky, he said you got a *trademark!* Y'all know what that means?"

Silky broke into a soft grin. "Lay it on me, little brother."

"It mean you in *business!*"

Silky exploded into a yowl of delight and began madly to flap the boy's palms, then picked up a towel and playfully flicked it at the newspaper. "Later for that bullshit," he announced. Silky's aim was perfect, and the tip of the towel snapped a hole in the page.

White Cons squealed with pleasure and dropped the newspaper. "Hey, Silky! Watch it, man! Hey!"

The boy danced out of range, and Silky took a couple of menacing steps after him.

"What chu doin', Silky? Hey! Be *cool!*"

At which point the front door swung open and Buddy Patella strode into the room. Everybody froze, including Silky.

"What the fricken hell goes on in here?" Buddy demanded. "You lazy crap-asses, get on back to work!"

The petrified ball boys scampered over to a sack of fresh towels and began to frantically stack them onto the trainer's table. Buddy then turned to face Silky.

"For shit's sake," Buddy scolded, "what ya wanna

horse around like that for? You wanna get hurt or something? Jesus H. Keerist! What a fricken ball club."

Silky tensed and defiantly stood his ground. His hands folded themselves into fists, his anger about to boil over just as Reed and Dave entered the room, and the moment passed.

Silky's body relaxed. He called out to Gold Pumas. "Hey you ... brother! Come here, I need me some breakfast. Go fetch me a Coke and two Twinkies." He turned and looked Buddy straight in the eye. "Two *chocolate* Twinkies."

# CHAPTER FIVE

OUTSIDE ON Eighth Avenue the sun was fighting to crack through the gray serried clouds, a struggle irrelevant inside the depth of Madison Square Garden. Outside the streets were heavy with noise, garbage and passersby, but except for the humming of a million miles of electric wiring, the basketball arena was tomb-silent. Every interior surface had been vacuumed and polished overnight; twenty thousand empty seats lay gleaming under the mercury lights. And Coach Wayne Smalley sat on the scorer's table and waited for his players to come filtering out onto the court. Wayne loved the still lifelessness of the deserted Garden. He loved the ghastly glow of the artificial lighting. His world was basketball, which happened indoors. Wayne couldn't care less if he never saw the sun again.

He was midway through his morning pack of cigarettes, his free hand fidgeting with the whistle that dangled around his neck. He stood up for a moment to stare dreamily into the vacant stands and for a moment almost fancied he could hear last night's cheers ringing out of the shadowless corners: "SMALL-LEE! SMALL-LEE!" Wayne had been halfway down the runway when he was certain he'd heard the crowd screaming out his name . . . "SMALL-LEE! SMALL-LEE!" Beautiful. And why not? He deserved it. . . .

He stubbed out a cigarette into the middle of the polished oaken table he was sitting on, and couldn't help shaking with a barely contained belly laugh. Let them try and fire him now.

"SMALL-LEE! SMALL-LEE!"

Wayne Smalley had no illusions when he first took his job. The Stars' general manager Joe Cunningham had been unmistakably blunt. Wayne was selected to succeed Red Holzman primarily on the basis of his presumed ability to control the volatile Silky Sims. If Silky continued to "misbehave," or if the Stars failed to win the championship, Wayne would be shown the door and the next victim brought in. Wayne, however, eagerly agreed to the terms and conditions, signing a one year contract worth fifty thousand dollars. As a sop to Wayne's coaching integrity Cunningham let him handle the Stars' collegiate draft, for which Wayne read volumes of scouting reports, viewed countless reels of films and made Kevin Harmon New York's number one selection.

The ball club that Red Holzman left for Wayne had all the elements of a dynasty—balance, explosiveness, speed and the potential for superb defense. Even though the Stars had been beaten by the Celtics in the previous year's semi-finals it was generally agreed that New York would eventually come to rule the NBA roost. All the Stars lacked was maturity and discipline, and given sufficient time the experts allowed that Holzman would have little trouble whipping his ball club into shape. It was

47

Holzman's long established practice to use a balky athlete's playing time as both reward and punishment. Holzman didn't bother with fines or personal confrontations. All he needed was the opportunity to exercise his own particular brand of laid-back authority and the Stars would be destined to eclipse anything that the Russellized Celtics had ever accomplished. But that was before the coming of Silky Sims.

Concurrent with Silky's incredible performance in the National Invitational Tournament, Madison Square Garden and all the Garden-based teams were taken over by an octopus corporation known as the Hudson Bay Company. A computer was immediately installed in the basement, the bookkeeping staff was doubled and an advertising agency was retained. Penguinlike men wearing horn-rimmed glasses and carrying black attaché cases were soon seen prowling about dressing rooms and the "closed" practices. A corporate decision was reached making Silky the Stars' top pick in the 1979 draft. Red Holzman was forthwith instructed to turn Silky into a basketball dreadnaught. Over a million dollars was spent hyping Silky as at least the second coming of Julius Erving. An imperative was laid on Holzman to play Silky thirty minutes a game during his rookie year. Holzman vehemently objected and threatened to quit before the season started. It was pointed out to him, however, that his contract was ironclad and that a lawsuit would clean out his life savings. Holzman had no choice but to remain with the ball club for one more year.

Silky was a sensation with the fans in spite of his capricious play and his off court antics. The Stars drew eighty-two consecutive SRO crowds and the revenue from the Home Box Office broadcasts of their games increased by forty per cent. Holzman was mercifully allowed to retire after losing to the Celtics. The computer figured that crotchety old coaches were a dime a dozen, but that players with the fan appeal of a Silky Sims were worth their weight in thousand-dollar bills. The machine in the Garden's basement further projected that the Stars had a good chance to win the championship no matter who their coach was. It followed then that Wayne Smalley be hired to control and nurture New York's latest supercilious superstar.

The strategy seemed to be working. So far this season Silky had been on his best behavior. He approved that Wayne's new system made him the focus of the Stars' offense. There had been no drug busts for the front office to hush up, no out of court paternity settlements, no public brawls with his coach, and no fisticuffs in exclusive restaurants. The pressure, however, was starting to get to Silky, his fragile self-restraint was about to break down. Silky had finished the regular season among the NBA leaders in scoring, field goal percentage, rebounds and foul shooting. His success puffed up his head, and selectively blotted out portions of his memory—such as where he came from and who he used to be. Even his mother called him "Silky."

Wayne Smalley was not a stupid man. He could sense Silky's coming explosion, and only hoped Silky could hold himself together until the play-offs were over. As long as the Stars beat Los Angeles, Wayne was certain that his position was secure . . . "SMALL-LEE! SMALL-LEE!"

Wayne ground out another cigarette. If New York won the championship, there was *no* way the fans would allow Cunningham to fire him. . . .

Twenty minutes before practice was set to begin Silky

and Larry Graham came dribbling onto the court. For a few minutes they casually shot and joked around. Both ignored the presence of their coach. Next Dave and Quinton showed up and the four ballplayers immediately convened another round of their perpetual shot-matching contest. The game was called "Horse," a schoolyard evergreen, but the pro version was a bit more complicated. According to the Stars' rules the only shots that had to be duplicated by the shooter next in line were the ones that went in without touching the rim. Silky was by far the most accurate shooter in the group; his field goal percentage of fifty-seven per cent was third best in the league. But either Dave or Larry usually won the competition because their shots had a higher trajectory. Dave was the only participant who took the game seriously. The other three players just clowned around and traded insults.

Watching them cavort through their game, Wayne smoldered in silence. Nor was he especially thrilled with Silky's outlandish practice uniform—a standard reversible practice jersey combined with a torn pair of sweat pants. Silky's hair was twisted into braided corn rows and a black watch cap covered the top of his head. Wayne figured that since a ballplayer didn't play with a hat on, he shouldn't practice with one. Wayne was also positive that the cap was meant as a personal affront to his authority. He was right. Things were definitely coming to a head.

Silky followed Quinton in the shooting order and they raked one another with a crossfire of insults, Quinton getting the better of the exchange but Silky remaining cocky.

"Sey hey, Q!" Silky shouted. "What you been doin', Pops? Sleepin' in between the subway tracks?"

All the other players broke up, but Quinton aimed a

withering glare at Silky. "You pussy!" Quinton snarled. "You wish you ever dreamed of doin' what I been doin' . . . shit! Get over here, motherfucker, I ain't got time to talk to you."

Silky immediately jumped into a spidery defensive stance in front of Quinton. Dave flipped Quinton a ball. "You ready, chump?" Quinton asked.

Quinton protected the ball behind his hip and faked in ten different directions at the same time. Then in quick succession Quinton hooked his left elbow under Silky's left armpit, bullied Silky with a hefty shoulder, bumped him with a hip, and kneed Silky in the thigh. And just as Quinton threw in a triple-pump lay-up, he threw his backside into Silky's solar plexus.

"It's *good!*" Quinton cackled. "And a foul on the chump!"

The first order of business was calisthenics. When Wayne finally blew his whistle the players congregated around the center jump circle. Compared to their coach the New York Stars were a disheveled lot. Silky was wearing his cap, Quinton wore a ragged Superman T-shirt, and Kevin Harmon's shorts were split down the seat. Wayne stood in the middle of the group looking nifty in a yellow Banlon shirt. Permanently stitched creases defined Wayne's gray cotton-blend pants and a brand new pair of leather Adidas twinkled on his feet. Wayne also wore a jockstrap over his BVD's. Wayne had served in the infantry in Vietnam and he still prided himself on his physical condition.

"Okay!" Wayne shouted. "Let's go. Ten jumping jacks." He led the team in the exercise, barking out a perfect cadence each time he clapped his hands high over his head.

51

"And . . . ONE!" Wayne commanded. "Hands up! Don't get lazy!"

Quinton rose up slowly on his toes and haphazardly flung his hands to the level of his shoulders, then slapped his hands against his thighs and farted.

"Move it! Move it!"

Reed stood totally motionless with his weight shifted off his weak ankle. The tape was too tight and Reed glared insolently at Wayne.

"Work it! Work it!"

The two taxi squadders were jumping up and down like demons, doing the drill in double-time.

"Get up! Get up!"

Silky was doing his own impression of Jumping Jack. Silky leaped as high into the air as he could. Then, at the very top of each mighty effort, Silky reached up with his right hand and gently tapped the moon.

"Extend! Extend!"

Tyrone was jouncing lightly on the balls of his feet and trying to jiggle his legs loose. He was paying no attention whatsoever to either his coach or his teammates.

"On count! On count!"

Kevin was tackling the exercise with his usual sloppy aggression. Kevin had the second highest vertical jump on the team and he banged his hands over his head with resounding thumps. One of Kevin's sneaker laces was untied and the plastic tips clicked against the hardwood floor.

"Move it! Move it!"

Larry Graham and Jeremy Johnson were absently waving their arms like holy rollers at a revival meeting. They were buzzing about their sexual menu for the three day stopover at the Salt Palace Plaza.

"Bust it! Bust it!"

Jack Mathias and Ardell Bartholomew worked side by side like a pair of synchronized mechanical dolls. They were both steaming and Ardell's clean-shaven head was glistening with sweat.

"Get it together!"

Dave was wandering dutifully through the exercise. He was trying to clear his mind and establish some kind of communion with his body. But Wayne's pitter-patter was too distracting. Nor could Dave keep his mind off Nancy.

"TEN! Okay!"

Wayne moved gracefully through a set of toe-touching exercises. He followed this with a series of push-ups, leg-rolls, back-stretches, sit-ups and leg-bends. Wayne didn't chide the players who habitually panto-mimed their way through the program, but he knew exactly who they were.

"O-kay!" Wayne grunted as he concluded the last of the leg-bends. "Let's go, three lines!"

The athletes moved up and down the court three at a time. They ran easily and the length of their strides increased as they ran. The pattern was the same, over and over again: Three players running, with the basketball shuttling among them like it was mounted on a greasy string, the man with the ball stopping at the foul line and passing it to one of his teammates for a lay-up, then back the other way. Every so often the players would jokingly call each other to task for bobbling a pass or missing a shot. The drill was designed to stretch and re-tune muscles, but it had been a long, demanding season and limbs were cranky and unresponsive.

For several minutes they continued to run with a listless elegance, then Ardell Bartholomew took a pass from Dave and rumbled to the basket. Ardell took off from the foul line like a redwood tree leaving a launching pad. He slammed the ball through the hoop, and it almost flattened out as it smashed against the floor.

"Big A!" Dave shouted.

"Ding-dong-DELL!" Silky yelled.

"All right!" said Jack.

"DO it, big fella!" Quinton hollered.

Wayne rejoiced at his players' spirit of togetherness. His chest swelled with inspiration. "Okay!" he screamed, and clapped his hands.

Ardell's brutal dunk shot magically invigorated the stiff, the lame and even the reluctant. The ballplayers now hustled briskly through the warm-up. Silky swooped through the air, gently deposited the ball into the basket from a height of two and one-half feet above the rim. Everybody kicked up another notch. Their bodies turned elastic. Now the players flew up and down the court, propelled by some secret wind-driven music. The sound of slam-dunks and vibrating rims counterpointed their random chimes of delight:

"DO it, L.G.!"

"Big dog!"

"It's the incredible Doctor Bags!"

Even Quinton's herky-jerky pigeon-toed gait was transfigured into a smart reggae beat.

"Q.! Climb that ladder, baby!"

All the players were soon loose and well-oiled with perspiration. "Last ones out," Wayne called. "Hit 'em both!"

Tyrone broke out of the chute in the middle with Larry Graham and Quinton on the wings. They sprinted downcourt, whipping the ball around in a blur.

Quinton loved it. Behind the back, under the asshole . . . he felt like he was back with the Globies again. But there was a nice little bit of pressure riding on him too. If he or Larry missed a shot, the entire team would have to run three extra "suicides" at the end of practice. Quinton was skating on a sweet edge and his bad knee felt free and easy.

Tyrone pulled up with the ball at the free throw stripe while Larry and Quinton cut sharply in toward the basket. Tyrone led Quinton straight to the hoop with a perfect bounce pass. Larry jumped up at the same time to slam home an unlikely miss.

But instead of simply catching the ball and shooting it, Quinton executed a half-step-and-turn and presented his backside to Tyrone. Tyrone's pass ricocheted off Quinton's ass and looped directly into the face of a surprised Larry Graham, who recovered with a corkscrew twist in midair, grabbed the unexpected pass and threw in a spinning backhand lay-up. On the return trip down the floor Larry dunked the ball with a vengeance.

"That's it!" Wayne shouted. "Okay! Way to push it!" He didn't like the showboating but at least it looked like the team would be up for tomorrow night's game. "Let's get a little scrimmage going."

Silky, Dave, Tyrone, Jack and Ardell comprised New York's starting, or "blue" team. The remainder of the squad played "white" with the two taxi men in reserve.

As his name was called, Reed limped over to Wayne. "Can't do it, coach," Reed said with an innocent shrug. "I think the tape's too tight."

"Okay," Wayne said with a smile. "Go back downstairs and tell Buddy to do it over."

And then Wayne lowered his voice. "Reed," he said, "I just want to tell you I'm hip you're the absolute guts of the ball club. I just want you to know that I know it. You're the one who makes the offense go. There's no way we can beat Jabbar without a big contribution from you. Right? So you've got to be ready."

"Yeah," Reed said evenly. "Yeah, okay." Then Reed turned and jogged off down the runway.

"J.B.," Wayne called. "Play white."

Wayne ran the two teams through a controlled half-court scrimmage. The blues were on offense and in preparation for the Salt Lake series they were compelled to use only the variations off the basic C and S plays. Tyrone snapped them out:

"Stack seven! . . . C two! . . . Box C! . . . Philly stack! . . . Stack C! . . ."

After twenty industrious but unemotional minutes, Wayne finally let them run fullcourt. They knew the plays as well as they ever would. As usual the blue team had the whites well in hand. Quinton and Tyrone slid up and down the court in idle tandem, but everybody else was working hard.

56

Wayne hated to admit it but he had to thank his pre-decessor for their enthusiasm. Wayne had opted to per-petuate Red Holzman's long-standing policy of having sequestered practices. Except for an occasional penguin admitted on a pass from the computer, no one was al-lowed to watch the team work out. The privacy filtered out distractions and forced the players to generate their own heat and intensity. In seclusion, they played for pride. Even Silky would dive for a loose ball, something he thought was too uncool to do in front of twenty thousand people. Closed scrimmages kept the ball club honest and scrappy.

"Watch it! Watch it!"
"Some help!"
"FUCKEN shit!"
"C two! C two!"
"On your left! Your left!"
"Bump here!"

Silky Sims and Larry Graham were almost an even match-up. They went at one another like fighters in an alley. Both had tremendous reservoirs of raw talent and unrefined energy, but Larry had the edge in experience. Larry was also bigger and stronger, and he used his body better. If he could catch Silky, Larry could usually control him. Most of the time Silky was able to beat Larry downcourt, but he was dragging this morning. Silky's nose was still sore from the cocaine he had snorted last night. Larry was embarrassing him and Silky's frustration was building up to something nasty. Now Larry was snatching a rebound out of Silky's hands, and stuffing it through the basket. Silky retaliated with an angry elbow that grazed Larry's ribs.

"Take it easy!" Wayne shouted. "Don't get *nervous* out there." . . .

"By yourself!"

"S four! S four!"

"You, Doggie!"

"Philly stack!"

"Me!"

As the players went through the scrimmage, Buddy Patella came bobbing up the ramp. Buddy was a fragile looking man and his nose was as sharp and thin as a blade on a weather vane. Several long strands of hair were secured across the top of Buddy's otherwise bald pate with Stick 'Em. The only color in Buddy's wan face came from his perpetual five o'clock shadow. He wore white tennis shoes, white pants and a blue cotton sport shirt that was open at the neck. The arms that protruded from the short sleeves were thin and knobbed at the elbows. But Buddy's hands were surprisingly large for someone of his slight physique.

Buddy had been the trainer for the New York Jets until five years ago when he'd decided to "retire" and work for a basketball team. An old-fashioned trainer whose idea of modern techniques extended only to whirlpool baths and Ace bandages, Buddy's most prized possession was an ancient red-stained popsicle stick that he used to reset broken noses. But Buddy's hands could poke and probe an injured limb and detect cartilage and ligament damage that no X-rays could ever reveal. And Buddy's powerful hands gave the best rubdown anywhere this side of a massage parlor. In fact, Buddy's hands were so strong that Quince once offered the possibility that he could palm his own head and lift himself right up off the ground.

Buddy had a copy of the *Dispatch* tucked under his arm as he ambled over to the scorer's table and sat down beside Wayne.

"Where's Reed?" Wayne asked.

"He's down there inna whirlpole," Buddy said through a stuffed cigar holder. "He says his ankle's saw."

"Goddamn," Wayne fumed. "Fucken prima donna."

"Well"—Buddy shrugged—"I can't say for sure and I wouldn't want you to quote me, but I heard Graham sayin' last week that Reed was still peed at you 'cause Brooksie is startin' and he ain't gonna put out for you 'cause you screwed him but good and you're takin' the food outta his mouth. Leastways, that's what I heard."

Wayne slowly shook his head with disgust.

"Comin' down!"

"Blue stack!"

"Get OFFA me, motherfucker!"

Silky was taking a hurried turnaround jump shot from his favorite spot along the left base line when Larry caught up with him just in time to whack him loudly across the forearm. The noise resounded through the empty amphitheater, and the ball popped harmlessly into the air. The players froze and turned to Wayne.

"Play ball!" Wayne said with a tight grin.

Wayne liked to have his players beat on each other every once in a while. They were forever bitching about the officials anyway, complaining that the refs never let them "play their game." Free-for-all scrimmages kept them hostile, helped maintain an edge of intensity. Just another one of Wayne's innovations he'd brought with him from Savannah State.

The players were quick to adjust their play.

"God DAMN!"

59

"C four!"
"Get that shit OUTTA here!"

Wayne bummed a cigarette from Buddy and furtively eyed the trainer's newspaper. The dead whistle had still another advantage—it gave Wayne the chance to look at Murray Klurman's story in the *Dispatch*.

"Through! Through!"
"Blue C!"
"One more time, motherfucker, and it's you and me!"
"A piece!"

Wayne skimmed through Klurman's deadpan account of the ball game, then came to a paragraph that demanded his undivided attention:

> It looks like Silky Sims is finally settling down and coming into his own. Sims seems to have outgrown his notorious rookie tomfoolery of last season. There's no question that Sims' basketball future is getting brighter every day in every way. Sims credits his added "experience" for much of his improved play. But that's only part of the story. A great deal of the credit has to shine on New York's rookie coach, Wayne Smalley. It was the personable Smalley who rescued Sims from the ghettos of Trenton and guided him to All-Americanhood at tiny Savannah State. It is also Wayne Smalley whose considerable coaching skills are now helping Sims to shape his own illimitable destiny as a pro. Depending on whether or not the Stars shine in postseason play, Smalley has to be one of the

> early candidates for Coach of the Year
> honors. Even with the hardship of Reed
> Carson's nagging ankle . . .

Buddy's sharp nudge summoned Wayne's attention back to the scrimmage. Silky and Larry were about to square off. Wayne immediately blew the whistle.

"Knock it off!" he screamed. "What the fuck you think this is, a fucken roller derby? Go 'head, white ball out."

Wayne handed the newspaper back to Buddy, but his head remained in outer space.

FUCKEN COACH OF THE FUCKEN YEAR!! OKAY!!

Followed by the sweet memory, one more time, of "SMALL-LEE! SMALL-LEE!"

The blue team was winning by only 9-7 when Tyrone suddenly came to life. Silky had been casually bringing the ball upcourt when Tyrone appeared from the blind side, poked the ball free, chased down the loose ball and scored an uncontested lay-up. The blue team bounced off the court while the losers, the white team, prepared to run their suicides.

The white team spread out along the Eighth Avenue base line, and waited. Then Wayne tooted his whistle and they began sprinting full-speed down the floor. Wayne blew it again when they reached the far foul line and they instantly reversed direction. They slowed now to three-quarter speed but they were all straining. Wayne blew the whistle and they changed direction once more.

Sometimes Wayne let them take only two or three strides before sending them upcourt again. Other times he waited until the lead man was almost back to the starting line. But each time Wayne ran the team through suicides he had to fight the impulse to blow the whistle only once. Theoretically the players would then keep running and running, until they crashed into the seats behind the far basket. There was no set limit about how long each suicide had to last, but there were films to be shown so Wayne let them run all five in just under three minutes, then instructed the full team to shoot their daily quota of fifty foul shots.

He also called Silky over to the sideline.

Silky's lanky muscles were still trembling as he approached the scorer's table. His eyes were sullen under hooded lids. His jersey was plastered against his chest. Even his sneakers were soaked through. A rancid odor was misting up from Silky's bare shoulders.

"There's no call for all that Bogart stuff," Wayne told him. His tone took both of them by surprise. "I thought you were finished with that shit."

"Yeah," said Silky. He couldn't keep his feet still. They tapped incessantly on the floor with a life of their own. "That fucken cat was all over me, man! You had the whistle in your mouth . . . sheyit, you're supposed to blow it, not *suck* it."

"Don't give me that," Wayne snapped. "You know what's going down. We used to do the same thing at Savannah. I don't call fouls, that's all. It's no big deal. It's just a psych. You know that."

"Yeah," said Silky. His feet froze and his eyes drew back into his head. "I know more than you think."

"What's that supposed to mean?"

"Nothin'." Silky said. "It don't mean nothin', Mr. Small-lee."

They both stared nervously at one another. Silky looked away first.

"Silkee . . ." Wayne said in a suddenly paternal, confidential tone, "what am I gonna do with you? Listen to me, man. It's just like it was at SSU. You're the heart and soul of the team. Everybody knows that. We go as far as you take us. You're everybody's main man, Silky. So you've got to set an example out there. You've got to be the leader. I'm hip that everybody's got a right to blow his cool once in a while. But you've got a bad history up here. Right? You've got to be very righteous."

"Yeah," Silky said. But a cautious anger was once again stoking his eyes. "Just tell me one thing, Wayne. How come you always cuss me out in front of everybody? That ain't righteous, man. That ain't *shit*."

"But didn't it work? Didn't you make the shot?"

Silky flexed his shoulders.

"All right," Wayne insisted. "Maybe it got you just riled up enough to give you that extra push. That extra little edge, you know? Shit, Silky, how long we been traveling together? I used to do the same thing back down at Savannah, right? And it worked then too, Didn't it?"

Silky remembered all the jive dinners with Wayne and his lady. He remembered last night and all the pussy. And he remembered the fans calling his name. SILL-KEE! SILL-KEE!

"Yeah," Silky said slowly. "But this ain't Savannah no more. This is New York City, you dig? The Big Apple. And I ain't no street nigger no more. I'm a superstar, Wayne! Man, I'm a fucken superstar." He said it quietly this time. With the intensity of conviction.

They stared at each other in silence.

"Go and shoot your foul shots," Wayne said, cold as ice.

# CHAPTER SIX

THE NEW York Stars floated through the crowded airport like a school of stately clipper ships sailing off to battle. In their wake they left a flotsam of greedy eyes, pointed fingers and whispered adulation. Most of the ballplayers had their faces locked into imperial masks. They were too busy digging their own fantasies to take notice of the commotion produced by their fleeting presence. Besides, as professional athletes they were well-accustomed to worshipful glances tracking their every move. Buddy Patella and Red Pumas buzzed unnoticed around the caravan, Buddy handing out the chewing gum and plane tickets, confirming reservations and arranging for ground transportation; Red Pumas shepherding the equipment trunk.

Dave Brooks trailed the pack by a good hundred yards, having paused to call Nancy as soon as the team got off their chartered bus. For a second goodbye and the sound of her kissing him over the telephone. Her voice made him feel warm and connected.

Dave knew flight #734 to Salt Lake City would depart at three-fifteen from Gate 29, so he could take time for the call and walk there by himself. There were risks, though—being separated made Dave more vulnerable to an autograph assault. In fact several passersby did turn and inspect him with momentary interest, but Dave's absurd marshmallow parka threw most of them off the trail.

The team was in his sight at the passenger gate when a hefty kid with glasses spotted Dave from behind. The kid, only about twelve years old but still in need of a shave, caught up to him and began riffling through an enormous NBA Players Guide. He also had a fancy leather-bound autograph book hanging from a piece of clothesline around his neck. Dave maintained an even pace while his chunky companion wheezed alongside, desperately flicking the pages of his book. Dave now gradually quickened his pace.

"Who are you?" the kid demanded as he ran to keep up. "Are you somebody?"

"No," Dave said. He walked even faster and the fat kid coughed and slowed down.

"Naw," the kid said. "You ain't nobody. You ain't got no suit bag. You can't fool me."

The kid suddenly speeded up and chased Dave through the X-ray checkpoint.

"You're a nobody, mister," the kid screamed. "You're a nobody that nobody ever heard of. When you die there ain't gonna be nobody at your funeral."

His teammates were already seated by the time Dave entered the plane. He wandered down the aisle, then paused above the vacant seat beside Reed, who was sitting at attention with his seat belt fastened. Reed looked up and smiled.

"It's the takeoff that's the most dangerous part," Reed explained.

Dave accepted the invitation and sat himself down. Reed immediately buried his face in the *Dispatch's* sports section. Dave also remained silent. The fat kid had upset him. Dave was being accosted by an increasing number of weirdo fans lately. The more the media began to rattle about a New York-Los Angeles showdown, the less privacy Dave had in public places. He also hated to leave Nancy, he ached to be with her. Still, he was glad to get out of New York.

Neither of the roommates spoke until the plane was airborne. "We made it," Reed said, then reached over and plugged his earphones into the console beneath his seat. Reed hated flying and always stayed glued to his seat during every flight the ball club made. He never watched the movie, he never ate the packaged food and he never even went to the bathroom. He just sat motionless and let the tinny music run through his head like an electric current. Noise was always soothing to Reed.

"Reed?" Dave finally asked. "Are you up?" It was a silly question. Reed was always up.

"Yeah, I'm awake. What's the matter?"

"I've been thinking . . . maybe it's a good idea if we took separate rooms for this trip. What do you think?"

Reed bolted up in his seat and popped the plugs out of his ears. "Why? What's wrong? What'd I do?"

Reed's defensive aggression instantly shrank Dave's resolve. "It's nothing. I just have a slight cold and I figured maybe you'd want some privacy . . . you know, to rest up your ankle. Hey, forget it, it was just a crazy idea."

Reed's hostility evaporated as rapidly as it had condensed. "Yeah," he said. "Maybe we should. All that Salt Lake pussy, hunh? Maybe I do need some privacy. All right. Let's split the cost."

"Right," Dave said.

Reed chuckled, leaned back and reconnected his brain with the Muzak machine.

The Salt Lake City franchise had turned into one of the NBA's most successful ventures. As a member of the American Basketball Association the Utah Stars had gone under in 1975. But the ball club had been reborn two years later in the aftermath of an incident that precipitated the collapse of the entire ABA.

For years the ABA had tried to get a television contract and CBS finally had been persuaded to broadcast the 1977 championship series between the Indiana Pacers and the Kentucky Colonels. But only one of the games ever made it to the screen. The opening contest was played in Lexington, and it was a close game all the way. Then one of the Pacers, Bahimba 10X, was called for charging. It was a pivotal call, and the replay also showed it to be a blocking foul on one of the hometown Colonels. In the following argument 10X collected seven technical fouls and was expelled from the game. 10X went berserk, and to the Kentucky fans' delight proceeded to beat up both officials and then both coaches. But a bloody riot ensued when 10X went into the stands after the venerable Adolph Rupp.

Two weeks after the debacle the NBA absorbed the Denver, San Antonio and Indiana franchises. The league also announced that the New York Knicks would merge with the New York Nets to form the "New York Stars." This move was widely interpreted as being a ruse to add Julius Erving to the Knick roster. The Nets ownership was permitted to buy twenty-five per cent of the new ball club and millions of dollars in corporate taxes were saved in the shuffle. The additional Home Box Office revenue on Long Island alone brought in ten million a season until Dr. J.'s knees gave out two years later. The "Stars," however, were still committed to play a token number of games in the Nassau Coliseum every season. The remainder of the defunct ABA's player personnel was collected into a revived Salt Lake City franchise, with more tax benefits accruing to the Utes' owners. . . .

A pretty blonde stewardess suddenly appeared to lean over Dave and flash him a vocational wink.

"Would you care for a pillow, sir? Or a soft drink?"

"No, thank you," Dave said, but he noted that a pin on her blouse identified her as "Denise Smyth." She winked again.

"Please let me know if there's anything I can do to make you comfortable, sir."

"Thank you," Dave repeated, and this time he even flushed a little. You can take the boy out of Michigan, but . . .

Denise next turned to minister to an old lady sitting directly across the aisle, bending over to fluff up the woman's pillow, and to show Dave a pair of baby blue ruffled panties. Dave closed his eyes and made believe he was asleep. It wasn't easy.

# CHAPTER SEVEN

THE MOUNTAINS that ringed the Salt Lake valley were the same shade of steel-blue as the sky overhead. The range was part of the Rockies; each mountain was still young, raw and bursting with kinetic energy. Their silver peaks shivered and dazzled in the sharp winter sunshine.

Murray Klurman stood on a traffic ramp in the middle of the airport. All the honking, fuming and bustling almost made Murray feel like he was back in New York. He rested his suitcase now on the sidewalk near the curb while he waited impatiently at an empty taxi stand, unaware of the spectacular scenery. Had he noticed the mountains, Murray would have imagined them to be plywood props erected by the Salt Lake City Chamber of Commerce. The only mountains that Murray knew were the well-worn, swaybacked Catskills.

There wasn't a cab in sight. Murray sighed and continued his vigil. He could hardly believe it. A taxi stand without a taxi.

"Rubes," Murray intoned through his nose. "Bunch of rubes."

Four huge limousines roared by on their way to the exit ramp. The procession contained the official New York Stars delegation, heading for the same hotel at which Murray was staying.

"Sure," Murray told himself. "And I can't even smell a cab!"

Murray knew better than to accept a ride into town with the team. It would be too obvious, and somebody was bound to get wise. Especially since John Burrows from the *Times,* and whoever the *News* sent, would undoubtedly be taking cabs. Probably the same one. But Murray liked making his way around strange cities by himself. The hassle was sometimes great enough to convince Murray that he was beholden to no one. There was another reason why Murray avoided the team limousines: he just wasn't particularly fond of professional athletes. Murray believed they were animals. Every single one of them. Murray knew it was the sportswriters who made them all rich and turned them into heroes. Most all of the interesting anecdotes and personality angles were fiction. Nobody believed any of it, except the fans and, of course, the players themselves. The beat men and the magazine puffers were more interested in good copy than the truth. But Murray cared about his craft. Murray believed that what went on inside his head was more amusing than what other people actually did or said. If a phony item made an athlete look good, then the player would be quick to acknowledge its authenticity. Like the bit Murray once wrote about Quinton Brown's visiting an orphans' hospital on Christmas Day. Quinton was actually famous for his hatred of children; the story was patently ridiculous, but Murray had needed some quick filler for a short column. Now, every year since then, Quinton was showered with humanitarian awards by boys' clubs, CYO's,

YMCA's and the like. Murray felt it was fair compensation. After all, whenever Murray happened to report something a player said that made him look bad, the player would swear that Murray was a liar. Even if Murray had the exact words on tape.

Sports reporting was a game of sleight-of-hand. Most athletes were either elusive lost souls who believed their own press clippings, or redneck jocks, or Mr. Cools. What was left of their heads revolved around their bodies. They lived inside of tiny rectangular shapes. Whistles shaped their instincts and they ran around in their underwear in front of millions of people. Basketball players had no caps, face masks, or shoulder pads to hide behind. They were monsters: too rich, too tall and too graceful. Murray was convinced he hated them.

Still, Murray was the first to admit that covering the Stars was a pretty good job. He'd certainly had his fill of all the other sports when he first broke into the business. For two very long apprentice years Murray was the basketball, football, hockey and baseball swingman for the *Dispatch*. Then one Christmas Eve fifteen years ago old Sid Schollander had a fatal heart attack while Murray was out covering his beat. New York was playing up in Boston and they won the ball game on Dick Barnett's shot at the buzzer. Murray turned in a sensational story and the basketball job had been his ever since. One week after he took over, Murray received a New Year's card from the Stars' front office. The greeting also contained an American Express card made out to "Murray Klurman." Over the years Murray never saw a bill, and never asked any questions.

Even Murray had to admit he had a good job. All he had to do was convince his ulcer. . . .

Murray paced up and down the sidewalk for another

ten minutes before a taxi finally came up to the stand. The driver had an ashen complexion and a sawed-off nose. Murray knew right away he was a Mormon.

"The Plaza," Murray commanded as he tossed his suitcase into the back seat, eased himself inside, and proceeded to stare blankly out of the window as the cab sped toward the city. The highway landscape seemed the same in every city in the league: clapboard houses separated by service stations and rapid-fire food chains; clothing hung out on lines; gritty lawns; shopping plazas and mammoth malls. Murray sighed.

Parochial nostalgia gave way to remembrance that he had no deadline to fret over today. His next story wasn't due until the stroke of midnight after the Stars-Utes game. Tomorrow's *Dispatch* was carrying an all-purpose mini-feature on Kevin Harmon that he'd written weeks ago. The article would claim that Kevin was a "hardworking and rapidly improving ballplayer." The truth was that Kevin was as slow as a slug, and almost as obtuse. The kid could jump and rebound but he could only move quickly in a straight line. The Kevin Harmon disaster had New York carrying the heavy end of a one million dollar, three year, no-cut contract. Kevin would love the article. So would Wayne Smalley and general manager Joe Cunningham.

Any other club in the league would have been raked by the local press for squandering a precious number-one draft pick. But the Stars were the only competitive pro team in New York. In recent years the Giants, Jets, Mets and Yankees (despite a flare-up of success in 1976) were all chronic losers. True, since the Rangers had come under the Hudson Bay Company's umbrella, their fortunes were on the upswing. And the Islanders had finished in the play-offs for five straight years. But the

Rangers and the Islanders were hockey teams. Nobody but their aboriginal fans cared what hockey players did to each other. So the Stars games provided the only sports glamor in town, and press credentials were most hard to come by. Murray didn't know what kind of arrangements the Stars had made with the rest of the media folk, and he didn't much care. He had his, which was, after all, the name of the game.

Murray's little essay on Kevin Harmon would explore the unusual quantities of milk, orange juice, megavitamins and bone meal pills that the young man daily consumed. It would investigate the weight-lifting program he religiously followed. And the picture running with the column would show Kevin palming his pet Great Dane. The concluding couplet: "Kevin Harmon certainly has a future. It's only a matter of time." . . .

The taxi rumbled along Freeman Boulevard, one of Salt Lake City's characteristically expansive streets. The avenues had originally been constructed to allow a wagon drawn by a team of oxen to navigate a U-turn anywhere in town, but the city's rapidly changing traffic lights now made crossing a street hazardous for its senior citizens.

The cab driver made a right turn through Temple Square, a busy intersection bounded by the famous Mormon Tabernacle, a municipal office building, the Zion's National Bank and a department store. In the middle of the square stood a gigantic statue of Brigham Young, Salt Lake City's founder and spiritual leader. The bronze statue was positioned so that Brigham Young's back was turned toward the Temple and his open hand was outstretched toward the bank.

Murray appreciated the gesture. This Mickey Mouse sportswriting racket was okay but it was only temporary. Murray Klurman knew he was an artist at heart. It had always been Murray's dream to be a famous novelist, even when he was a snot-nosed journalism major back at Northwestern University, and he'd actually been working on a novel for the past few years. He was going to call it *Cast Not a Shadow,* the best of everything he'd known or thought in his life, bound to be a best seller. The composition of the first line had taken almost two months: "It was a darkling and stormy nite."

As soon as he tried out the soft bed in his hotel room Dave decided to take a nap. He quickly undressed, dove under the covers and let his hands glide over his washboard stomach and muscular torso. During the season a professional basketball player was forced to take notice of every strain, every twinge and every aching muscle, and now Dave pulled the covers up to his chin and began kneading the lingering Charley Horse in his right thigh. He also squeezed his genitals and suddenly felt guilty, alienated. His head was a muddle, and his soul pulsed with prohibited desires.

He was glad Reed was willing to take a separate room. He needed time to think, to take inventory. He found it difficult to concentrate on anything internal in the off-court presence of one of his teammates. Mostly they seemed to gabble at one another like they were being interviewed on television. Without exception, they made him feel uncomfortable.

In fact, the Stars were artificially bound together with a gaudy ribbon of fraternity. All the corners of everybody's idiosyncrasies, resentments, competitive drives and jealousies were securely circumscribed and rendered impotent. As professional athletes they were continually competing with each other for playing time, money, media exposure and, in some cases, women.

Without their spurious sodality they would have soon been at one another's throats.

"Brotherhood" also insured a common frame of reference. Conversation was limited to basketball, parties, chicks, what a shit the coach (any coach) was, and the athletic/fiduciary superiority of their own alma maters. The Stars also whispered about drugs and money, but any other subject was an unlisted number. Each player lived in his own sphere of influence, and his teammates knew almost exactly where the boundary lines were laid. If Tyrone held court at Toots Shor's, Quinton had squatter's rights at Harry O's. The only time they all shared the same off-court geography was when they were compelled to make appearances at public relations gatherings. And the only time the team hung together in any real sense off-court was when they traveled—nobody had any turf rights on the road.

Because Dave felt a need to socialize with his teammates, the transition into the pro game was a difficult one for him. Dave always performed better on a closely knit ball club. At one time he thought there might be a link between himself and Silky. Savannah State was a small school and Silky was the only other Star to have escaped the undergraduate basketball extravaganza. But Dave soon discovered that Silky was devoted to making up for lost time, lost glory. . . .

Dave was too brain-weary to plumb his soul. Instead he absently rubbed his sore thigh and fell asleep, dreaming that the baby was a boy. And that Nancy was thin and sexy again.

Reed switched on the television set the moment he entered his hotel room. He really didn't care what was on but he was partial to situation comedies. The canned laughter seemed to justify his paranoia. If it was up to Reed, the tv could have stayed on twenty-four hours a day. Even when nobody was in the room.

Reed's ankle was tingling. He decided to take a short nap before checking out the lobby.

Murray found his own way up to his room and tossed his suitcase on the bed. His cologne, mouthwash, hairbrush and hairspray were the last things he had packed. He made a ten minute pit stop in the bathroom, then hit the lobby.

"Look out Salt Lake City," he murmured as he stepped inside a vacant elevator. "Here comes Murray the K!"

The hotel lobby was neatly decorated with furniture made entirely of black plastic wrapped around gleaming chrome bars. The floor was carpeted in a pale blue. It was a chilly-looking place, but it was also the only game in town.

The room was swarming with about two dozen females. There was a group of coeds from the nearby state university and a couple of high school pom-pom girls. There was an off-duty cocktail waitress, several bored housewives, an aspiring Hollywood starlet and three black hookers. The rest of the crowd was made up of bar floozies, secretaries, librarians and schoolteachers. All the ladies were eyeing three members of the New York Stars: Larry Graham, Jeremy Johnson and Silky Sims, whose suitcases and suit bags were clumped on the floor near the front desk.

Larry was sniffing after a pom-pom. She looked to be about seventeen. He stood in an athletic slouch, his mink coat draped around his shoulders. The girl's eyes were open wide, and her head was already nodding.

Off to the left, Jeremy was applying charm to a snub-nosed divorcee in a white uniform. As he hovered over her, he pressed his cock into her ribs, then craned his neck to spy out the shape of her ass and upper thighs.

"Tough enough," he said. "Lookin' all right. What you do here, baby?"

"I'm a cocktail waitress," the blonde said. "And I'm waiting on you."

There was a stolid leather couch off to one side of the room, partially hidden by a potted palm. Murray Klurman slid inconspicuously around the edge of the crowd, then let himself drop into the middle of the ancient sofa. He barely had time to settle himself when he looked up to see Silky backing a freckled redhead right up into the other side of the palm tree. Murray ducked his head back.

"Yeah, mama," Silky was saying. "You the baddest looking fox in sight."

"What's that mean?" The girl's face broke into a flush. "What's that? Some kind of ghetto talk? It sounds funny. Nobody out here ever talks like that."

"Is that a fac'?" Silky said. "But, c'mon, tell me now. What do people out here talk like? Lemme hear some of your local jive. C'mon. Let's hear." Silky put his hands on the girl's shoulders.

"Well,"—the girl started to fidget with her fingers— "I guess we talk the same as you. But it just doesn't sound the same. I don't know. Maybe I shouldna come here."

Silky laughed lightly. "But you're here, ain't you,

red? So c'mon and tell me. Tell me what kind of thing all a you talk about."

"Well. We talk mostly about school, about parties, about—"

"I'll bet you talk about other things too, red. Let me guess. How about talking about boogying with all the brothers? Ha! Yeah! Now don't you be blasé with me, red. You know my name, girl?"

"Sure," the girl said boldly. "Everybody knows you're Silky Sims." She looked up at him and suddenly burst into a mischievous giggle. "How come they call you that?"

Sims put his arm around her and started leading her to the elevators. "It's a long story," he said.

Murray shook his head. Animals. Rapists. He'd bet anything that old-timers like Bobby Wanzer or Slater Martin never acted like that. But these guys today, they were pituitary freaks. Maybe it was the bomb. Murray leaned back and wondered what ever happened to Bob Kurland.

The crowd seemed to be flowing into the bar. As it thinned out some, Murray could make out Dave Brooks standing in front of the magazine rack.

Dave had dozed for a while, but had been too restless to sleep. He was thumbing through a copy of *Sports Illustrated* as a young girl of perhaps fifteen tiptoed up behind him and stood poised for a moment in back of him. Murray noted her young breasts pushing their way through her tight black sweater. Wouldn't mind making off with a nice little piece like that himself. . . .

"Hi ya, Dave," the girl said cheerfully.

"Hello," Dave said. Without missing a word of the story he was scanning, he set his hands in autograph position. But the girl offered nothing to sign.

"What're you doing tonight?" the girl asked.

Dave looked up sharply. "What's your name?"

"Elizabeth."

Dave's face suddenly crisped. "How old are you?"

"Seventeen, what's the big—"

"Bull," Dave said. "What the hell are you doing here?"

Elizabeth looked at him with her overaged fourteen-year-old eyes. "I'm not doing nothing, I'm just looking for a little—"

"For a little trouble," Dave snapped. "Now you get on home, little Miss Elizabeth. You hear me? And if I ever catch you in here messing with ballplayers again I'll whip your hide and call your momma to come fetch you. . . . "

Elizabeth stared at him, finally shrugged, turned and made her way out the front door and into the street. A supersquare, she decided. Not to be believed. Screw him, she'd hit the action later.


Murray stood up and stretched his arms. He was suddenly very glad he was still a bachelor. He fought back a yawn. The time lag was making him drowsy. He glanced at his watch. Too late to take a nap. Only one thing left to do.

On his way to the Zebra Lounge, Murray saw Dave vanish into an elevator. Nice kid, Murray told himself. Good ballplayer too. But too quiet for his own good. And bad copy. Dull. Never says more than he has to. Sounds like a mama's boy too. Then Murray's ulcer belched.

"Guts," Murray said. "Gotta have guts."

"What's that, Mr. Klurman?"

"Hunh? Oh. Nothing. Ummm. Let me have a Scotch and water, will ya?"

# CHAPTER EIGHT

DAVE BROOKS was lounging on his bed and reading a magazine when room service knocked at the door with dinner.

"Come in," Dave called out.

The bellhop opened the door and strode into the room bearing a tray balanced on one hand. The youngster nervously placed the tray on the dresser and handed Dave the bill. His duty done, the bellhop's face collapsed into an embarrassed mess. He was too intimidated to talk but he pulled out his high school autograph book and silently handed it to Dave. There was a ballpoint pen attached to the spine of the book with a piece of blue ribbon.

"What's your name?" Dave asked.

"Matthew," the boy whispered.

Dave wrote out a personal greeting before signing his name, then added on a two dollar tip to the bottom of the bill.

"You a ballplayer, Matthew?"

The bellhop shook his head and hurried out of the room.

Dave liked that.

He carried his dinner over to the bed and began to peck at his salad. He was tired, and he needed more than food to revive him. He glanced at his traveler's alarm clock. It was almost nine-thirty back in New York. Nancy would be curled up on the couch in her bathrobe, doing the *Times* crossword puzzle. The record player would be spinning out a cushion of music. James Taylor. Or maybe the new Carole King album. Dave hated traveling.

On the spur of his melancholy, he decided to call her. It was an hour earlier than usual; well, her surprise would sweeten his mood.

Just to make sure it wasn't a wrong number or a computer malfunction Nancy let the telephone ring three times but she knew it was Dave after the second ring.

"Hi, babes," Nancy said with a tease in her voice.

"Nancy. How did you know it was me?"

"Can't imagine. How was the flight? How are you feeling?"

"You first."

"Oh, pretty good. I had some back pains for a while but they're just about gone now. I was just relaxing. I miss you, Dave . . . How was the workout this morning?"

"Not too bad. Except the films were a drag. For a change. It's a crazy scene. The lights are out and Wayne's up there talking a mile a minute and half the guys are nodding out. But I'll tell you, Wayne sure does know what he's talking about. It's amazing. He can take apart a ball game like a surgeon. He knows everything that happens out there and he's a real good teacher. Trouble is, it just doesn't come out right. You know? All he does is talk numbers and jive. Nobody really *listens* to him."

"Except you," Nancy said with another tease stretching out her voice. "You sound tired, didn't you get any sleep on the plane?"

"I couldn't even tell," Dave said. "I think so. Maybe I dreamed I was sitting in an airplane. Oh . . . Reed and I decided to take separate rooms so I'm by myself. That's why I'm eating dinner up here. It's too nuts downstairs, everybody's prowling around. I went down for a magazine and I've been inside the room ever since."

"What are you eating?"

"Chef's salad plate, real exciting stuff. Part of the glamorous life of a professional ballplayer . . . Jesus, I miss you, Nancy. It gets harder and harder to be away. I get scared sometimes. . . ."

"Shh, why don't you sack out early tonight?"

"I'm going to. I'll watch the news, catch the scores and then conk out."

"Max stopped in to see if he could do anything. He even wanted to do a whole load of shopping. He's really sweet. And there haven't been any kids hanging around. It's been a good quiet day."

"I wish I was there with you," Dave said. "Oh, yeah. I sort of had a talk with Wayne today."

"What do you mean 'sort of'?"

"Well, he buttonhooked me on the elevator."

"What'd he say?"

"Oh, nothing, just some stupid thing about me taking a shower before his speech last night after the game. You know how he loves to play Knute Rockne? Nothing to worry about. So everything's under control, hunh? Hey. Tell me something, you criminal. You use your dictionary on the crossword puzzle yet."

"Absolutely. I await your sentence."

"Yeah. Listen, I love you, Nancy."

"I love you too. But this is ridiculous. We're trying to cut down, remember? You won't be a famous and fabulously wealthy basketball star all your life. Call me tomorrow after the game."

"Right. 'Bye, honey. I love you."

"'Bye, Dave. Love you too."

Dave kissed the receiver as he hung up the phone, then lay back and closed his eyes.

Hail the conquering hero.

Wayne Smalley had been in the elevator with the blonde stewardess Denise Smyth, a fine looking specimen even in civvies. Wayne was smiling, ear to ear. He'd lectured Dave for five floors, all about "insubordination" and "setting an example" and "respect . . . " He savored the memory: Dave stepping out of the elevator, Wayne pushing the hold button and staring at him, straight in the eyes. "Better watch your step, this is my ball club now and I won't tolerate . . . insolence."

Dave Brooks, nice guy. No question, they'll kill you every time. Given half a chance. No chance, then, Wayne Smalley decided.

# CHAPTER NINE

SILKY ALWAYS felt uncomfortable inside the visitors' dressing room at the Salt Palace. Everything was too neat, too antiseptic, too starkly functional. The floors were covered with a fibrous gray carpet, the metal lockers were an institutional green. The place reminded Silky of the reform school where he'd lived when he was thirteen (sent there when he slugged a junior high school shop teacher who'd made fun of his plaited hair).

Despite the unpleasant associations Silky was the first player into the room. He undressed quickly and hung his clothes on padded wooden hangers he always brought along on road trips. He sat down and carefully pulled his away uniform out of his Adidas bag—the jersey was royal blue with white lettering and red trim. Silky ran his hand over the raised numeral on the back; lucky seven was the only number Silky'd ever worn. . . .

Before Silky had joined the Stars, the number seven belonged to Dave Brooks, but Silky refused to sign any contract that failed to guarantee him his favorite number. The Garden's front office was thrown into a panic. A hassle was avoided, however, when Dave simply agreed to wear another number. Silky was appeased but confused—he could never understand how any player could be so cavalier about his number.

Number seven fit Silky perfectly. It was sleek and smooth, with a little razor hook at the end.

The result of another subclause in Silky's contract was revealed on the back of his jersey. White script letters traced out the word "Silky." Except for Quinton Brown's famous "Q," the rest of the team carried their last names on their backs. New York's logo was written across the front of the uniform: "S-T-☆-R-S." Silky pulled the jersey as taut as he could, then bent over and fastened the pearl snaps under the crotch. . . . His custom-made uniforms were also fine-printed in his contract. . . . He walked over now to the other side of the room and studied himself in a full-length mirror. He loved the way he looked in his uniform: smooth as glass, sharp as steel. A black diamond.

As the rest of the team arrived they exchanged a few moments of festive greeting, but the dressing room soon settled into silence. There was another game, another trial by blood. Private lives were to be temporarily swallowed, forgotten. For the next two and one half hours the players' lives would be recorded on instant replay. For some of them preparing for a game was a monumental effort. Dave Brooks had his chair turned to his locker; he sat motionless, hypnotized by the pungent darkness within. Ardell Bartholomew was similarly huddled before his locker, silently ranting over his Bible. Jack Mathias sat as an angry statue, clenching and unclenching his massive hands. Kevin Harmon was memorizing the layout of his cuticles. Reed Carson was doing the "Word Jumble" in the local newspaper. Tyrone White pored over the sports section. Even Jeremy Johnson and Larry Graham were subdued. Now was not the time to interfere with other people's privacy.

Quinton Brown was the only player who was totally relaxed. Quinton had been in the league for twelve years and could avoid turning on his game schizophrenia until the opening center jump. At thirty-seven Quinton was the oldest active player in the NBA. . . .

When he was eighteen years old Quinton Brown was the most sought after schoolboy All-American of his time. Quinton played for Aviation Trades High School in North Philadelphia and led his team to consecutive state championships in his junior and senior years. He averaged 53.1 points a game in his senior season and at least doubled every high school scoring record on the books. With his bustling, hooking moves Quinton could even drive against zone defenses. Players seven and eight inches taller couldn't block his shots. An article in *Sport* magazine called Quinton "the best roly-poly, stop-and-go, bump-and-pump basketball player the game has ever seen." During his high school career Quinton averaged almost twenty-five free throws a game. He threatened to revolutionize the sport.

Virtually every college in the country tried to recruit him. From the middle of his junior year Quinton was besieged with letters, telegrams, phone calls, personal visits from coaches and dinner invitations from wealthy alumni. Quinton once came home from a ball game to find the legendary recruiter Swifty Frizzell hiding under his bed. Everybody wanted Quinton: UCLA, Indiana, Maryland, Kentucky, St. John's, North Carolina, Marquette, North Carolina State, Notre Dame, Arizona State. Quinton even got a letter from a correspondence school in Jackson

Hole, Wyoming. He was showered with promises of money, women, cars and drugs. Three colleges told Quinton he could name his own coach. The competition was frenetic, and the basketball public eagerly awaited Quinton's decision.

Two days after his high school class was graduated Quinton startled America by choosing an obscure school in Albuquerque, New Mexico, called Southwestern University. Nobody could believe it. Southwestern did come across with good money and fancy fringe benefits, but Quinton certainly could have done better. Southwestern, however, offered free rides to all of the other starting members of Quinton's high school team. The idea of playing for four more years with his familiar supporting cast was irresistible to Quinton. So was the thought of taking a nowhere school and transforming it into a major basketball power.

After his first five games at Southwestern, Quinton was the collegiate superstar of the decade. In a game dominated by inaccessible giants, it was refreshing to see a relatively short player rule the college game. Quinton was also chubby and homely. He was the perfect underdog and basketball fans everywhere loved him. The public clamor to see Quinton play was so great that a Southwestern game was featured on national television at least once a week.

Quinton ended the first season leading the country in scoring with a mark of 49.4 points per game. He also set an all-time NCAA record by shooting 724 foul shots in just 31 games. At a home game against Michigan State he proceeded to foul out seven of the Spartan's ten man traveling squad. His teammates worked around Quinton like a bebop machine, and during their collective freshman season made it into the NCAA semi-finals.

Southwestern was beaten 78–75 by a Marquette team that eventually went on to win the NCAA championship, but Quinton scored 63 points. Nobody ever suspected that it would be Quinton's last ball game as a collegian.

The roof caved in a month after the season ended. It was announced that neither Quinton nor any of his playmates had ever graduated from Aviation Trades. An enterprising writer named Murray Klurman matched everybody's high school records against the transcripts that Southwestern had received, and reported that Quinton had actually possessed a higher points-per-game than classroom average. In lieu of a diploma Quinton had been awarded a "Certificate of Attendance." Southwestern was called upon to forfeit all of its victories and to return its full share of the NCAA play-off revenue. Quinton and his supporting cast were immediately expelled.

Not twenty-four hours after the scandal broke, there was more trouble. A car registered in Quinton's name was driven into a liquor store window in downtown Philadelphia by one of his perpetual teammates. The police also found a large brick of cocaine hidden in the trunk. Quinton, of course, had put up the front money for the purchase, but as soon as he got wind of the accident he called the local precinct and reported that his car had been stolen several hours earlier. Both the NBA and the ABA issued announcements to the effect that neither Quinton nor his teammates would be eligible for the draft until the criminal investigation was completed, whereupon Quinton immediately sued both leagues for restraint of trade. The Philadelphia district attorney found no evidence linking Quinton with the drugs and no indictment was issued. The collegiate draft was already completed by this time, so the courts declared Quinton a free agent. But the pros were still wary of him and only four teams were desperate enough to make him any offers. After much quibbling and another threatened law suit, Quinton finally signed a six-year no-cut with the floundering Detroit Pistons. Because of its extraordinary length and security, the pact was only worth $125,000 a year.

Quinton worked out to be a good pro but not an outstanding one. The pace of the game was simply too quick for him. He played in Detroit for five years and averaged just over twenty points a game. During that span the Pistons made the play-offs once and Quinton played in the All-Star game twice. He continued to score an enormous percentage of his total points from the foul line.

Even as a collegian, Quinton never took care of his body. He partied at the drop of a suggestion, he did far too much dope and he ate nothing but tuna fish, potato chips, soda pop and candy. Midway through his last season with the Pistons, Quinton was driving out to the hoop when his left knee suddenly popped out. The injury required extensive surgery. Afterward, the doctors told the Detroit brass that Quinton's career probably could be saved, though knees, as everybody knew, were tricky propositions. The brass considered, declared the operation a success, and two weeks later dealt Quinton to New York.

Quinton sat out the following season while his knee mended. He went barnstorming with the Harlem Globetrotters as soon as he received medical clearance. Three of Quinton's high school teammates were also with the Globies at the time (the fourth was still in jail). But Quinton somehow managed to get back into a reasonable facsimile of playing condition. Over the course of the subsequent NBA season Red Holzman, a man who used his head, turned Quinton into a specialist. Quinton played twenty minutes a game in batches of one and two minutes. He was a definite liability on defense, but Holzman used him whenever he wanted to hang another foul on a particular opposing player. It worked. Quinton had been a fixture with the Stars ever since. . . .

Even with his seniority, Quinton was wary of interrupting the pre-game stillness. Quinton, however, led the NBA in complaints as well as drawing fouls, and he now proceeded to fatten *that* percentage as he sidled his folding chair over next to Silky.

"My knee is killin' me, man," Quinton informed in a hoarse whisper. "It must be the altitude. Or the humidity. Or the fucken salt."

Silky nodded his sympathy but tried to keep his mind on the game. Silky had to concentrate on Kim Covington—six foot eight, 240 pounds, tough man. The last time they played the Utes, Covington had thoroughly embarrassed Silky. Silky would have to come out cutting and slashing. But Quinton had to be treated with respect. When Silky was a rookie it had been Quinton who introduced him to the lively ladies, the connections and the good time parties around the league. It never did anybody any harm to be on the right side of Quinton Brown.

"Yeah," Quinton said as he bent over to lace up his sneakers. "I'll tell you somethin'. It's been seven years since I hurt my knee, and the damn thing still hurts. Sometimes. But I'm still a lucky dude for sure."

"How you figure that?" Silky asked.

"Cause it didn't end my career, man. I still been drawing paychecks all this time. Plenty of other cats get instantly retired when they hurt their knees."

Silky got up and began to step nervously around his locker. He wondered where Wayne was. All of Quinton's talking was making him fidgety.

"As it was, man," Quinton continued, "I had to do rehabilitation stuff five times a week for a whole year. I had to lift weights and run in the park like a damn fool. It was a bitch, Jum! And I didn't even know if I could ever get it back together again. You dig? That was the main drain."

"That's you," Silky said with an edge on his voice. "Nothin' ever hurts me, man."

"I can dig it," Quinton said wearily. "A course I was always heavier than you. The doctor told me when I had the operation, he said it was the extra weight. But the cat also said it was the playgroun' that does it too. Runnin' on all that concrete give your legs a beatin'. He tol' me that all that time in the playgroun' gets you in the end. But the doc still said I was lucky."

"What you talkin' nonsense?" Silky snapped.

"Listen up, man. The thing the doc tol' me was I was lucky I wasn't never a jumper. I mean, even back in high school you couldn't barely slide a piece of paper between me and the floor. You dig? The doc said that jumpers get fucked up the worse. Ain' no lie. But you cool, Silk. Like you say, nothin' hurts. You still young and strong. You just got to be careful you don't break no leg fallin' offa no chick. You hear?"

Silky laughed in spite of himself. But all of Quinton's flap was too distracting. "I hear you," Silky said as he started for the trainer's room. "If I ever broke my leg, man, they'd have to shoot me."

Quinton echoed Silky's laughter. But Quinton knew Silky had it all wrong. They'd shoot Wayne.

# CHAPTER TEN

THE STARS had just made their appearance on the floor and the players were trotting through their warm-ups:

Jeremy Johnson's jump shot swished through the net. Wayne Smalley was a racist white pigfucker and Jeremy hated him. Bang! Another jay from twenty feet. So Jeremy had gotten stoned before the game. Pop! A turnaround from the base line. J.J. felt good. Good enough to go out there tonight and score thirty against those suckers. Swishshsh! Like a rush of air. The Utes were a shitty team. Bingo! From the coffin corner this time. He had gotten stoned just to spite Wayne Smalley. Bang! Off the back rim and in. Paleassmuthafucka! J.J. couldn't miss a shot if he tried. He knew he should be the starting center instead of that crazy man Jack Mathias. Rip! From the top of the key!

Wayne sat alone on the bench watching his players warm up. Wayne was particularly interested in seeing if any of them were screwing around. J.J. and Silky sometimes got it into their heads to shoot their foul shots left-

92

handed. Wayne was going to fine them if he caught them, but everything seemed to be cool. All of the players knew the game was on tv.

Wayne was also trying to spot any player whose shot happened to look unusually good. He was interested in seeing how loose Quinton's knee was, in discovering if Jack's shot was working, in trying to measure how much Tyrone's bad wrist was hurting him. Wayne, a very observant man, registered J.J.'s hot shooting immediately. He also didn't particularly like Jeremy's attitude, he planned on sitting the big seven-footer as long as possible.

While Wayne was overseeing the warm-ups Melvin Withers, the tv color man, came up and sat down beside him. Wayne's mouth drew back to uncover a gleaming array of perfect white teeth . . . he'd had them all capped right after he signed his contract with the Stars.

"Melvin!" Wayne beamed. "Good to see you, what's up?"

"You can do us a big favor," Withers said softly. "We had this local writer with a book to plug all set up for the half time interview, but his wife just called to say he's got the flu. We'd like to know if you could help us out."

"Sure, be glad to."

"Appreciate it," Withers said. "We'll need you a little early then." Withers stood up to leave.

"No sweat. Send somebody down to get me just before we go on. No trouble. Any time. Glad to . . . "

"Thanks, buddy. See you later."

Thank *you*, buddy. . . .

Bango! That one didn't touch a thing but string. J.J. was feeling no pain. There was dust in his nose and smoke in his lungs. Everything was right with the world.

Then the buzzer ripped off the top of J.J.'s head. And he remembered that he'd be seeing most of the game from the bench.

J.J. walked dejectedly over to the bench and filled the seat next to Reed Carson.

"LADIES AND GENTLEMEN! WELCOME TO THE SALT PALACE! WHERE TONIGHT, THE UTES TAKE ON THE NEW YORK STARS IN THE OPENING GAME OF NBA'S SEMI-FINAL PLAY-OFF SERIES!"

Wayne considered his tv appearance at half time. They'd played a couple of taped interviews near the beginning of the season, but this would be live. He wanted to give it his best shot . . . the future coach of the year (*Jesus,* he could almost taste it) couldn't flop on-camera. He needed, for example, to lead off with a funny story. He didn't feel funny.

"AND NOW INTRODUCING THE STARTING LINEUP OF THE VISITING NEW YORK STARS"

The stands were packed with a Standing Room Only crowd of twelve thousand. Except for a scattering of college kids in blue jeans the Ute fans were dressed up for going out. They watched the proceedings very attentively, and they seemed to be a little startled by their own cheers.

"AT ONE GUARD, NUMBER EIGHT, DAVID BROOKS"

Dave hustled out to the midcourt line. He posed with one hand resting on his hip while the other hand ran a towel over his face and neck. Dave's mind was a blank, but it tingled with excitement. The right combination for now.

"AT THE OTHER GUARD, NUMBER SIXTEEN, TYRONE WHITE"

Tyrone slowly chewed his gum and trotted carefully out onto the court. Tyrone's yellow eyes roamed slowly over the section where the ballplayers' people were sitting. His two seats caressed the shapely behinds of two black models whom Tyrone had flown in from New York.

"AT FORWARD, NUMBER SEVEN, SYLVESTER SIMS"

Silky Sims shuffled out, churning his flexed arms in tight circles. He touched hands with Tyrone and Dave, shook his wrists loose, commenced bouncing sprightly on the balls of his feet. "Sylvester?!" he mumbled to himself.

"AT THE OTHER FORWARD, NUMBER TWENTY-FIVE, ARDELL BARTHOLOMEW"

Ardell loped out with his hands already cupped and ready for contact. He bopped and slapped the hands of his teammates and they each chanted a muffled greeting: "Yeah'm." "Dell!" "Hummmn." "Yo."

"AND AT CENTER, NUMBER TWENTY, JACK MATHIAS"

As before, the starting players offered up their naked palms to exchange a blessing with Jack. But Jack came off the bench roaring and steaming. He went down the line pummelling every outstretched hand in sight.

**"THE COACH OF THE STARS, WAYNE SMALLEY"**

Wayne stood up and hollered out to his men. "Let's go! Bring it in!" Then Wayne clapped his hands several times to stoke their enthusiam.

**"AND NOW, A FINE SALT PALACE WELCOME FOR THE UTES STARTING FIVE!"**

Upon hearing their cue, the "Utettes" emerged from a ramp and high stepped onto the court. They were a group of six unemployed chorus girls who had been imported from Las Vegas for each home game. The girls accompanied the introduction of each hometown player with a buoyant Lindy hop and a virginal waving of pompoms. The fans cheered weakly for the ballplayers but they hung tight on the cheerleaders' moves. Then two of the Utettes detached themselves from their formation and marched primly off to chaperone the color guard: three Boy Scouts carrying a state flag, a city flag and Old Glory. Flanked by their escorts, the boys sheepishly toted their burdens out to the center jump circle.

**"WON'T YOU PLEASE JOIN IN SINGING WHILE THE ORGANIST PLAYS OUR NATIONAL ANTHEM? THE STAR SPANGLED BANNER."**

Wayne stood erect and cleared his throat. He still needed a funny story.

**"OH, SAY CAN YOU SEE BY THE DAWN'S EARLY (muthafucka) LIGHT? ... O'ER THE LAND OF THE FREE (Kill) AND THE HOME OF THE BRAVE."**

"AND NOW, LADIES AND GENTLEMEN. LET'S PLAY BALL."

The Stars jumped off to a quick ten point lead on the back of five straight baskets by Silky. New York's backcourt maintained constant pressure on the Utes guards, and most of Silky's points came on syncopated fast breaks.

With the score 16–6 after only three minutes, Salt Lake called a time-out.

"Good," Wayne said. "Good. Good. Just got to keep it going. Silky . . . overplay Covington to his right and he won't be any trouble. Way to push it. Jack . . . you gotta help out on the weak side a little quicker. Right? Got to keep thinking out there. Okay. Now let's hump up and blow them right out of the fucken building. Okay? Let's run a Blue Stack. Everybody got it? Silky? Jack? A Blue Stack. Okay! Let's keep thinking. No guessing. Okay!"

The Blue Stack was Silky's favorite play. It called for his setting a pick off the ball for Dave. Then Silky was supposed to bump his man into a double-pick and wind up with an open ten footer from the base line. It was a surefire play. But as Silky braced himself for the initial pick, Dave's man ran right into him and knocked Silky to the floor.

Nick Hatcher immediately blew his whistle.

"No, you don't, Sims! You moved into the man!" Hatcher scampered over to the scorer's table. "Number seven," he said. "Blue." Hatcher placed his hands on his hips and took one giant step to his right. "Charging."

"No!" Silky protested. "No!"

"Shut up, Sims. I called it a foul, it was a foul. That's a warning."

97

"UTE BASKET BY COVINGTON. THEY TRAIL TWENTY-ONE TO TWELVE."

Kim Covington bullied his way past Silky for a couple of baskets and the Stars game suddenly went flat. New York now had to work their patterns to try and find shooting room, but the Utes doubled up on the ball and jammed up the passing lanes. The Stars offense soon degenerated into either Silky or Tyrone going one-on-one. For the rest of the half, Dave Brooks rarely handled the ball.

Kevin Harmon leaned back into his seat and lifted his right leg until its entire length was parallel to the ground. Kevin then loosed a thundering fart. Everybody on the bench began to whoop and wave towels. Wayne paused to turn an uncomprehending eye down the ranks, then quickly returned his attention to the ball game.

"BASKET BY SIMS NEW YORK LEADS, TWENTY-FIVE TO NINETEEN."

"Do it, Silk!" Jeremy Johnson yelled. As he clapped his hands, J.J. accidentally bumped his elbow into Reed Carson's shoulder.

"What the fuck are you, crazy?" Reed said. He got up and moved to another seat.

"ONE OUT OF TWO FREE THROWS FOR CARTER. THE UTES STILL TRAIL, TWENTY-NINE TO TWENTY-TWO."

Kim Covington had Silky backed into the pivot. Silky planted a cunning elbow into the small of Covington's back, but the bigger man wouldn't yield.

"One!" Buddy Patella shouted from the Stars bench. "Two!" How long? How fricken long!?"

Covington came out a step to meet the pass. He took

one ferocious dribble to the middle, flinging a bruising forearm into Silky's chest and sweeping toward the hoop. The contact rocked Silky back on his heels. Covington cocked his shooting hand and Silky fought for enough balance to jump. The shot was released. Silky skied. Silky's hand flicked at the ball like a lizard's tongue stabbing at a pebbled insect. The shot was maimed, and it fell harmlessly out of bounds.

As Silky landed, his shoulder nudged into Covington's outstretched left elbow. Covington let out a loud grunt and took a dive.

> (A player shall not hold, push, charge into, impede the progress of an opponent by extended arm, knee or by bending the body into a position so that it is not normal.)

"On the arm!" Hatcher sang as he danced over to the official scorer. "Number seven. Blue. In the act. Covington shoots two."

Silky stomped his foot and took an angry step toward the referee. But Dave grabbed Silky by the elbow and calmed him down.

Kevin Harmon was so caught up in the game that he forgot what he was doing. The score was getting tight, so the probability was that Kevin wouldn't be used at all. Kevin was the third center and he only played in laughers.

Kevin had no idea he had just bitten his right thumbnail down to the quick.

"One, Miss'ippi! Two, Miss'pi! How long? You fricken turkey!"

Jack Mathias stood poised on the foul line. Even though the ball was dead, Jack held his arms straight up over his head. The posture gave him good rebounding position. Jack had read all about it in *John Wooden's Secrets of Winning Basketball*.

Jack wasn't sure of the name of the player who was shooting the free throws, but just before the ball was released Jack convulsed his head and his shoulders in an attempt to distract him. The shot went in anyway. As the ballplayer aimed his second shot, Jack moved again. This time the ball rimmed the basket and kicked out. Jack dipped his arms and leaped to take off the rebound. It was already his fifth of the game.

"BASKET BY BARTHOLOMEW. THE STARS LEAD, THIRTY-ONE TO TWENTY-FIVE."

Silky grabbed the ball, executed a nervous fake to his right and then his autonomic ganglia took over. Silky's pet move was imbedded in his tendons: a couple of short dribbles to his left, then jump to find his shot. Covington caught up to Silky just as the ball was being flicked from its boney cradle. Covington's shoulder smashed into Silky's side and Silky went down, his flywheel shot spinning off the heel of the rim.

"Foul!" Silky screamed. "That's a foul!"

(The mere fact that contact occurs does not necessarily constitute a foul. Contact which is incidental to an effort by a player to play an opponent, reach a loose ball, or perform defensive or offensive movements, should not be considered illegal.)

"It's a foul only if I call it," Hatcher said. "Quit bitching, Sims, and play ball."

"TWO FREE THROWS BY JAN BARNES AND THE UTES STILL TRAIL, FORTY-TWO TO THIRTY-NINE."

Silky was still fuming and cursing as he sat down. With Larry Graham now in at forward, the Stars patterns soon became even more mired in confusion than before. The only plays that Larry knew well were those that called for his taking the shot. Dave and Tyrone had to yell instructions to try and keep Larry out of the way. If the Stars continued to have trouble scoring, Larry's sinewy strength and maniacal aggression did slow Covington down.

"STARS BASKET BY WHITE. THE SCORE IS TIED AT FORTY-SIX. THERE ARE TWO MINUTES LEFT IN THE FIRST HALF! TWO MINUTES!"

When an exhausted Kim Covington was finally given a breather, the Utes sent Jonah James into the pivot, who was quick to beat the tiring Mathias with two straight turnaround jumpers.

The pass went inside for a third time and James dribbled and jockeyed for a better angle. But this time Dave Brooks was ready. Instead of trailing his man through the middle and out the other side, Dave dropped off and attacked James' dribble. A half-lunge, a dancing wrist, and the ball was knocked loose.

Several players changed direction in a flash but Tyrone was first to the ball and corralled it into a dribble without breaking stride. Then it was a foot race downcourt between Tyrone and a blur of white uniform. Tyrone's instincts instantly collated the speeds, the vectors and the macho. He could have pulled up at the foul

101

line and waited for a cutter: he knew without loking that Dave would soon be flying by his left hand. But it was a matter of honor. A matter of blood. Tyrone arched his back and leaned away from the collision. Just as he sprang toward the basket, a white uniform crashed into him from behind. The jolt forced Tyrone into a new flight pattern, but he made the adjustment easily and flipped up a left-handed toss that leaned into the backboard and fell dead through the hoop. Tyrone then broke his fall with his sore right wrist.

There were twenty-six seconds remaining in the half when Quinton reported in for Tyrone. Quinton strolled leisurely onto the court, rotating his shoulders and picking his uniform away from his body. "Who you got?" he asked Tyrone as they passed. It was number six, Jan Barnes. Quinton did a half-squat and pulled at his jockstrap, bopped fists with Barnes and wiped his hands on the back of his opponent's jersey.

The only time Quinton touched the ball, he heaved up a Goose Tatum hook shot from just past midcourt, the ball slamming off the backboard as the buzzer sounded.

The Utes led, fifty-three to forty-eight.

Melvin Withers adjusted the microphones and whispered with the cameraman while Wayne Smalley twitched with eagerness. Wayne alternately pulled at the front of his sport jacket, smoothed a hand through his hair and straightened his necktie. The red light atop the camera winked at him and Wayne turned on his smile.

"And now, fans," Withers said, "we have a special half-time treat for you. Here with me at courtside is a man who has been a vital factor in continuing the Stars winning tradition. A man who is already being hailed by the press as the NBA's coach of the year. Here he is, fans. The often irrepressible, always unpredictable coach of the New York Stars . . . Wayne Smalley."

Wayne ducked his head, signalling good-humored modesty while the Ute fans sat on their hands. Screw them, thought Wayne. This is for the big time. This is network, for the future coach of the year . . .

"Thank you, Melvin," Wayne said. "It certainly is a pleasure to be here and have the opportunity to chat with you and the wonderful Stars fans back home."

"Tell me, Wayne," Withers said. "What are some of your impressions of the first half?"

Wayne suddenly hunched up his shoulders, pulled his lips into an exaggerated sneer, and poked at Withers with an imaginary cigar. "It was a tough half for the Stars, see? A tough half, see?"

Wayne then smiled. "That was my Eddie G. Robinson impression of the first half. But seriously, Melvin . . ." Seriously, he was right all along—he needed a joke.

Bradley Hulsapple hadn't missed a Ute home contest all season long, but tonight's game was extra special. Last Wednesday Bradley's entry slip had been drawn in the Utes Vacation Shoot-Out Sweepstakes. During the halftime intermission Bradley would be trying one precious shot from the midcourt line. If he were successful Bradley's name would be in the papers and his entire family would be sent on an all-expenses-paid trip to San Francisco.

Throughout the week the significance of his dramatic field goal attempt had blossomed in Bradley's adolescent brain. If he made the shot, Bradley was convinced that he and Mary Lou would be selected as King and Queen of the upcoming junior prom. Which in turn would be the turning point of his life.

Bradley had been practicing all week long. He knew he couldn't miss. All he had to remember was to relax and follow through properly. His dad had been working with him too. Everybody, in fact, had been helpful. Mary Lou hadn't even objected when he'd insisted they arrive at the Salt Palace three full hours before game time, giving him the chance to practice for almost a half hour on the very same rim he'd be aiming at later on. He had wowed the early spectators with his remarkable long-range shooting. He couldn't miss.

As Bradley's name was announced, he flushed and walked stiffly to the middle of the court. He had watched with pleasure as all of his predecessors became rattled when their names were called; he remained resolute. None of the fanfare would distract him. Out of the corner of his eye he caught a glimpse of Mary Lou sitting on the edge of her seat, fingertips drawn up to her mouth. Bradley, of course, wouldn't allow himself to turn around and smile at her. He was primed and anxious to be put to the test. His golden future lay waiting. All he needed was a basketball.

One of the Utettes came wiggling up from Bradley's blind side with the ball in her hands. Bradley heard her footsteps, but he turned his head the wrong way and his arm inadvertently brushed against the largest breasts he had ever seen, or felt.

Bradley's shot fell a good ten feet short.

Because of Wayne's interview, the Stars could appear on the court ten minutes ahead of the home team. But Jeremy Johnson dallied unnoticed in the dressing room.

104

He hadn't seen any action in the first half and was assuaging his anger by smoking another joint.

Wayne didn't trust his bench at all. Especially during the play-offs. He felt that his starting five should be able to go at least forty-five minutes each. Nonetheless he was forced to make two changes in New York's lineup to begin the second half. Silky had four fouls, so Larry Graham started at one forward. And Buddy informed Wayne that Tyrone's jammed wrist would cause him to sit out the rest of the game. "I don't think he needs X-rays," Buddy said. "Maybe he'll miss a game or two, is all."

Wayne nodded and summoned Reed Carson.

"Control," was Wayne's advice. "Pick your spots. And run a Philly Stack the first chance you get."

With Reed now playing along side him in the backcourt, Dave Brooks' finger was on the trigger of New York's offense. Dave was quick to call one of Reed's plays, and Reed beat his man for an easy lay-up. Dave then came right back and assisted on a short jumper by Reed off a five on four controlled break. For the next few sequences Dave kept a close watch on Reed's movements as he tried to breathe some continuity and discipline back into the Stars attack.

Reed scored still another basket, the shots were falling and he once again lived in a Reed-made universe with the strings of his own fate held securely in his own hands. He coolly regarded his faceless opponents like a scientist observing a batch of fruit flies.

Dave and Reed sent each other silent body signals—they gave and went, they zigged and zagged. The two of them shared the Stars' first twelve points of the second half. Their communion was instinctive and overwhelming, with Dave passing up a complicated lay-up to dish off a free six foot pop to Reed. They vibrated on the same frequency, shared a consummation.

On the next series Dave switched the play to Ardell, hitting him with a lead pass that burgeoned into a stuff. Some music for them. The Stars were dancing again, and the ball game warmed up.

"BASKET BY BARTHOLOMEW. THE UTES STILL LEAD, SEVENTY-FOUR TO SEVENTY."

Then the magic show suddenly turned into a clumsy pantomine. Reed began to force his shots and they wouldn't fall. He tried to strongarm the flow of the ball game and wound up struggling in its wake. He turned the ball over twice in a row. His concentration was spent and he helplessly bounced off a pick he never saw, caroming into Kim Covington just as the big man was pulling up for a shot.

"If! If!" Hatcher shouted as the ball teetered on the rim. The shot fell out, but Covington was awarded two free throws.

The call catapulted Buddy off the bench. "Way to protect the white hope!" he hollered. "Who the hell you think he is? Frigham Young's grandson?"

"BASKET BY BROOKS. THE UTES LEAD SEVENTY-NINE TO SEVENTY-SIX."

Larry was dragging so Wayne moved to reinstate Silky. He locked one hand onto Silky's upper arm and escorted him over to the scorer's table.

"Run a 24T," Wayne said. "Then try a Double Louie or a Stack Seven."

Silky barely paid attention as he strained toward the

court. Wayne dug his fingers deeper into Silky's bare arm.

"24T, Double Louie or a Stack Seven."

Silky wrenched out of his coach's grip. "Offa me, motherfucker," he said, then hustled into the game.

"BASKET BY GEORGE BOONE. UTES LEAD EIGHTY-THREE TO SEVENTY-EIGHT."

The Mad Snotter struck in the middle of the fourth quarter. Reed, collapsing on the bench during a time out, blindly reached for a towel. Somebody obliged by placing one in his outstretched hand. Reed blotted his face, his forehead making contact with a living wet . . .

Were they trying to tell him something?

Jack Mathias fouled out with 4:32 left in the game and the score tied at 104. Wayne signaled for Jeremy Johnson, by now flying high, who, on his first trip down the court, stumbled over the foul line and picked up a painful floor burn. J.J. returned to the bench, bleeding and laughing. Wayne had little choice but to send Kevin Harmon into the game, a center.

As the ball game now rushed toward an end, Silky went wild. He singlehandedly shot the Stars back into control. With 1:35 left to go New York had the ball and was up by three points. A hoop should wrap it up. Dave milked the twenty-four-second clock, then beat his man to the middle with a smooth change of pace dribble. Jonah James quickly deserted Kevin and jumped out to pick up Dave. But Dave faked the shot and bounced a waist high pass that led Kevin straight to the hoop. The pass, perfectly thrown, brought Kevin visions of a savage dunk that would fair shake the building. Except the ball grazed the tip of Kevin's right thumb as it came up off the floor, the flash of unexpected pain yanked Kevin's hand away. The pass sailed out of bounds.

Kim Covington smelled the fates, drove for a gritty three point play that tied the score and fouled Silky out of the game.

The Stars, dead, went on to lose 115 to 111.

And Wayne still needed a funny story.

# CHAPTER ELEVEN

JOE MALONEY had won NBA championships with the Chicago Bulls and the Phoenix Suns, and an ABA title with the San Antonio Spurs. Maloney was the dean of the professional basketball coaches, but nobody took him seriously. He was in his twenty-fifth year in the business and the Utes were his sixteenth ball club. The ballplayers around the league called Maloney "the Chameleon," and the other coaches referred to him as "the Survivor." Maloney was universally considered to possess an out-of-date, ragamuffin basketball mind. Wayne had paid absolutely no attention to Maloney. Wayne went into the Salt Lake series expecting the Utes to run the same offenses and defenses they'd shown during the regular season. But to the would-be-future-coach-of-the-year's astonishment, the Utes had come out in a two-three zone defense which had shut down New York's Stack offense. Wayne had been had by a beat-up second-rater.

Wayne, stunned by the unexpected loss, negotiated a blonde from the lobby and repaired to his room. All throughout the following day he alternately brooded, screwed and racked his brain. He had to devise some new trigger for the Stars' moribund offense, and he had to do it in a hurry. Another loss . . . out of the question.

Trays littered the floor of Wayne's hotel room, a single empty bottle of champagne lay on its side on the dresser. Wayne was sitting up in bed, toying with his magnetic basketball court. The blonde lazed beside him, flipping the pages of Wayne's *Sports Illustrated*. Her name, she said, was Velma LaRue and she was a thirty-five-year-old waitress at a nearby rollerama.

Velma was born and raised in Greensboro, North Carolina, but she'd been living in Salt Lake City for nearly fifteen years, having been rudely deposited there by a tin-horn movie producer who was taking her by train to Hollywood to make her, he said, a star. Velma's first, and only, movie was a porno special filmed entirely inside the producer's second class compartment. By the time the train pulled into Salt Lake City, the producer had all the footage he needed and Velma's contract was terminated.

Since then Velma had supported herself in her fashion. She told Wayne she was twenty-seven and a reservations agent for TWA. Who checks? Wayne called her his "hot tamale." . . .

Velma leaned over now and rubbed her still-sprightly breasts up against Wayne's bare shoulder. "C'mon, sweetie, I got to be at work in a couple of hours."

"Okay," Wayne said as he shrugged her off. "Okay. Be right with you." Game time was coming up and Wayne hadn't come close to solving Maloney's defense. He winked out his most bewitching smile. "I just got to take care of some business, honeybunch," he said.

Velma was too moist to be put off so easily. She twined her arms around him and stabbed her salient breasts into Wayne's back. "C'mon, sweetie," she whispered with a practiced hoarseness.

"Don't *pester* me!" Wayne snapped. "I told you I had something to do, didn't I?" His ruddy face tensed into a brief smile. "*Okay?*"

He turned away with annoyance, his feverish brain instantly fussing with his portable basketball court. His impatient hands poked the tiny X's and O's with the abstract dedication of a monk working his prayer beads. The shiny metallic surface was an alchemist's slate where perfect ideas and their impeccable fulfillment were brewed. Like most of his colleagues, Wayne entertained little respect for his ballplayers. It was no trick for him to translate their hulking bodies into diminutive white circles and black crosses. In fact, it was a pleasure.

Wayne also mistrusted his players. He thought they were spoiled children living on the Big Rock Cocaine Mountain—who destroyed the beauty and precision of his immaculately designed patterns with their incessant free-lancing. He only forgave them when the Stars won.

There were only three ballplayers whom Wayne had well in hand. One was Ardell Bartholomew, the finest rebounding thoroughbred in the game. Wayne had no trouble controlling Ardell. He always spoke softly to him, his face melting with piety. Wayne planned to drive Ardell until he was ready for the glue factory. That's what horses were for. Jack Mathias was more of a quarterhorse. He was a gem of a fourth round draft pick whom Wayne had plucked out of a can of USC game films. Jack was humble and eternally grateful for everything that had ever happened to him. The only other player who usually wore the bit without complaining was Dave Brooks. Dave always played hard, long and under

111

the proper restraints. But Wayne was still bitter over Dave's insolence after the Seattle game, when Dave had showed him up in front of the entire team. Wayne was itching to punish Dave, to find an excuse for fining him.

Wayne's lungs bit sharply into a cigarette, and a searing reflex bent him into a cough. "Goddamn," he choked, "son of a bitch!"

His hacking rhythm was instantly picked up by the ringing of the telephone. He cursed again as he reached across Velma and lifted the receiver. He hated to be disturbed when he was working.

"Hello!" he barked.

"Hello yourself!" Buddy snapped just as fiercely. "I got bad news. I got to get Tyrone's wrist X-rayed. I'm here at the whachacallit arena fooling with this here mechanical ice pack they got put in here. It's a piece of shit. But I think it might be busted . . . Tyrone's wrist."

"Goddamn! Just what I fucken need."

"Yeah. But maybe it ain't broke anyway, because it didn't swoll up until this morning. I'm taking him over to the hospital just to make sure. But I can tell you right now, either the which or the way, they ain't no chance Tyrone can play tonight. If it ain't busted after all, he can probably play the third game back in New York. Probably is all I'm saying. But if it's busted, then Tyrone's out for the season. But like I say, I don't think that maybe it ain't broke . . . you know?"

"Yeah, yeah," Wayne said restlessly. "Okay. Run him over there quick and call me back here as soon as you find out something."

"Oh, yeah," Buddy said, "I almost forgot. The Utah PR guy? You know, the feller with the big nose?"

"Redmond, what about him?"

112

"Well, I called him about seeing the tape of last night's game like you said I should. But the guy told me the video tape machine is broken down. He said it just happened this morning."

"Bull!" Wayne said. "That sneaky fucken Maloney."

He slammed the receiver home and crawled back across Velma, who took the opportunity to snuggle against him as he passed.

Wayne yelped as though assaulted, grabbed up his ouija board and hopped out of bed. "Be right back, got to take a pee. Goddamn!"

On his way out he snatched another cigarette from a crumpled pack on the dresser. "Fucken prima donnas," he grumbled. "The bastards'll do anything just to mess me up."

Once inside the bathroom Wayne screwed himself into the toilet seat and placed the metal board across his lap. His body was tingling with aggravation and betrayal. He had a craving to castigate every player on the team, even his horses. Maybe he'd have Buddy roust them all out right now, and he'd march them over to the gym and make them run suicides until their tongues got floor burns. The only language they understood was pain. Horses were also made to be whipped. But the tide of his anger quickly bilged over into a sigh of frustration. Nobody but Ardell, Jack and Kevin Harmon would ever show up for such an impromptu practice. Everybody else would simply roll over in bed and eat the $150 fine.

Wayne was also much too afraid of his ballplayers to ever attempt such a stunt. At five-eleven, their physical presence alone was enough to intimidate him. They were so huge, so powerful and so graceful. He could match their granite egos, but he was also dwarfed by the sheer mass of their self-esteem. He'd give the team a new offensive wrinkle and a blistering pre-game speech. Try to save his skin. Period.

Velma was climbing out of bed just as Wayne reentered the room. "I'm sorry, sweetie," she said, "it's been fun and all that but I got to take a shower and get dressed to go to work. At the airport, you know?"

All of this basketball monkey business was starting to get Velma very bugged. A whole lot of fuss about a bunch of grown men running around in their underwear. Worst of all, Velma was beginning to think that Wayne was a cheapskate. Just like those bumpkin professional hockey players she sometimes dated.

Wayne watched her slither off into the bathroom. His eyes traced the clean, hard lines of her body. He was tempted by her glistening pubic hair, her plump, marble-hard ass. He wheeled around and grabbed Velma just as she was stepping into the shower. Amid a barrage of tickles, squeezes, bites and promises, he managed to coax her down to the floor of the bathtub. Then he turned on the shower.

Velma leaned back and pressed herself into the wet procelain. She loved getting laid in cramped quarters. It brought back the glory of her youth. The warm rush of water made her thighs blossom. And the lips of her cunt whispered to Wayne of emerald thrills. She stroked Wayne's cock as he crouched over her. In an instant they were both groaning and undulating with bittersweet pain. Then Velma suddenly grabbed hungrily at Wayne and he had to jump to catch her orgasm. Their torrid consummation boiled their spines into jelly.

They rolled and toiled in a variety of sexual agonistics for another hour. Afterward, when Velma was already dressed and gone, Wayne once again gathered himself over his basketball ouija. But this time the pieces were moved in the grip of inspiration, and shortly thereafter Wayne had flashed out an entire new offensive set. He'd met the challenge. Joe Maloney would strangle in his own crafty net.

Wayne christened his new plan the "Velma series." It was especially designed to keep the middle open and let everybody go back-door.

# CHAPTER TWELVE

ANY PLAY-OFF game involving a pro team from New York always generated headlines. But the likes of Elton John, Dustin Hoffman, John Lennon and Kinky Friedman could be expected to be on hand to cultivate any post-season doings in the Stars' Garden. Over the weekend, games number three and four at MSG were being prime-timed into instant culture by ABZ-TV, so a horde of media gnats swarmed over the Salt Palace doing preliminary work and raising a mound of dirt.

A phalanx of photographers in unkempt corduroy jackets flopped and kneeled around the margin of the court. The sideline press table teemed with freeloaders, free-lancers, sychophants, wire servicemen, magazine slickers and other variants of prying scriveners. Not even the fans' twittering restlessness could cover the hubbub that rose from the courtside dais.

Seated in the place of honor, his folding chair astraddle the midcourt line, was Murray Klurman. Himself. Murray nodded cool and majestic greetings to selective passersby while he munched upon a pack of Tum-

116

mies. The players were still warming up but Murray already had a case of deadline bends. The chair to his right was empty. An index card taped to the table told Murray the place belonged to "Ms. Dorothy Evans—ABZ-TV." Murray belched politely into the back of his wrist.

Dorothy was a campaigning five footer who handled all the interviews for the network's half-time package. Her trademark was a milk box upon which she conducted her powwows with the players. The public adored her. Murray thought she was mousey looking. Also a pain in the ass.

Out on the court Jeremy Johnson's jump shot was talking to him. "Bang!" it shouted along the base line. "Dush," it whispered from behind the foul circle. Jeremy's lean, skeletal fingers instinctively softened and adjusted each shot. Under the ointment and the bandage, his floor burn was throbbing. J.J. moved stiffly about the court and his reddening resentment welcomed the rolling pain.

The buzzer sounded, herded J.J. over to a sullen, accustomed seat on the bench. . . .

Silky was primed for the ball game. He was riding the same wave of ego-cannibal that once made him the king of the schoolyard. Silky was out to humiliate Kim Covington, to destroy his opponent's personality.

It was a tribal matter, mostly, but Silky's street-slick eyes registered the flashers at the press table. . . .

Reed Carson shuffled out on the court licking the tips of his fingers. With Tyrone still nursing his wrist, Reed was expecting to play most of the game. His goal was to score twenty-five points on twenty shots.

Reed had thrown up in the locker room, and his ankle didn't bother him at all. . . .

Dave Brooks exchanged a Masonic handshake with George Boone.

As the referees checked with the official scorer, Dorothy Evans slid into her assigned seat. She rubbed shoulders and smiles with Murray as she settled her typewriter into working position. It was a brand new battery-powered machine made almost entirely of aluminum and fiberglass. Dorothy slipped a page neatly under the cylinder and her polished fingernails began to chitter away at the keyboard. She wished she had a drink.

Murray's tender stomach sent up another smoke signal. He inched his chair away from Dorothy. Murray planted a foot securely on each half of the court and laid his fingerprints into the worn keys of his own machine. He synchronized his physiological and psychological time with the game clock, then exploded into blood-red numbers as another ball game gathered itself and began.

1Q
12:00
NY–0
SLC–0

Wayne fumed in anticipation as the players crouched under the ball. He had diagrammed the Velma series at least twenty-five times and the team had run through all four options for over an hour. He also was sure they'd screw it up and run their hully-gully all over his dotted lines.

"Think!" Wayne yowled, "goddamn it, think!" He lit his first cigarette of the game. "You bastards," he whispered.

Silky easily won the opening tap, diverting the ball to Dave. The Stars then set up in a hurry, each of them running a different version of the same play. All the helter-skelter disrupted the Utes defense, and Jack ended the sequence with a short angle jumper. The shot was off, but Silky leaped high to confiscate the rebound and stuff it home.

1Q
11:48
NY–2
SLC–0

With the notable exceptions of Covington, Boone and James, the Utes roster was studded with ABA riff-raff. But all of Joe Maloney's ball clubs had one characteristic in common: patience. Maloney always attempted to crucify his opponents on the twenty-four-second clock.

The Utes set up their offense slowly and deliberately. George Boone, the trigger man, shouted out a play that Silky almost recognized. The chalk diagram flitted through Silky's head as he battled Covington through a gauntlet of picks and a forest of hostile elbows. But Silky's hands were empty and they twitched for the comfort of a basketball. Before he knew it, Silky was pinned behind a screen and Covington had an open shot from the foul line.

It was already too late, but Silky jumped and spiked Covington's shot to the deck. The fans gasped and an official made a goal-tending call.

Silky didn't even bother to complain. His game was in town, he was feeling good, and he knew he was looking even better.

1Q
9:43
NY–11
SLC–7

In the pit and tar of the three-second zone, Jack and Moses James fought an aboriginal contest for territorial dominance. Instead of playing defense, they collided. Instead of rebounding, they smashed each other's bones to gristle. It would take both big men a while to adjust themselves to everybody else's ball game. In the meantime, the officials let their primate mayhem continue unabated and unwhistled.

1Q
6:20
NY–18
SLC–12

Silky evolved another mutation off his favorite stutter-right-shoot-left maneuver. His elbow grazed Covington's nose as he sent a gyroscopic jump shot twirling through the net.

"Look out sucker," Silky taunted. "You gonna get burned tonight!"

1Q
2:18
NY–25
SLC–17

Tyrone White sat stonefaced on the far end of the Stars bench. He wore a pair of rust-orange knit pants and a brown turtleneck sweater. A golden quarter moon dangled from a braided chain around his neck. Tyrone's mind had turned to ice, and he retained no images of the ball game in front of him. Tyrone was a spectator, a civilian. The game was being played outside of his body.

2Q
11:36
NY–33
SLC–23

As soon as Kim Covington neared the top of the key, Silky pressed into his skin.

"Panama Red," Covington shouted to his teammates. But Silky's chest was in the way and Covington couldn't turn to make the entry pass. With his free hand Covington hacked his way clear to the foul line. Silky pushed again, and suddenly Covington's eyes flared up and the play was forgotten. He broke into a dribble and began to sashay and strain toward the basket, looking for his own shot. He faked several times, then cuffed the ball in his left hand and wheeled sharply to his right. Silky jumped into his lane, tugged at Kim's jersey and fell over backward, pulling the Ute forward down on top of him.

"That's a charge!" the official screamed with righteous clarity.

2Q
7:43
NY–40
SLC–29

There was a time-out and, except for Jeremy, the entire New York bench rose to meet and congratulate their teammates. Even Tyrone, yawning, climbed to his feet.

Wayne knelt over his lodestar Tinker Toy while he endeavored to explain the Velma series once again. The players looked and nodded agreeably, but nobody knew what he was talking about. They didn't want to abstract their bodies into Wayne's abbreviated alphabet.

As the players moseyed back onto the court, Silky pulled on Dave's arm.

"Later for that boolshit," Silky drawled. "Just clear me out a side."

121

2Q
5:57
NY–46
SLC–34

Silky came body surfing down the court on a solo breakaway. The blue three-second zone lay open to him like a carpeted runway. He launched himself from the foul line. He spun his body around full-circle in midair and then slam-dunked with both hands.

2Q
4:02
NY–50
SLC–36

Kim Covington picked up his fourth foul trying to climb Silky's back in the rebound tussle. Maloney immediately replaced Covington with Paul Tierney, a hardy 6'9″ rookie out of Dayton. But Silky made mincemeat of the new man. In fact, for the rest of the half Silky played a mile above the rim and had it all his own way.

By half time Silky had twenty-one points and the Stars led 59 to 45.

A special half time smorgasbord, free food and free booze, attracted most of the courtside squirearchy. Amid the sparkling, ravenous gaggle, Murray and Dorothy found themselves pressed together between a herring salad basketball and an egg salad chicken.

Dorothy Evans was a recent Vassar graduate with a degree in creative writing and an uncle who was well-screwed into ABZ-TV's board of directors. She wore blue jeans and a baggy sweater and she sipped at a tumbler of raw Scotch. Whenever Dorothy got tipsy she loved to flirt with older men.

"If it isn't Murray Klurman," Dorothy said with a little girl's smile. "The Tiresius of the basketball world."

"Tiresius?" Murray said. "Who'd he play for, love?"

Dorothy smiled. "Really, Murray, I've always wanted to ask you something but somehow I never got around to it."

"Why not?"

"I don't know. Maybe those famous sour smiles of yours put me off."

Murray laughed slowly and laboriously. In spite of himself, he found Dorothy's perky charming manner very appealing. "Ask away," he said. "I'm all sweetness and light."

"Tell me, Murray. Straight injun. Do you think that women reporters should be allowed in locker rooms?"

Murray shrugged. "Once you've seen one, you've seen 'em all."

Dorothy smiled in appreciation of Murray's wisdom. "Do you know what John Burrows told me?" she said. Dorothy dug a notebook out of her purse. "He talked about the fall of the Roman Empire. He said that the first symptoms of moral decay were carnal promiscuity and sexual lassitude. Then he asked me how I'd feel if somebody wanted to interview me in my bathroom."

"That's pretty funny," Murray said, unconvinced. The very name of one of Murray's peers and competitors—especially one from the *Times*—straightened his demeanor. Nor did he relax until Dorothy put away her notebook. "But let me ask you something, toots. What's a nice girl like you doing in a business like this? You're not one of those groupies or something, are you?"

Dorothy trilled a laugh and clinked her glass of Scotch against Murray's ginger ale. "No thanks, you chauvinist pig you," she said, and a merry lilt rubbed the sting from her words. "But I'll tell you a deep, dark secret if you promise not to tell."

"Strictly off the record," he said.

"All right. Now, I'll agree with you that it's a wacked out business, but we're all crazy anyway. I mean, after all . . . who the hell wants to be normal. It's so dull. . . ." Dorothy's wicked smile tickled Murray's underwear. "But the secret is that basketball really turns me on. As a sport, I mean."

"As an indoor sport?"

"Up yours," Dorothy said. "Don't tell me you watch little Olga Korbut on the tube because you like gymnastics?"

Murray blushed through his tan.

"You're probably too close to the game to realize it," Dorothy said, "but to me basketball is really beautiful, truthful and, most of all, erotic. That's why women are the biggest fans."

"Erotic?" Murray said in disbelief. "Yeah. Erotic like a horse race. Listen. I thought all you college dames liked football players."

Dorothy laughed and her eyes bubbled with a delicious mystery. "Just because you're so cute," she said, "I'll tell you another secret. All of those big, muscle-bound football players are a bunch of faggots. That's something that every woman in America knows. But basketball players are sensuous, vivacious. They're god-sized and godlike. They're balanced, they're pluperfect, they have all the moves."

"Feh!" Murray said as his stomach fizzed. "I've been in the land of jocks for seventeen years, little girl, and believe me I know what makes them tick. All of them, from basketball players to jockeys . . . they're all animals."

Murray fumbled in his pocket for another stomach

124

pill just as a red light flashed on above the bar. The second half was about to start, and the crowd began to file out of the press room. Murray and Dorothy dallied behind.

Dorothy shook her head. "This is all too depressing," she said. Then she bent over and planted a dry kiss on the tip of Murray's nose.

"Back to work," she said sternly. "Who do you like?"

Murray's features folded into a loose arrangement of creases and sneers. "New York's a balloon," he said. "The Utes can't lose."

Ben Ellis started instead of Kim Covington as the second half got rolling. Ben was a veteran player with quick feet, a hanging belly, a pair of Popeye forearms and a smooth rap.

"How you doin'?" Ben said as he clasped Silky's hand in the center jump circle. "Tell me, my man. Is it still snowin' in New York? How's your new pad comin'? I'll bet it's dyn-o-mite! How's Tee's wrist? Silky, my man! You sure were lookin' fancy in the first half . . ."

3Q
11:05
NY–61
SLC–51

Silky had the ball in the corner with one eye glued to the hoop. He tried to hop into his move but Ellis' hand gripped his hip like it had a handle. The pass was closed, Silky's dribble was used and the clock was counting down. But Silky heard an echo from the schoolyard beating live underneath his confusion. . . . When in doubt, shoot. . . . He forced up a shot that grazed the side of the backboard and turned into a brick.

125

Several players on both benches erupted into help-less, whooping laughter. Silky's ears burned, and he missed his next three shots as well.

3Q
7:28
NY–66
SLC–58

Reed did a rocker step near the head of the foul cir-cle, lifted one foot a scant half-inch off the floor—exploded into full stride with the other foot. His man was caught off balance, and Reed skipped to the hoop for an easy lay-up.

3Q
5:15
NY–73
SLC–80

Quinton was in for Dave so Reed's hungry hand was the one that shaped the Stars offense. He hit a twenty-footer from the right side. He connected on a high arch-ing moonshot over a leaping Moses James. He could feel the ball game sliding under his control, and he milked the little pocket of time for as many points as he could.

3Q
0:39
NY–89
SLC–80

Reed was working on a streak of five consecutive field goals and was horny to try for six. But Silky's hands were also twitching as he snared a rebound and headed resolutely down the court.

"Give it up!" Wayne screamed. "Velma, Silky! Velma!!"

Ignoring him, Silky took a wild rambunctious shot from twenty-five feet out that split the net. Wayne jumped up and beat his hands just as an official with a crew cut blew his whistle.

"Charge!" the official said. "No basket!"

Wayne stomped his feet in rage. "Charge?! You sonofabitch! Charge?! You flathead cocksucker!"

"That's a technical!" the official said.

4Q<br>
10:57<br>
NY–91<br>
SLC–87

Quinton and Dave were now paired in the Stars backcourt. Quinton huffed and wheezed along the base line, trying to draw foul number five on George Boone. He was sure he'd succeeded as he made his move to the basket and Boone sledged him with a forearm, knocking him off balance.

"Foul!" Quinton screamed as he stumbled out of bounds.

(The player is out of bounds when he touches the floor or any object on or outside a boundary. For location of a player in the air his position is that from which he last touched the floor.)

"That's a force-out!" the flat-top referee said. "Blue ball right here!"

"He fouled me, man!" Quinton insisted. "Either I stepped out or he pushed me out! That's a bullshit call!"

"That'll cost you a hundred!" the official said, and snapped his hands into a quick T-formation.

"Sheyit," Quinton said. But he knew better than to argue with officials, so he quietly walked away. On the bench, Wayne fumed and sputtered.

4Q
6:20
NY–97
SLC–97

Covington, back in for Ellis, immediately dragged Silky into the hole, grabbed a pass and went straight up for a turnaround without even paying Silky the respect of a fake. Silky, caught napping, recovered in a hurry. He leaped into the air, and this time he caught Covington's shot while it was still climbing, his stovepipe arm stretching out and ticking the ball off its intended course.

The same official called it goal-tending. Wayne jumped up and bounced off the ceiling.

"You homer!" Wayne shouted. "You asshole! You've been screwing up all night!"

The official sucked on his whistle and tried to stay cool. He knew that another technical foul on Wayne would mean automatic expulsion from the ball game.

"Screwing us all fucken night!" Wayne insisted. "The last fucken crew-cut in America and he winds up with a striped-shirt and a fucken whistle in his mouth! You suck!"

"Technical foul! Take a walk, Smalley."

"What!" Wayne said, and his passion caught pneumonia. He had never been ejected from a ball game in his entire coaching career. It didn't take Wayne long, though, to convince himself he had deliberately drawn

128

the technical to rouse up his team. Before he left the floor he conferred with Buddy.

"Take over," he said. "Go with the starters all the way and try to get them to run something if you can. You have three time-outs left. Call one now and talk to them. Tell them I'll be watching on the closed circuit tv in the press room. That ought to fire them up."

"Yeah," Buddy said wearily. "I'll tell them. . . ."

A suddenly somber ball club gathered around their trainer. There was no doubt that the crunch was on and that everybody's private wars were now up against the wall. Buddy wiped a sweaty hand over the top of his head, his powerful fingers leaving red tracks on the shiny skin.

"I don't know what the fug to tell you guys," Buddy admitted. "The man said you should try and run something. Anybody got any ideas?"

"Let's run the Velma stuff like the coach said," Jack suggested.

"Aw, fuck the coach and fuck Velma!" Silky spat. "All's I know is that dick-head ref won't let me play my fucken game."

Ardell Bartholomew shrugged when his teammates' eyes sought him out. "Whatever you cats decide is solid with me," he said.

"Gimme the ball," Reed said greedily. "I'll turn it around. I swear it."

"Fuck you," Tyrone murmured anonymously from the rear of the huddle.

The buzzer sounded and Buddy listlessly clapped his hands. "Just go out there and hustle," he said.

Dave now reached out and deposited his two up-turned hands into the center of the huddle. His empty fingers curled and beckoned a welcome.

"Let's get it together," Dave said quietly.

The moment froze and threatened to pass, but Quinton leaned over and laid his pudgy palms on top of Dave's. One by one, all of the other players slid and glued their hands onto the pile. A warm pulse beat through them.

"Let's go," J.J. said. "Let's whip them mothers."

4Q
6:19
NY–97
SLC–100

Dave brought the ball upcourt while the rest of the team milled about and waited for someone to tell them what to do.

"Stack two!" Dave said. "Stack two!"

Dave passed the ball to Silky on the wing and they traded electric blinks. Dave started loping mechanically to the other side of the court, then swiftly changed direction and dashed to an open spot in the foul line. Silky's bounce pass was already there and waiting for him. Dave toughed out a short dribble before drawing a crowd. He left his feet, faked a shot and drilled a pass to a wide open Silky. The shot snapped home off the backboard.

"Nice! Nice!" shouted Buddy. "Way to burst your balls out there!"

The Stars began responding to Dave's body signals and eye contact. They moved around the floor at Dave's unspoken suggestions, and they willingly trusted him with the ball.

Jack took a pass off a break and canned a shot from twenty feet out. Silky went backdoor and Dave delivered the ball on the money for a slam-dunk.

4Q
5:21
NY–103
SLC–102


Reed plugged on from ten feet and Dave ran a pretty pick and roll with Ardell. Each player had ten hands, five heads and one will.

4Q
4:08
NY–107
SLC–104


The Utes were on a two-on-one break, George Boone boring in on the Stars' lone defender, Dave Brooks. Dave hopped in front of Boone, forcing the Ute guard to rein-in his momentum long enough to change his direction. As he did, Dave jumped to the side and stuck Boone like a picador lancing a charging bull. The ball was poked free and Dave pushed it upcourt on his way to an uncontested lay-up. Except Dave pulled up at the foul line and waited a beat until Reed jackaled up behind him. Reed's eyes bugged with disbelief as Dave plopped an easy two points in his lap.

4Q
2:19
NY–114
SLC–108


The Stars frolicked through the remainder of the game. The final score was 121 to 112, and the Stars hugged each other as they danced off to the locker room.

# CHAPTER THIRTEEN

MOST OF the clubs in the National Basketball Association traveled on regularly scheduled airlines—the Red Eye Special to and from the coast; the Sunrise flight out to Denver. The New York Stars and the Los Angeles Lakers, however, flew by charter. So the Stars and their camp followers left Salt Lake City ninety minutes after the final buzzer, while the Utes weren't able to depart until six-forty-five the next morning.

Throughout the flight Wayne sat in the press section and repeated on demand the pious, self-serving speech he had delivered to the team in the post-game locker room, carefully omitting the confused harangue on "spirit and pride" he had laid on the players, especially after Quinton told Wayne that he sounded like an A & P commercial. For public consumption, Wayne confined himself to an explanation of how and why he had deliberately gotten himself ejected from the ball game.

While his coach jabbered away and his teammates peacefully snoozed, Dave sat awake, his eyes tightly closed. The glow from the game had burned out, and Dave was feeling chilly.

It was snowing when they landed at Kennedy International at 3:00 A.M. Dave waited on Reed while the rest of the party ate up all the taxicabs.

"I don't like this crazy Yankee weather," Reed said. "On account of we have practice tomorrow afternoon I think I'm gonna stay in town tonight. You're welcome to hang around. There's plenty of room."

"No, thanks," Dave said.

The only cabs left were gypsy jalopies driven by hostile looking men with scarred, shadowy faces. Dave knew that Reed's girl was stashed on West Seventy-second Street, so he asked to be dropped off at a subway station.

"Any time," Reed said. "Glad to oblige. Hey, roomie, you done okay tonight."

As he descended the steps Dave zipped up his parka against the cold, sharp and moist subterranean air. The fusty concrete floor of the station was overlaid with swirling paper sweepings, including a torn fragment from the back page of the *Daily News* announcing the results of the Stars-Seattle game: "SILKY SNUFFS SONICS, 105-104."

A paunchy middle-aged man was working the change booth, the entire structure encased by a padlocked fence with bars across the counter. John Girandella wore a grimy brown uniform and a shiny badge. The Seventy-second Street station had been his regular post for the past twelve years. He looked up now, bleary-eyed and unseeing, as Dave approached.

"How many?" he asked.

"One, please," Dave said. Dave rode the subways often but never carried any tokens. They were too light, and somehow, too sterile—chits for a machine.

The opening through which business was transacted stood at a height perfectly suitable for normal customers, but to claim his token Dave had to bend conspicuously. His hovering, lingering bulk popped John Girandella's head up with instant alarm.

"What you want, mister?" John said. "You got the right change. Right?"

Dave nodded and headed over to the turnstiles, while John did a pronounced double take.

"Wait a minute, mister!" John said urgently. "Yeah! You're Dave Brooks! I seen you on tv. . . ."

Dave eased into a loose, tired smile.

"How are you friend?" Dave said. "Do you suppose you could tell me what time the next uptown train's due?"

"Nobody knows," John said, "but it'll probably be coming in soon . . . holy mackerel! I can't believe it's you. I thought all you ballplayers rode in cabs and fancy cars. Holy mackerel! I saw the game tonight. Hey, that Silky Sims is really terrific, ain't he?"

"He sure was," Dave said.

"Hey, hey, Dave! Don't run away! Ain't nothing coming for a while yet. Let's talk a little 'til your train comes. Jeez, Dave, I'm sitting here all night from ten to six in the morning like I'm blind. . . ."

"Sure," Dave said. He walked over to the cage and leaned against the bars. "How do you like it inside there?"

"It's great! I got my radio and a couple of sandwiches. There's a lot of room in here. You'd be surprised. . . . Hey, there's one thing you gotta do for me, Dave, you gotta sign me an autograph. . . . Hey, lots of famous people coming through here. Seventy-second Street is a very popular place. . . ."

The clerk pushed a nub of pencil and a soiled napkin through the slot. "Yeah," he said, "the old scooter Phil

Rizzuto was in here about five years back, and last September I saw Paul Simon. But you're my biggest celebrity up close, Dave. Let me tell you, I'm a real big fan of yours, me and all my friends. I just wanna ask you one thing though . . . are you guys gonna beat the Lakers? That Jabbar is something, ain't he? But is he really that good? I mean, is it just cause he's so tall—"

"Jabbar, my friend, is the best there ever was," Dave said. "He'd be great if he was a foot shorter."

"Yeah," John said, "that's what I said. Jabbar is something, got that sky hook, don't he? Hey, Dave, how you guys gonna stop him? I mean, what's Smalley got up his sleeve? C'mon, you can tell me, I won't say nothing to nobody. I swear it on my mother—"

A sound of tortured steel came roaring out of the tunnel, and Dave could feel the dusty air already getting nervous.

"Have to go," Dave said, "that's my train."

"Hey, Dave!" John said desperately, "you gotta shake my hand! C'mon, you gotta do it. Phil Rizzuto did it!"

The clerk tried to force his right hand through the slot, but it wouldn't fit.

"Come on outside," Dave suggested. He could see the train's headlights flashing into the station. "But hurry."

"What's that? Wha'd you say? *Me walk outta this here booth?* You must be crazy, man. Hey! How do I know for sure you're really Dave Brooks? Uh, uh, mister! Hey, for all I know you're some kind of nut, one of those homicidal maniacs. . . . Oh no, buddy, you ain't no real Dave Brooks, just look like him. Get the fuck *lost*, creep. You didn't fool me one bit."

The walls of the subway car were spray-painted in-

135

side and out with a hundred garish designs, each one of the twisting patterns centering around the artist's name: "The Stroker," "Gorgo II," "Pancho Vanilla," . . . The screaming, desperate colors made Dave wince.

Except for a wino sleeping in the far corner, the car was deserted. Dave had ridden the subway often enough to understand that these beaten, decrepit old men were harmless. Hopeless. Whenever one of them asked him for "some spare change," he just naturally emptied his pockets, and felt terrible.

He closed his eyes now and slept. The deep subway rumble massaged his aching body. The warmth of machinery came seeping through the molded plastic seats and loosened his back. He slept for several minutes, until a sudden sharp screech of metal-braking-metal bolted his head upright, and when the noise passed once more was lulled into a tender sleep.

When the doors opened on Eighty-sixth Street a heavy-set black woman got on, closely followed by a youth in a raveling Navy peacoat. The woman quickly settled herself near the wino, but the youth carefully surveyed the car before choosing a seat. He was in his late teens, clean-shaven and, except for his coat, neatly dressed. He also wore a pair of mirrored sunglasses. He finally slumped into a seat directly across the aisle from Dave.

Dave napped intermittently, trying to wade into the shallow, unfocused patch of sleep that lingered just beyond his reach. Several drowsy images dragged themselves across his wispy dreams: Wayne Smalley's chattering teeth in a glass, a grafittied ABA basketball being dribbled by a team of eight-foot robots . . . and then a menacing, real-life shadow.

Dave snapped open his eyes to see the peacoated

youth sitting beside him, and holding a straight edge razor to his neck.

"My name is Desperado Dan," he said. "Gimme your wallet or I'll cut your throat."

Dave moved wide-eyed, and gingerly, to pull out his wallet from his hip pocket. He half-thought he was still dreaming.

"Don't try nothing funny," the youth warned as he flashed his blade. "Don't make me cut you. Just slow down. That's it. Easy does it. Now give it here."

The youth slid Dave's wallet into his coat and started backing slowly toward the doors.

"Remember, sucker," the youth said. "You just got mugged by Desperado Dan. That's me. Don't forget to tell the cops it was Desperado Dan. . . ."

The train clanged to a halt and the doors split open, but the kid paused momentarily to look back at the scene of the crime . . . "Hold on. Hey, don't I know you? Ain't you . . . ? Yeah! It's my man, Brooksie!"

The youth let the door close and came lunging back over to shake Dave's hand.

"I'm real sorry, man. Real sorry. Hey, you know? I didn't realize it was you. Man, I never would have bothered *you*, man. . . . You should ought to have said something right away. . . ."

Dave shook his head in relief. "How about my wallet, Mr. Desperado?"

"Oh yeah!" He forked it over with a sheepish, almost gentle child's hand. "Hey, man—" he smiled "—could I get your autograph?"

"Sure," Dave said, being grateful for the switch from mugger to fan.

The boy reached back into his jacket and extracted a

small spiral-edged notebook and a Bic pen. "Sign it to me, okay? Sign it to me personal. You know? Not to no Desperado Dan. Hell, that ain't my real name. I just saw that in a John Wayne golden oldie, you dig? My real name . . . don't you never tell nobody . . . my real name is Jose Garcia Weatherspoon. That's my real name. No shit. I work in a car wash during the day. Windshields is my specialty. But I do this at night sometimes. For kicks. You know. The *News* even had my name in it last week. Yeah, man, I'm famous just like you. I grabbed some old lady over on the D train. But she said my name was Desperado *Don.* Would you believe it, man? Some people are so stupid. You know? . . . Hey, Dave! You know what? Since you're so famous and everybody knows who you are . . . could you do me a big favor, man? Just tell the cops you was robbed by me. Desperado *Dan,* I mean. Not Jose Weatherspoon. Jesus, what a name, right? But, hey, listen! Don't do it if it'll get you in no trouble, man. You know? I mean, it's a real pleasure just to meet you. Hey, you guys win or lose last night?"

Desperado Dan stayed on the train for two more stops. Before he left he copped a poverty plea and Dave dug out a five dollar bill, which Desperado Dan promptly asked him to autograph.

"I can sell it for maybe six and a quarter," he said as the subway doors slowly hushed across his face.

"New York, New York, it's a wonderful town . . ." Dave hummed the words, but he wasn't smiling.

# CHAPTER FOURTEEN

THEIR CHARTERED flight out of Salt Lake City made the Stars a lock in game three. Wayne convened a practice on Friday afternoon, tinkered with the game plan and drilled the team in the Velma options. Afterward they watched films for another hour and a half. The Utes, on the other hand, didn't reach New York until three-fifteen that same afternoon. After being stacked up and having to circle the airport for nearly an hour, and then battling the rush hour traffic, the travel-dusted Ute party didn't arrive at their hotel until seven o'clock. Joe Maloney could barely squeeze out a thirty minute shooting practice the morning of the game.

The Las Vegas point spread was a syndicated feature that regularly appeared in all local papers. It was conspicuously printed on the back pages of both the *Daily News* and the New York *Dispatch*. Even the two game officials knew that the Stars were favored by nine and a half points.

The NBA's corps of referees was backbone to the

league's integrity, character and credibility. And they were all honest men. The supervisor of officials made public claims that all of his men possessed "the judgment of Supreme Court magistrates." By virtue of having logged twenty-one years and over ten thousand miles with a whistle in his mouth, Nick Hatcher was the NBA's Chief Justice.

Nick was trim, swarthy and forty-three years old, but thanks to his mania for physical conditioning he could easily pass for a man in his early thirties. As the league's senior official, Nick's whistle always had a vote-and-a-half whenever he worked. He earned $36,000 a year and he loved his wife, his kids and his job, not necessarily in that order. Over the past few years Nick had also developed a passion for nifty clothing. When his natty threads were properly hung from his five foot seven inch wire-hanger body, and when his false teeth were in place, Nick was a considerable sharpie. Nick and his family now lived in suburban New Jersey, though he'd begun his career officiating YMCA games in Flatbush; his mother, two sisters and three brothers still lived in Brooklyn. Each time Nick worked the Garden, the Stars front office slipped him ten extra "comps"; even for play-off games when MSG was SRO. Especially.

Inside the minuscule officials dressing room Nick dutifully went through his usual pre-game procedure: ran in place for five minute double-time bursts; did sets of knee-bends and hamstring stretchers; gobbled honey balls by the handful.

Nick's zebra-shirted partner for the upcoming ball game was a quick twenty-nine-year-old, ex-collegiate athlete named Phil Keller. The younger man had been working the pro game for only four years, but his lively style and blond good looks were rapidly making him one of the league's most colorful basketball officials.

Neither official cared very much for the other. Keller felt that Nick was over the hill, too slow to cover the ground. He also resented Nick always being the "lead official." The young man would like nothing better than to make Nick look bad on national television.

The two men made their preparations in silence. Ten minutes before game time there was a loud knock at the door. Nick did another hasty round of knee-bends, while Keller did a fast weave in front of the mirror, spraying the finishing touches to his hair. Nick carefully insinuated himself into his black warm-up jacket and, mindful of the protocol of his seniority, stepped up to the younger man.

"Good luck," Nick said with a professional air. He knew the kid was a showboat who constantly had to out-run his mistakes. "Let's have a good ball game."

Keller laughed through clenched teeth.

A burly, armed Pinkerton led the two officials through the congested halls and tunnels and up the ramp. The fans acknowledged their appearance with a few obligatory boos and catcalls.

"Ya bums!" shouted one.

"I never hoid a no two blind mice!" shouted another.

Keller glanced up at the smoky abuse and laughed easily. He loved it. Until a foghorn of a voice came booming out of the artificial twilight: "Hey, you fucken thiefs! You faggot-commie bastards! . . ."

The brutality of it locked Keller's knees and pulled him up short, filled him with thoughts of presidential assassinations, political bombings and kamikaze murderers. He stood frozen until Nick backtracked to pull at his arm.

"Let's go, rabbit ears," Nick gloated. "We've got work to do."

In addition to baiting officials and opposing ball-players, the Stars fans also prided themselves on the sheets of noise they could generate. The Garden crowd especially delighted in drowning out larger and larger portions of the national anthem with their famous cheer of "Defense! Defense!" The situation had come to a head several years back when Houston was in New York for an important play-off game. The fans, at a fever pitch, had managed to engulf "The Star Spangled Banner" just after "the rockets' red glare." Ever since then the Stars home games had been serenaded in with "America the Beautiful."

While the Utes were being introduced, a small black youngster in a Stars T-shirt came running up to their side of the court.

"Hey Boone, you goon," he shouted. "Fuck your mother."

Nick skillfully spun the game ball in his hands until he received the go-ahead signal from the network spotter. Then he summoned the spotlight by lifting the ball overhead like a sacrificial lamb, dipped his body under the ball and twirled it high into the air.

Silky and Jonah James bounded up after it, grunting with the effort. Silky's lively fingers got there first, and he tapped the ball over to Reed.

The Stars hustled smartly downcourt and worked a Velma backdoor play against a sluggish Utes defense, Silky sneaking past his man and converting a pass from Dave into the game's first score.

142

At one time, George Boone was the finest guard in the defunct American Basketball Association. But like Jim McDaniels, George McGinnis, Charley Scott and other ABA expatriates before him, Boone had difficulty trying to establish his game in the NBA. The new set of officials was not accustomed to Boone's moves and talents, so their first impulse was to whistle him into a box.

Boone now received a pass near the extended foul line, and Dave jumped right on him, attacking every dribble. The Ute guard spun sharply to the hoop and fired up an off-balance shot, his follow-through grazing his arm against Dave's shoulder. Keller, who had center court responsibilities, flattened out his hands to indicate incidental contact. But Nick stepped up and blew Boone down for an offensive foul.

Silky levitated his man with the first head fake, then dipped underneath and broke toward the basket. But Jonah James materialized from the weak side just in time to make Silky change his shot. A pair of hungry hands and a basketball challenged each other a foot above the rim. Nick Hatcher peered up past the two contorted bodies, at a leather spheroid being manipulated almost six feet above his own eye level, through a haze of smoke and grit. Silky pumped twice, extended his arm another couple of inches and slithered the ball home off the glass. No contact was made.

Nick blew the whistle and called a foul on James. Once Nick had told the story with numbers to the scorer, the sequence became immutable history. Bad history, but history.

"Lucky guess!" shouted a fan.

Jeremy Johnson sat on the bench wedged between Quinton and Kevin. Quinton was telling jokes and doing a play-by-play, but J.J. wasn't interested in his teammates's hully-gully. J.J. was mulling over the idea of waylaying his coach with a tire iron in a dark alley.

The Utes shot a meager thirty-two per cent from the field during the first quarter, and the Stars jumped out on top, 29 to 19.

Ardell grabbed an offensive rebound in a crowd and bounced right back up. Three opponents conspired to clobber him and Ardell missed the shot. Keller, positioned along the base line, was screened out so that he heard the foul rather than saw it. Nonetheless he tooted his pipe and began to snap out an educated guess.

"I got it!" Nick shouted to him. "My call! Number thirty-seven, blues, James, with the hip. Bartholomew is shooting, two for two."

Keller handed the ball to Ardell at the foul line. He would have called the foul on Kim Covington. He would have been wrong, but he still resented Nick showing him up.

Tyrone White sat on the end of the Stars bench, his feet propped up on the twenty-four-second clock. He was temporarily a leper, and his teammates were sly to avoid him. For all they knew a sprained wrist was contagious.

Silky nailed down a twisting fifteen-footer from the right side despite Kim Covington's defensive hounding.

"Dust in your eyes," Silky said. "You chump, you can't stop me."

Silky then turned and broke into his nonchalant

trance-dance down the court, and barely saw Covington roar by him to take a lead pass and toss in a soft lay-up. Wayne was not shy in calling Silky's attention to the play: "What the fuck are you doing? Don't turn your fucken head, Silky! You'll fucken unscrew it!"

Jack Mathias set a solid pick on Ben Ellis' blind side ... Ellis recovered in time to hammer a short, blunt forearm against Jack's sternum. Jack muscled up and tried to hold his position but Ellis clubbed his way through. Ellis had been Bogarting people for the last nine seasons. His educated savagery was the key to his reputation as "a good defensive player and fine rebounder." His forearms paid his rent and fed his children. Jack Mathias was only a rookie.

Nick called Jack for setting a moving pick. . . .

The Stars led at the half, 57 to 42.

UCLA ran up a record of 89 and 3 with two national championships during Tyrone White's varsity career. The advance word from all the pro scouts was that Tyrone was the finest penetrating guard since Kevin Porter, and the DC Darts made him a first round pick. Tyrone paid his rookie dues behind the Darts' perpetual all-stars, Bill Chandelier and Don Cherry. He played well enough when he got the floor time but never quite well enough to make it into the starting lineup. Still, Tyrone didn't mind laying low until he got the feel of playing pro ball. He minded his own business and did some coke when it all got too heavy. But Tyrone was a Watts-child and he refused to be bossed around. He never carried any of the veterans' suitcases, not even Wes Unseld's. When his teammates saw that Tyrone was willing to go to war, they let the whole hassle drop out of sight. Unseld branded him "the Ghost" and everybody walked wide circles around Tyrone.

After another year of sitting, Tyrone realized his career was on a treadmill. When the Darts front office refused to trade him, Tyrone considered his options, telephoned the club's owner and threatened to rape his daughter. The next day Tyrone was dealt to Philadelphia for Fred Carter and a medium draft choice. The new surroundings did little for Tyrone's playing time. The 76ers' backcourt featured Doug Collins and Lloyd Free, and Tyrone was still an insurance policy. His incendiary pride finally simmered over, and he began having violent arguments with his coach. From Philadelphia Tyrone was sent to Portland, and then on to Kansas City. Over the years he came to be thought of as the best fourth guard in the league—not third but fourth. . . .

From K.C., Tyrone was traded back to Philadelphia and, after a three-month stay, was deposited with the Pistons. In Detroit Tyrone dabbled briefly with the Black Muslims and learned to carry a gun, which was all too much for the Pistons brass to deal with and before his second training camp with the ball club it was announced that Tyrone had failed his physical examination. No details were given.

Tyrone was now thirty-one years old. He languished on the waiver pile and on the blacklist for ten months while he worked as a liquor salesman in Los Angeles, where he finally received a phone call from Red Holzman.

During their initial meeting Holzman stunned Tyrone by offering a one-year, no-cut, no-trade contract. "I don't care what you do with your private life," Holzman said. "I don't care who you see, where you go or how late you get to sleep. Just play hard and don't call attention to yourself and we'll get along. There's a home for you here if you want to work for it."

Holzman's rap sounded like the real thing to Tyrone. During training camp he watched, listened, followed orders, and said nothing. By the time the exhibition season was under way his game was sweet as candy. He started alongside Frazier and completed his first season with New York averaging a steady 16.2 points and 4.1 assists per game. He also ran the show whenever Frazier took a rest. Tyrone's quietude survived Holzman's retirement, and his 23.8 scoring over the past season shouted happy tidings into his new coach's ear. Wayne didn't mess too much with Tyrone.

Nobody did. Throughout all his changes, Tyrone's disposition remained acerbic. He volunteered information only to his agent, his lawyer and his accountant. The only other occasions on which Tyrone spoke up took place whenever a teammate or a reporter couldn't resist asking him a question. He avoided media appearances, but he didn't resist them. There were rumors, however, that he never brushed his teeth to help ward off the press.

Despite the dour reputation, Dorothy Evans was mounted on her milk box and about to conduct a quickie live interview with Tyrone White.

"Tell us, Tyrone," Dorothy said with a pumped-up smile, "what is the exact status of your injured wrist?"

"It hurts."

"Yes," Dorothy said, "I'm sure it does. The word out of the league office is that it's a bad sprain."

Tyrone nodded agreement.

"Is it feeling any better?"

"Than what?"

"Better than yesterday?"

"Yes."

Dorothy stared merrily into Tyrone's bottomless eyes. "The score doesn't show it," she beamed, "but the Stars have to miss your scoring and your leadership in the backcourt. . . ."

Tyrone shifted his weight and waited to hear a question mark.

"Uhm," said Dorothy, "do you think you'll be ready for tomorrow's game?"

"Ask me tomorrow."

"Tell us, Tyrone, to what do you attribute your recently newfound success here in New York at this stage of your pro career? And why did you have so much trouble with all the other coaches and teams you played for?"

"That's a difficult question for me to answer"—from mumbles to professor—Tyrone said, his eyes brightening momentarily. "I mean, I could create wherever I played. I mean, even in K.C. where the team was always at a deficit. And I always liked playing pro ball. I mean, it gives me the chance to talk to the youths in the ghet-to. Where I was born and where my roots are at. But that's a difficult question, Doris. Maybe you better ask somebody else."

"Thank you, Tyrone White."

A stare from bottomless eyes.

Quinton drove the base line, clearing his path with a series of muffled elbows and hidden shoves. He'd been using the same *modus operandi* for twelve years, but young Phil Keller would have none of it. Keller was the one with the future, and the ballplayers would have to conform to his standards, to his version of how the game should be played. . . . Keller dashed over to the scorer's table, did a bump and grind for the tv cameras, and called Quinton on a charge.

"Fucken blindman!" a fan observed.

Nick wasn't too happy with his partner's call either. Quinton was an old-timer, an NBA curio who had long ago earned the right to make his own rules. From his station near the midcourt line, Nick came right back and piped an offensive foul on Boone. Nick and Keller exchanged hostile glances as play resumed. And George Boone, catching the wind, didn't attempt going to the basket for the remainder of the game.

Silky tried an off-balance shot, jumping only off his right foot, but Covington wasn't fooled and jammed the ball back into Silky's hand. The crowd twittered with disbelief as Nick signaled for a jump ball. But Silky was upset, badly embarrassed, and threw himself into a sulk. Snatching the ball up off the floor, he turned his back on the official. Nick was about to slap a technical on Silky when Dave sidled up behind his frustrated teammate.

"Give him the ball, brother," Dave said as he tapped Silky's rump. "Show him the second half of that move later on."

Silky shrugged, forced a husky laugh and tossed the ball to Nick.

"Say, hey, Hatcher, your mother eats bat shit!" Hatcher sighed, fighting off the rabbit. . . .

Quinton's left knee buckled as he tried to change direction, and this time Nick had no alternative but to call him for traveling. In fact, Quinton's knee hadn't been working properly for the past six years. He was accustomed to playing in pain, and trying to compensate by

149

moving to his left with extreme caution. Mostly, though, he relied on an athletic instinct conditioned by the intelligence of his pain. It kept him alive.

The Stars were up by twenty early in the fourth quarter when Wayne called down the bench for Jeremy Johnson. But J.J. heard nothing. He was too busy stewing in his own chimeras of revenge and vindication. Larry Graham had to reach over and pat his knee.

"It's you," Graham said.

He finally rose to, "Sit down, Johnson . . . ya bum, ya!"

In five minutes of playing time J.J. accumulated three blocked shots, two goal-tending violations, four personal fouls, four offensive rebounds and six points. He ran around the court like a crazed ostrich. And then, in an instant, J.J.'s nervous energy seemed to have emptied itself out. His body suddenly went listless, his timing went on vacation; passes bounced off his limp hands, his legs turned to Jell-o. J.J. was still shaking when he returned to the bench.

Nick was calling a hacking foul on Larry Graham, planting himself in front of the official scorer and beginning to flash the familiar hand semaphors. Suddenly Keller was jumping dramatically between Nick and the scorer.

"No foul!" Keller yelled, "no foul!" He turned and yelled again, right into Nick's face. "No foul! I got the call. A three-second violation before the foul took place. Blue ball out of bounds."

Nick turned red-faced, hesitated, and finally ran upcourt. Keller—a slow-boot punk.

Quinton now conducted the New York scrubs

150

through garbage time. Finding himself leading the slowest fast break in history, he did a stutter-goosestep coming down the lane—his left foot extended and his dribble still alive, he actually skipped once on his right foot . . . a move meant as an insult to his opponents.

Also a signal to them that they were dead. The game got loose and sloppy down the stretch, neither official being anxious to drag it out. In the closing minutes the Utes did manage a late burst behind a fullcourt zone press. Boone's twenty footer at the buzzer meant the Stars had failed to cover the spread: final score was New York 118, Salt Lake City 109.

Two to go.

# CHAPTER FIFTEEN

SILKY SIMS was successful, famous, affluent, handsome, street-slick, street-dumb and just turned twenty-two. He lived in a seven-room penthouse on Fifth Avenue and Sixty-seventh Street. The most inexpensive suite in the richly appointed building sold for fifty thousand dollars. Silky's apartment had cost twice that much, a sum equal to his original bonus for signing with the Stars. When he was a kid, Silky used to sleep in the same room with Lamar, his older half-brother, and his two younger sisters. These days Silky slept in a master bedroom that featured a mirror instead of a ceiling and a heart-shaped waterbed.

But sometimes the worm squirmed in Silky's soul and he had trouble sleeping.

It was ten o'clock on Sunday morning and Silky was still floating heavily in the middle of his bed. Adorned in black silk pajamas, his head cushioned by a pair of stuffed black satin pillows, his eyelids pressed tightly together . . . he had nonetheless been awake for hours.

152

The fourth game of the Stars-Utes series was scheduled for that afternoon. Silky was averaging twenty-seven points over the first three contests, and he was being acclaimed as an authentic all-star by the press. But in the luxurious seclusion of his bedroom—where he had but to open his eyes to gaze at himself full-length—Silky floated and brooded.

The fact was that Silky never played well indoors in the daytime. Sunlight hoops meant playing on asphalt behind a gaping hole in a bulging fence, with red bandanas tied around sweaty foreheads and a pile of dog shit on the foul line. Uniforms, whistles, wooden floors and nets were for nighttime. The Stars afternoon ball games were unnatural creatures, and Silky was afraid to the death of playing poorly. In his mind failure and humiliation were two heads of the same gruesome beast—his young, confident universe always rutted out when he didn't play well.

He even thought for a moment of sitting out the game . . . of claiming that his back hurt or that his stomach needed pumping . . . of staying home and watching the game on the tube . . . of dreaming himself into Sunday night. . . .

The harsh ringing of the telephone reddened the inside of Silky's head as he sloshed into a sitting position and rubbed his eyes open.

"Hello, Silky? It's Sy. . . ."

Silky's body yawned silently. He looked straight up, relieved to note that though his hair was matted his good looks had survived still another night.

"Sy Kersh . . . your agent . . . sorry if I woke you. . . ."

"Yeah," Silky said through fuzzy teeth. "What you want?"

"Silky, I hate to call you so early on a Sunday morning but I just got your latest redecorating bills, another three thou for a mirror over the fireplace! That's kind of a whopper, Silky! Wouldn't you agree that's going a little too far . . . ?"

"Yeah," Silky said absently, reflecting that Clyde Frazier never had a mirror in the living room—with the flickering fire turning him and *his* lady of the moment into frolicking, fornicating, golden gods. Not even the Dipper's million dollar pad in Los Angeles had one in the *living* room. "Yeah, like I got real good taste, you know?"

"I know," Kersh said quickly, "I realize that. And nobody deserves it more than you. But, Silky . . . we've been through all this before . . . you've got to slow down, man. You're not a millionaire yet. You can be, you will be. But not yet. You hear me? That's me warning you, Silky. Sy Kersh. Remember that. Just read your bank book. There's no more checks from the ball club until after the play-offs. You're running out of bread. . . ."

Kersh's hints stuck like burrs into Silky's skin. Whenever Silky's appetite outdistanced his paychecks, Kersh always seemed happy to lend him some ready cash. To date, Silky owed his agent nearly fifty thousand dollars. It had all started when Kersh "advanced" Silky the money he needed to purchase his fancy penthouse. But over the intervening two years Kersh had become much more than Silky's agent. When Silky became negligent in paying his bills, Kersh took over the responsibility—for an extra three percent.

"Yeah, yeah," Silky said as he plopped around and fired up a cigarette. He couldn't believe he was really broke. . . . Hell, he hadn't seen a cockroach in two years.

Kersh must be running something down on him, but right now he was feeling too tight to worry about it.

"Listen, *Seymour*, why don't you just get on your horse and round me up some more bucks? It's simple as that. That's part of your job too, ain't it?"

Silky stood up alternately to scratch and fondle his genitals. "What about that soda commercial? What's happening with that?"

"We're still negotiating," Kersh said, "but they're really impressed with the way you've been playing lately. Especially that Seattle game. That shot you hit put you in the middle of a lot of people's heads. It was terrific, Silky, I mean the spin and everything. So we're getting close, you're going to be real big, kid. Leave it to me and just be patient. Soon."

The impending ball game loomed again in Silky's head. He climbed to his feet, dragging the phone over to the window. "Mister Silks can take care of himself with the brothers," Silky said. "You let me worry about the playing. Just you get gainfully employed and churn me up some bucks. In a hurry, hear?" He drew back the curtains to see the sun glittering like a razor blade.

"Silky, baby, I'm out there working and sweating for you all day. And that's the God's honest truth. Matter of fact, that's the real reason why I called, I got you a big tv spot doing a thing for a national distributor."

Silky jumped eagerly away from the sunlight. "Outasight, man," he said. "That's solid, brother. Now you cooking. Tell me what it is man. They want me to model some clothes or something, right?"

"Sure, sure," Kersh said hastily. "The spot pays a thousand for about a half hour's shooting. A thousand, Silky. Plus you get residuals, limo service door-to-door

155

and lunch at Twenty-One. . . . But I got to let the man know by this afternoon—"

"Yeah! Yeah! All right! All root! But lay it all over me, man, What is it? A car? A superstar rent-a-car? Yeah, that's it! . . . Tell me, man . . . hey, man, how come you ain't telling me . . . ?"

"It's for the Hand-O-Matic Corporation," Kersh confessed. "One of the fastest growing companies in the country."

"Yeah, keep talking."

"They make automatic hand washers."

"Say what?! What the fuck is that? Hand washers?! Are you jiving me, you dufus?"

"No, no, on the level. A thousand up front with lots of residuals . . . maybe two, maybe three G's all together—"

"Later for you, man," Silky said. "I don't want nothing to do wif no chump-shit like that, man. I want a car or some clothes stuff. What you doing to me, man. What you doing to me, man. What you getting me involved with that jive-shit for? Mannh!"

"Believe me, Silky," Kersh said confidently, "it's a start, a good start. I know the business. Believe me, trust me. I know what I'm doing—"

"Yeah, I'm sure you do." All the hustlers working the street swore the very same thing.

"What can I tell you? Look, Silky, I got a call on another line. All I can say is we're almost there. Just play good and stay out of trouble. I'll be in touch."

"Yeah, catch you later. . . ."

Silky hung up the phone, his mood deepened. His eyes tried saluting himself once again in his overhead looking glass, but he refused to be cheered. He turned and walked stiffly into his wardrobe room, idly reminded that this afternoon's game would be the Stars' 101st of the season. His closets choked with flashy clothing and expensive finery, his shelves and hangers all lined in black velvet, he now stepped inside the largest closet and picked out his outfit—a patchwork leather suit. Suited his mood.

"Hand-O-Washer," Silky intoned with disgust. "Fucken parasite Jew."

Taking a silent, slow, sullen shower, he prayed for rain to come and brighten his day.

As usual Silky had to hustle to reach the Garden on time, and was only five minutes ahead of a two hundred dollar fine when his taxi pulled up in front of the players' entrance and he carefully extracted his long, spindly frame from the rear seat. A knot of black street urchins immediately heralded him by name:

"It's Silky, man!"

"Silky!"

"Hey, you! Silky! Gotta have your autograph, man!"

Light on their merry heels came the rest of the foaming, jostling mob, including an excited young father dangling his infant son, a dozen tourists, a number of ladies looking for a look, and a passel of undifferentiated bystanders. They surged in on Silky now with their demands that he sign library cards, newspapers, bus transfers, score sheets, racing forms. . . . And Silky, who loved to wallow in the public, obliged as many as he could, signing half of the requests with his right hand and half with his left, all the while relentlessly slicing his way through the crowd toward the large metal door.

As he did so a gang of black kids hopped and skipped all around him, each youngster seemingly awed with Silky's presence, that in turn made him proud of his own future. The boys seeded the springtime air with their random chatter.

"You a good player, Silky!"

"How did you grow so tall, man?"

"My brother Reggie say you even better than Docta Jay!"

"Hey, Silky! Can you touch the top of the basket ...?"

A clean laugh bubbled up into Silky's nose as he remembered when he was one of their insistent company ... coming early to Knicks games, even when he didn't have a ticket ... jabbering away at The Pearl, at Dr. J., or at Clyde ... at whoever the hell would jabber back at him. ...

Back at them ...

Silky dug the fact that his trip also belonged to his people. So he teased, tapped and slapped his way toward the door.

"Hey, little dude," Silky said to a smudged black face, "where's your front teeth at?" He turned to another. ... "Hey, Stretch, my man, how old are *you* ...?"

An eight-year-old suddenly popped up alongside, running to keep up. "Watch this!" he said. The youngster wore a green Welfare parka, and his patched dungarees were several sizes too small. He spun a balloon of a basketball on his fingertip. "Check it out! I betchu can't do that!"

"We got to have a party for you, small fry," Silky said, "to have your pants meet your shoes!" Then he reached down and whisked the ball out of the youngster's hand.

"Stuffed!" shouted a taller boy. "Doobie got hisself stuffed!"

"Doobie got chomped!"

"In yo' face, Doobie!"

Silky scooped the ball off the sidewalk and signed his name plus "With best wishes to Doobie" across its smooth, worn surface.

As Silky approached the door, he flung a last look back over his shoulder. The core of black kids was already halfway down the block, screaming, dribbling the ball, and chasing each other in and out of the slow Sunday morning traffic. Abruptly, chillingly, Silky somehow felt older than he'd ever felt before. He recalled the face of a dead child named Sylvester, and for an instant longed to join the reckless, carefree sport he'd left behind.

"Just under the wire," a security guard said. "You're the last one in."

The door clanged shut behind Silky as the bright yellow darkness sucked him in. . . .

## NEW YORK STARS (123)

| | MIN | FG | FT | RB | A | PF | TP |
|---|---|---|---|---|---|---|---|
| Bartholomew | 39 | 7-13 | 5-9 | 17 | 2 | 4 | 15 |
| Sims | 35 | 4-19 | 4-6 | 5 | 0 | 5 | 12 |
| Mathias | 40 | 6-9 | 1-1 | 15 | 3 | 3 | 13 |
| Brooks | 42 | 8-14 | 2-2 | 8 | 9 | 4 | 18 |
| Carson | 35 | 12-23 | 3-3 | 2 | 2 | 1 | 27 |
| Brown | 19 | 4-6 | 8-9 | 0 | 4 | 4 | 16 |
| Graham | 18 | 4-11 | 2-4 | 7 | 1 | 2 | 10 |
| Harmon | 6 | 2-3 | 0-2 | 4 | 0 | 3 | 4 |
| Johnson | 8 | 2-5 | 0-0 | 6 | 0 | 3 | 4 |
| White | ----------DID NOT PLAY---------- | | | | | | |

## SALT LAKE CITY UTES (108)

| | MIN | FG | FT | RB | A | PF | TP |
|---|---|---|---|---|---|---|---|
| Covington | 44 | 4-12 | 4-6 | 12 | 4 | 4 | 12 |
| Carter | 30 | 3-7 | 0-1 | 6 | 0 | 3 | 6 |
| James | 41 | 8-17 | 9-13 | 18 | 1 | 4 | 25 |
| Boone | 45 | 7-21 | 6-8 | 5 | 5 | 5 | 20 |
| Barnes | 25 | 4-10 | 2-4 | 2 | 2 | 5 | 10 |
| Ellis | 24 | 5-8 | 3-3 | 8 | 2 | 3 | 13 |
| Fullmer | 7 | 3-4 | 1-1 | 2 | 0 | 2 | 7 |
| Lassner | -----------DID NOT PLAY-------- | | | | | | |
| Ramsey | 23 | 5-9 | 3-5 | 4 | 1 | 3 | 13 |
| Tierney | 7 | 0-1 | 2-2 | 1 | 1 | 0 | 2 |

```
NY   33  31  26  33 - 123
SLC  21  27  23  37 - 108
```

Attendance - 20,146

One to go.

# CHAPTER SIXTEEN

NEW YORK. (UPI)—Silky Sims scored 17 points in the 4th quarter to lead the New York Stars to a 124-111 series-clinching fourth win over the Salt Lake City Utes. Sims' explosion broke open a tight ball game and many of his crowd-pleasing shots had the loyal New York fans on their feet.

Sims finished with a game-high total of 42 points and 19 rebounds. Dave Brooks also contributed a career-high of 12 assists to the Stars victory.

The win entitles New York to face the seemingly invincible Los Angeles Lakers for the NBA championship. The Lakers reached the finals by routing the DC Darts in four straight games. The championship series begins in Los Angeles on Wednesday evening.

Kim Covington led the Utes with 29 points and 17 rebounds.

Salt Lake City

Covington 12 5-5 29, Carter 4 0-1 8, James 9 6-9 24, Boone 8 5-6 21, Barnes 2 3-4 7, Ellis 4 1-3 9, Fullmer 2 0-0 4, Lassner 1 1-1 3, Ramsey 2 2-3 6, Tierney 0 0-0 0. Totals 44 23-32 111.

New York

Bartholomew 6 3-4 15, Sims 16 10-12 42, Mathias 4 2-2 10, Brooks 3 3-3 9, Carson 9 3-4 21, Brown 3 5-7 11, Graham 1 0-0 2, Harmon 2 0-1 4, Johnson 4 2-4 10. Totals 48 28-37 124.

| Salt Lake City | 28 | 30 | 24 | 29 - 111 |
|----------------|----|----|----|----------|
| New York       | 31 | 29 | 33 | 31 - 124 |

Fouled out: Boone, Mathias. Technical foul: SLC coach Joe Maloney. Total fouls: Salt Lake City 41; New York 33. A: 20, 146.

The final game of the Eastern Division playoffs was an hour into the record books. Several ballplayers were already long gone from the Stars locker room: Since Tyrone failed to suit up, he'd made a congratulatory whisk around the room, then breezed out the door. J.J. and Larry left together, while Reed and Jack each exited alone. Wayne took off right after the television cameras were dismantled. A covey of reporters had pinned Silky on his stool for a half hour, but he'd since moved on too.

Only four players lingered inside the room: Ardell, sitting unshowered in front of his locker; Dave, shaking his long legs into a pair of faded blue jeans; Kevin, wearing only his uniform shorts as he leaned over the whirlpool, bathing his quick-bitten right thumb; Quinton, squatting on his chair like a peanut-butter Buddha. All of the players were noticeably happy, but they were also uncommonly muted and still.

For the most part the media flood had likewise subsided from the dressing room, only three continuing to prowl about: Dorothy Evans, Joe Cunningham and a visiting dignitary named Roland Skyler Boyngton.

Boyngton was the front man for the conglomerate that ruled the Stars. His official title was provost of the New York Stars board of directors, but his duties were strictly functionary. The provost's previous experience included four Purple Hearts in Vietnam, six years as PR man for Grand Union, five years as cat's paw for a roller derby league, starring roles in three spaghetti Westerns and a one term stint as the mayor of Miami Beach. Boyngton had frosted brown hair and rugged good looks. He exuded honor, glamor and charm, and his command mission was to promote morale, loyalty and harmony among the employees. He had spent most of his visit shaking hands and wishing well. . . .

"Congratos," Boyngton said to Ardell. "You played yourself a fine ball game."

"Thank you, sir." Ardell had played forty-five hard minutes, and his molten muscles and fresh bruises still needed towelling.

"Just terrific," Boyngton went on. He inspected the troops only on state occasions and liked to demonstrate a personal interest in the players' physical and mental well-being. "You boys ready for the Lakers? . . . How are you feeling?"

"Fine, sir." Ardell gargled up a glob of organic gelatin and spat it into his towel. "Just fine."

"Terrific," Boyngton said. "Nice talking to you."

Joe Cunningham, New York's general manager, next shepherded Boyngton over to the whirlpool.

"How are you feeling, son?" the provost asked Kevin Harmon with a concerned smile.

"Can't complain, sir," Kevin said, "just as long as we win."

"Terrific. That's really terrific. Nice to chat with you. Keep up the good work."

Dorothy Evans, busy doing spot interviews with members of the team, was lacking sessions with Dave, Kevin and Quinton, but she was running short of tape. She smiled blandly now at Quinton and headed quickly over to Kevin.

"We need some voice-overs for the Laker series," Dorothy chirped, "could I ask you a few things?"

Kevin smiled uneasily and swished his fingers in the warm, heaving water. He had yet to shower and was embarrassed by his own body odor.

"Great," Dorothy said, and switched on her tape machine. "Tell us, Kevin Harmon, what do you think of the Star's chances of beating the Lakers? Most experts don't give you guys much of a shot."

"Well," Kevin said cautiously, "I'm sure we'll be okay once Tyrone comes back. But I guess we'll have to play them one at a time."

"I see." Dorothy peeped into the tub. "What's the matter with your hand?"

"Oh," Kevin said, "it's a . . . I'm soaking my shooting callous. You know. Like the kind you get when you shoot. They're no good for you. If it gets too hard, the balls kind of jerk off to the side and you're in trouble. It's really the balls . . . they're pebbly and kind of rough. . . . So you get a callous on your shooting hand. You know."

164

"Thanks," Dorothy said brightly, trying to conceal her shock and outrage. She wasn't entranced by Kevin's discussing his horrid little masturbation problem. But then she considered the socko human-interest of his confession. She would have to check it out with her producer. . . .

Boyngton followed his guide over to another corner of the room. "Dave Brooks," Cunningham whispered.

"Certainly," Boyngton pealed. "Dave Brooks! Great game. Terrific performance. How are you feeling after such a rough tussle?"

"I'm feeling right fine, sir. How about you?"

Boyngton flexed his war hero grin with the unexpected opportunity. "Pretty good, actually . . . for a man my age, that is. I still swim a mile at the club every chance I get, but lately I've been getting these pains . . ."

Cunningham cleared his throat.

"Nice talking to you," Boyngton said. . . .

Quinton stood in front of his stall, his chunky body clothed only in leopardskin underwear and a pair of argyle Supp-hose. He swung open his locker door and saluted himself in the tiny mirror attached to the inside. He was feeling good right down to his bones.

Quinton's minimum play-off share already amounted to $20,000, with more in the offing should the Stars beat the Lakers. When his retirement became a fact at the end of the season he would also be receiving a severance lump of $144,000, and a $20,000-a-year pension would commence once he turned forty. But New York's latest victory had extended Quinton's active career for at least another four games and seven days. Despite his paunchy features Quinton never had any difficulty attracting his share of sandy foxes and serpentine ladies—so an extra week also meant another dozen or so chicks to play with.

Most of the ballplayers had taken specific notice of the presence of a female in their locker room, several dressing in the bathroom and most being careful to wrap towels around their privates. Quinton alone refused to modify his post-game routine as he strutted his naked carcass in front of Dorothy, winking, leching, fletching and trying to search out the bottoms of her oblivious eyes.

Quinton was feeling feisty and the blood fizzed in his veins like champagne. He leered now at Dorothy as she huddled with Dave.

Dorothy had caught up with Dave just as he was packing his Adidas bag. "Would you mind answering a few questions?"

"Sure," David said, "be glad to."

"Tell us, Dave, what's the taste of winning like? How does it feel to be better than anybody else?"

"I can't say." Dave laughed. "And besides, we really haven't won much yet. The next go-round is the one that counts."

"Tell us, Dave. So far this season the Stars have played twelve exhibition games, eighty-two games in the regular season and ten play-off games. At this stage what effect, if any, does the long season have on your concentration?"

"Well," Dave said slowly, "I don't know. . . . I don't mean to duck your question, but it does seem to me like steelworkers and farmers have longer seasons. . . ."

Ardell was showered and dressed in a jiffy. He nodded over to Dave and slicked hands with Quinton on his way to the door.

"Dell!" Quinton shouted. "What's the good news, brother?"

Ardell's taut, African face surrounded an easy smile. "Jesus is crucified, risen and coming again."

"Amen to that," Quinton said loudly. . . .

Boyngton and Cunningham pulled up in front of Quinton's station. "Terrific work, P."

"That's Q," Cunningham prompted.

"*Q*," said Boyngton. Of course. That's what I was going to say. . . . Got to mind your P's and Q's if you're ever going to amount to anything . . . eh? . . . But how are you Mister Q? I see you have an ice pack on your knee. How are you feeling?"

Quinton's long, thick fingers engulfed the hand the provost proffered. "The knee ain't never too good," Quinton said mischievously. "Sometimes I wisht I could drill a hole and pour some oil in the motherfucker. . . ." Quinton's free hand snaked out and lightly kneaded a corner of Boyngton's yellow denim leisure suit. "But I sure do dig your ropes, man. I once had me a Honk Konk chink used to do me up some shit almost as good, man. And that ain't no lie, jummm! Dapper, is what it is . . . dapper."

Boyngton leaned away. "Nice talking to you," he said. Quinton declined to release his sweaty palm. "Nice chatting with you," Boyngton insisted, a tremor breaking into his voice.

Quinton laughed and relaxed his grip. And before Boyngton could make good his escape, Quinton reached up and handed him back his wallet.

"Smokin'!" Quinton howled.

Boyngton brushed past Dorothy as he hurried off into the hallway to count his money. . . .

Dorothy had tape enough for only one more interview, for an apparently unavoidable session with Quin-

167

ton. But then Quinton blew her a secret kiss from across the room and Dorothy opted to have another stab at Dave. She headed him off at the door.

"Dave? Do you think I could ask you a couple more questions? I won't keep you but a minute."

"Sure."

"Tell us, Dave . . ."

Quinton pulled on his nylon windbreaker, donned his shades and ambled over to the trainer's table, where Dorothy sat writing down some quick notes. She was wearing a bright red "Press" button pinned above her heart. There was no one else in the room.

"What do you say, mama?"

Dorothy looked up in absent surprise. "What's that? You talking to me?"

"Sure am, bitch. You been checking me out ever since last Thursday night."

"What are you talking about?"

"Come clean, bitch. They don't call me Alex O'Henty, the pussy expert, for nothing."

Dorothy craned her neck and regarded Quinton with undisguised loathing. Followed by her eyes filling with the strained signs of unmistakable boredom. Quinton snickered and dropped a gigantic hand that covered her media badge. He smirked again as he squeezed her breast.

"What are you doing?" Dorothy shrieked. "You bastard! You animal! Don't touch me! You're not supposed to touch me!"

"It said 'Press,' " Quinton reported as he walked out the door. "So I pressed."

# CHAPTER SEVENTEEN

IN MURRAY Klurman's previous incarnations he was a spider, an otter, an eggplant, a Central Park pigeon named Eugene, and an English setter. From them Murray retained only the dimmest recollections and the most inexplicable habits. But Murray really believed himself to be nothing less than the living reincarnation of James Joyce. The sports arena was Murray's subject, and his task was to forge the basketball consciousness of his race, making art of wax, sneaker laces and feathers. As a writer, Murray felt certain he was riding a complimentary ticket into a heavenful of universal geniuses and transcontinental gurus.

But in the meantime . . . Murray was lying under a sun lamp on a padded bench in the bathroom of his modest three-room flat on New York's swinging East Side. His eyes scanned the sports pages of the *Times*, sopping up numbers and names.

"What do you know?" Murray asked himself, "Silky's averaging twenty-seven for the play-offs . . . son of a bitch . . . ain't that something?"

Sometimes Murray just nodded his head with vigorous postnipotence. Sometimes he clucked meaningfully.

But with the infra-rays sizzling Murray's bone marrow and baking his will into vapor, he had to chatter to himself to stay awake. . . .

"Look at this! Spring training already . . . trade . . . ? Wait a second! I don't believe it! Catfish Hunter for who? Nix! Nix! Bad trade for the Yanks. Unbelievable . . ."

But despite Murray's efforts, the newspaper slowly sagged and crinkled into his chest. And Murray dozed. . . .

First he dreamed he was crawling around behind his eyes, spinning webs from ear to ear. Next he dreamed he was a stone.

But the fail-safe mice in Murray's brain reminded him of the paper shadow that stood between his tanned, greased skin and the electric sunshine. Murray shrugged himself awake. . . .

"Look at this! Three hockey players sentenced to jail terms . . . unfuckenbelievable! Animals! Ten years to life. . . ."

Now Murray dreamed of Sara, his ex-wife . . . divorced only ten years ago; a ball-nagging, tight-lipped, coffin-twated Jewish Princess from Long Island's North Shore. He still paid her a hundred dollar bill every week to help support her and the boy. . . .

"L.A. . . . minus seven and a half against New York. . . . Too long, way too long. . . ."

Murray's timer pinged just as the sound of a vacuum cleaner whooshed past the open bathroom door. He blinked his plastic eye shields into his hand and checked his watch. Only six hours left before the next deadline, before his inexorable fate grazed his neck and drew blood. Or before he put together another secret master-piece.

Murray raised himself slowly off the bench and slouched into the living room. "Goddamn it, Mildred!" he complained in a mild huff, "how the hell can I concentrate around here with that damn machine going? Can't you do that later?"

Mildred, who lived next door, was a slender woman in her mid-thirties, with short brown bangs, glistening gray eyes and a ready blush. She was the head of Columbia College's reference library. Mildred had never married. She'd met Murray four years ago in the incinerator room.

"I'm sorry, Murray," she said as she snapped off the vacuum.

"I was working on my novel, for Christ's sake. Working a couple of things out in my head. I'm developing negatives, so to speak. I'm dealing with shadows and shapes. Lots of shadows. Most of the action takes place at night. . . ."

Mildred nodded, and her heart-shaped smile flickered with love and understanding. "I'm sorry, Murray."

"But now my damn chain of thought is broken—"

"I didn't mean to disturb you, but I've got to go . . . soon. I thought that I'd tidy up while I had the chance. . . ."

"Yeah," Murray said. His fragile new burn was making his stomach itch. "I know, I know. You told me enough times."

Mildred had a date. A computer-arranged appointment. The whole thing had started out as a lark several months ago. Murray had even helped Mildred fill out the questionnaire, bringing some wine for the occasion.

They'd had a merry time. Mildred had been out to put down a 7 under "Personal Attractiveness," but Murray, even though he knew it was a lie, talked her into giving herself an 8. They had made tender love after that. . . .

Tonight, Mildred actually had a date with one Robert Swart, a thirty-eight-year-old lawyer and widower, and as she returned the vacuum to its closet and unfastened her apron, Murray's relentless glare of betrayal stalked her down, trying to make her feel like an ax-murderer. Mildred didn't like Murray very much, she just loved him.

"Murray." Mildred spoke his name sweetly but wearily too. "We said all along it was all right to go out with other people. You were even the one who insisted."

Murray waved his hands in casual self-defense. "Yeah, yeah," he said, "so what's the big deal? I didn't say nothing, right? Go out and enjoy yourself. You're entitled. . . ."

Murray followed Mildred into the kitchen, his bleeding pride turning her face more and more crimson.

"Have a great time," Murray said. "Sure. Maybe you'll even get laid. You ain't my wife. What do I care?"

Stung, Mildred bit her lip and tried to keep her hurt from turning into anger. "I can't sit here forever," she said, "watching tv by myself and listening to you screaming and cursing and writing your articles—"

"Stories, Mildred. Stories. And my novel. They're what I do, Mildred. What I am. And I have to do them the way I have to do them. . . . I can't expect you to understand it. . . . The process of creating. . . . Oh, the hell with it, I've got to take a shower. Will you be here when I come out?"

Murray emerged from the bathroom fifteen minutes later neatly secured into a terry-cloth robe. Mildred had

172

already set the table and was poised to leave. Murray's Tuna Helper casserole was set on a New York Stars place mat and his official New York Stars coffee mug was filled to the brim with chocolate milk. There was also a daisy arranged in an empty Gatorade bottle.

"Looks delicious," Murray said as he sat down. "Real nice . . . not burnt like the last time."

Mildred hovered over him, reluctant to leave, afraid to stay. "You going to be home tonight?" she asked. "There's a good movie on channel seven later . . . *Guys and Dolls.*"

"I ain't interested in movies. They're not a valid art form. You know that. Besides, I got a story to write and some calls to make." Murray absently scratched the back of his right ear. "We're leaving in the morning, you know. I probably won't see you until the weekend."

Mildred bent over and mashed her dry lips into his, and Murray tried to force his tongue into her mouth. As she wriggled away, he pinched her ass.

"Have a nice time," they said in unison.

The Smalleys rented the downstairs of a two-family house in Bayside, Queens. Their resident landlord was a retired postal worker who knew nothing about basketball. Actually, he and his wife suspected that Wayne earned his living making porno films. What else could he be doing watching all those films in secret with the door closed?

The downstairs domicile included a kitchen-dining room, a living room, a master bedroom, two smaller bedrooms and a bath-and-a-half. The base rent was four hundred dollars a month. For another fifteen dollars the landlord permitted Joan to work and tend a garden in the backyard. Back in Savannah the Smalleys had owned a brick colonial on a two-and-one-half-acre plot, but Wayne's one year contract with the Stars ruled out the immediate advisability of buying a house. Joan, however, wouldn't tolerate bringing up her children in an apartment building, and the Smalleys actually considered themselves fortunate to have some dirt, flowers and trees at their disposal, with Madison Square Garden only twenty-five minutes away.

It was closing in on evening now, but Joan was still crawling about in her vegetable bed, turning over the topsoil with a hand spade. She toiled in a slow sweat as she tried to take advantage of the last luster of sunlight. But the gnats and mosquitoes were also out tending the night air, and she had to pause several times to rub the red spots from her eyes.

Joan's features were as sharp as a seagull's, but fetching and engaging even in profile. She brushed at her rusty-brown hair and wondered what had ever made her believe she would like living in New York. True, the career opportunity for Wayne was a bonanza and not to be slighted, and at first even the landlord seemed like a friendly sort. They'd moved into the city in May, and while the summer was still young, Wayne took them all exploring and sightseeing. . . . They circled Manhattan on a boat, they picnicked in Central Park, they feasted on snails and cat's tails in Chinatown. But training camp opened in mid-August, and Wayne had mostly been living on the road ever since. When he was at home he moved around the house like a distinguished visitor.

At the far end of the yard, four-year-old Glenn and his six-year-old sister Meridian were pulling at each other's toys. Downstairs in the basement one of the landlord's kids was practicing the drums. The sky was deepening into a leaden field of soiled reds and grays.

"Merrie," Joan called out. "*Share* with him." For God's sake, she added to herself. For mine too.

The little girl began to whine in self-defense, "But mommy, he took my—"

"Merrie! I don't care what he took. You're his big sister. You have to care for him. . . ."

She needed a beer. God, how she hated New York—hated it for turning her man's love to vinegar, her children into jackals and her own life into boredom and frustration.

Wayne, also making a pit stop in the kitchen, encountered his wife with a worn-out smile.

"Where are the kids?" he asked casually, sniffing the refrigerator as he loaded a plate. "Ready for bedtime soon, huh?"

"They're out in the yard, with me."

Joan was wet with grime and dehydrated, deodorized chicken manure. Wayne grunted and zeroed in on a freshly made chocolate cake.

"Wayne! Mitts off the cake. It's for Merrie. She's having a birthday party in school tomorrow."

He nodded dumbly, his deep thoughts on Kareem Abdul-Jabbar . . . the strange goalie's mask he now wore . . . his unstoppable claw-hook . . .

"How much longer will you be working?" Joan asked. "The kids haven't seen you all day."

"Listen, honey," Wayne said, "honeybunch . . . it's the championships. The whole ball of wax. We both have to tough it out a little longer . . . gut it out, know what I mean . . . ?"

Meanwhile he pilfered the children's Yankee Doodles in lieu of the cake. "I may be up late," he said, and vanished back into his lair.

The bare floor was littered with ashes, crumpled paper, bits of chalk and wasted cigarettes. The shades were down, the air was close and stale. A movie projector sat on a bridge table, shooting a dusty yellow beam at a blind silver screen. The room's only other furniture was a large portable blackboard and a folding chair.

As Wayne entered, the rewind reel was flapping down the loose end of the last Stars-Lakers game of the regular season. He'd already seen the film at least a dozen times, but he threaded it through once again, then sat in the folding chair and watched Kareem Abdul-Jabbar close the lane, press the foul line and seal off the sky. . . .

Kareem was generally conceded to be the greatest, most dominating basketball player who ever lived. For the past ten years Kareem had sailed along averaging thirty points a game and leading the NBA in minutes played, blocked shots and intimidations. He led the Milwaukee Bucks to a championship in 1971, and to a seventh game loss at the hands of the Celtics the following year. Although Jabbar had been traded to the Lakers in 1975, Los Angeles failed to make the play-offs for four seasons running. The critics and doubters came pouring out of the woodwork: writers who could stomach neither Kareem's lifestyle nor political philosophy; fans who thought Kareem excelled only because he was black and seven feet four inches tall. They charged that Jabbar was loafing, that he paced himself too much, that he lacked a killer instinct. They pointed out that Oscar Robertson had still been operating in the Bucks backcourt back in 1971 when they won with Jabbar. Others were of the opinion that the game had simply passed Jabbar by; that basketball was a team sport, and that the whole always amounted to more than the sum of the parts.

The Lakers' owner, Jack Kent Cooke, heard the same rumblings. He responded by collecting the best parts money could buy: George McGinnis, John Drew, Doug Collins and Phil Chenier. The Lakers were now an all-star team. And Kareem's new crew fit around him like atomic particles with antagonistic charges. Even though Jabbar rarely spoke to his teammates, a fragile, mysterious truce held the ball club together. Kareem Abdul-Jabbar was still only thirty-three years old. He remained "the big guy." The biggest. He had promised to retire as soon as he won another title, which encouraged his teammates to run loose, have fun and bide their time.

Jabbar responded with the most illustrious year of his career. Night after night he went out and came back to average forty-five points, seventeen rebounds, eight assists and seven blocked shots per ball game. Out of sight. Definitely. Kareem also led the league in personal fouls, time on the court and offensive rebounds. The Lakers had finished the regular season with a record of 72 and 10. . . .

The game in Wayne's machine fluttered on, and once again Jabbar wheeled, grabbed, swatted and stuffed the Stars into submission. The final score was always 138 to 116.

Halfway through the second showing, Joan knocked on the door to announce that the children were ready to be kissed and sent to bed. Glenn and Merrie stood pink and scrubbed in the doorway. They were wearing matching Mickey Mouse pajamas, and for a moment, Wayne wished that the season was over.

"Say goodnight to daddy."

But before the children could climb onto their

father's lap, the telephone rang. It was Murray Klurman.

Wayne scooted the kids away and bared his smile to the receiver. "Hi, Murray. How are you, what's the scoop?"

"Nothing much, just looking for a story . . . something to fill up a column during a travel day. By the way, I just happened to be filling out my ballot for the Coach of the Year award and I thought I'd give you a call to see what was shaking."

"You mean they vote before the finals?" Wayne asked in surprise.

"Yup. Don't ask me why, I don't make the rules. But about this story . . . I was thinking of doing something serious, something important. You know, with real sociological implications. Maybe about pressure and deviant behavior. Something significant. So, if you could tell me . . . what's really happening on the team? Anything unusual? Everybody getting it on?"

"Sure. All together. Harmony. Everybody pulling for one another. Great team spirit. Boola boola."

"Listen, kid," Murray said, "my bubba once told me, 'Don't never try and bullshit a bullshitter.' You capiche what I'm saying? . . . Nobody busting your chops? No fights in practice? No arguments over chicks? No racial tension? No one hanging out by themselves? Everything's off the record, but I need an angle. Anything. In a hurry. Capiche?"

*On the screen, the black-white-and-tan image of Dave Brooks misses a complicated lay-up and commits a needless foul in the scuffle for the rebound.*

"Hangs out alone?" Wayne asked. "What do you mean?"

"You know. Never messes with chicks. Doesn't

fraternize with the other players. A loner. Eats by himself maybe. . . ."

"A loner," Wayne said. "Yeah, I think I know what you're driving at. . . ."

*Dave pauses at the free-throw line to wipe the sweat that cascaded down his face. Dave always wears an absorbent headband and a pair of terry cloth wrist bands. Not like the other boys.*

"Maybe like Dave Brooks?" Wayne said.

"Yeah, sure . . . you're right!" Murray picked it up. "Come to think of it, I never remember seeing him with a chick on the road. Who's he room with?"

"Reed Carson."

Wayne was beginning to feel uncomfortable. On the screen Dave was now bouncing a gorgeous feed into Jack for a stuff.

"What can you tell me about Brooks?"

"Nothing much," Wayne said quickly. "You see what I see. He plays his steady game. Sometimes he makes things happen, sometimes he disappears out there. But I got to say he never makes too many mistakes. In fact, I think he had the fewest number of turnovers on the team. . . ."

*Dave wipes his hands on a towel as he takes the ball from an official and puts it into play.*

"But I think . . . you said this is off the record. Right?"

"I swear on my mother," Murray said.

"Well, I do think that too many players get away with murder. No bed checks. Wearing jeans and crap to games. If you know what I'm saying?"

"Yeah? So?"

"So . . . I think that maybe Mr. Brooks is getting a

179

little swelled in the head now that he's suddenly a starting player. I'm telling you the truth. It's in the record book. I wouldn't make it up. Just look at what he did last year and this year."

"Got it right here," Murray said. "Here it is . . . thirteen minutes and two-point-three points . . . this year, forty-five minutes and fourteen points."

"You'd just think that a guy would be a little more appreciative of his opportunity, and of the faith his coach showed in him. That's all I'm saying. But, other than that, he's a real nice kid."

"Sure."

"Now . . . what it really comes down to, is that I consider myself more of a teacher than most of the other coaches. You'd be surprised at how many pro players don't even know the most basic fundamentals. . . ."

"You're right," Murray said, "I would . . . but I got to jump and get cracking. Just want to let you know I'm plugging for you. I was also a good friend of Red Holzman's, so I know what you been through with Silky. And thanks for the tip on Brooks. I'll make sure to protect your confidentiality, coach. . . ."

By the time Wayne got off the phone the kids were overtired and cranky waiting for him in their cramped bedroom.

"I don't want to go to bed!" Meridian shouted.

"Don' wanna!" echoed Glenn.

They both ran to Wayne as though Joan were the Wicked Witch of the West. Wayne patted their heads, kissed their cheeks and tapped their bottoms.

"There, there," he said. "Mind your mother."

Wayne and Joan exchanged strained, tired glances as she tried to shoo the children into bed and he swerved into the kitchen to replenish his supplies.

Coach of the Year! It had to be!

Wayne opened the refrigerator and boldly pulled out the chocolate cake. Coach of the Year. Coach of the Decade. Coach of the Century. Wayne stared at the cake. Maybe he'd demand a five-year contract. They'd buy themselves a ranch house in Huntington.... He snatched a gob of icing onto his index finger. Joan maybe wasn't much of a stuff, but she sure could cook. Coach of the goddamn fucken son of a bitching year! He was dipping his finger for another helping when the kids suddenly came dashing into the room.

"You're eating my cake!" Meridian shrieked.

"Mommy said!" Glenn screamed. "Mommy said! Bad daddy!"

The children ran off crying and wailing in search of their mother. Wayne took to his heels and locked himself in his room.

Coach of the Year....

On the day before the final championship series began, the following story appeared in the New York *Dispatch:*

*KLURMAN'S KORNER*—Who's Got the Best Pot?

One of the highlights of the cultural year in ancient China was the annual pottery contest. The venerable judges had their own method of selecting the winner. If a potter cared enough to lavish his art on the part that nobody would ever see, he was given the Blue Ribbon.

That's exactly the same kind of meticulous effort the Stars will need if they are to defeat the Lakers in the championship round of the NBA's play-offs. New York will have to be at its best or any hope of bringing back a title to the Big Apple goes out the window.

As the teams square off in the Fabulous Forum tomorrow night, the Stars will be buoyed by the return of Tyrone White to the lineup. Dr. Fujimoto, the team's physician, gave Tyrone a clean bill of health yesterday. White, the number six scorer in the league, missed three of the five games in the series against Salt Lake City, and the Stars offense was noticeably erratic. His return should invigorate New York's attack at a time when they need it most.

But if White is well enough to start, then somebody must sit. Who will it be: Dave Brooks? Or Reed Carson? In this humble Korner of the sports world the opinion is that Carson should get the nod. Numbers tell only part of the story: in the recently concluded showdown with the Utes, Brooks averaged 12 points per game, Reed averaged nearly 24.

But professional basketball players are more than digits on a stat sheet. They have personal problems just like the rest of us subway-riders, problems they feel are just as important as the ones that afflict us mortals. Even though they live in the public eye, ballplayers are American citizens and are entitled to their privacy.

Dave Brooks is surely no exception. Teammates call him a "loner." Ex-roommate Reed Carson vouches for that. "Dave just stays off a ways by himself," says Carson.

We should remember, however, the word of the late great Em Tunnell of the football Giants, who used to say, "Different streets for different feets."

Wayne Smalley, the Stars brilliant rookie coach, is only interested in his players' on-court activities. "Dave is a solid ballplayer," Wayne says. "He led the team in having the least number of turnovers in the regular season. But sometimes Dave disappears."

Carson is quick to agree with his coach. "Dave and I have been roomies on the road for almost a year," Reed says. "I always thought we got along pretty good. Then last week, just before the Utes series, Dave told me he wants to room alone. I guess some guys just have to be by themselves. Dave is a fine ballplayer. Everybody in the league respects his ability."

Reed also believes that the competition in the backcourt is good for the club. "I don't care who starts," Reed says, "as long as the team wins. If we can get it together, we can give the Lakers a run for their money. And you can quote me on that."

Whatever Coach Smalley decides to do, the long-suffering Stars fans deserve a no-nonsense effort from *all* of the players. New Yorkers aren't used to anything but the best. In more ways than one. . . .

# CHAPTER EIGHTEEN

THE FORUM was engorged with over seventeen thousand people: enthusiastic basketball fans, shimmering movie stars, two-bit producers, jangling hippies, Bingo Beach messiahs. Walter Matthau sang the national anthem, and Telly Savalas crooned "God Bless America."

Then a spotlight introduced the starting lineups.

For New York: Jack Mathias, Ardell Bartholomew, Silky Sims, Reed Carson and Dave Brooks.

For Los Angeles: John Drew, Phil Chenier, Doug Collins, George McGinnis and Kareem Abdul-Jabbar.

The teams took the court while the assembled witnesses chanted madly to themselves.

Abdul-Jabbar's jaw had been fractured three summers earlier in a UCLA alumni game. Ever since, Kareem's frog-goggles had given way to a form-fitting goalie's mask. His eyes were set back behind protective ridges of fiberglass, and a plastic hump guarded his nose. Kareem looked like a ferocious praying mantis. At the center jump circle Jabbar's long warrior arm descended from the sky to wrestle with—and devour—Silky's right hand.

Silky, however, refused to look up. Instead he stared at the big man's sneakers. Silky had been coiling for the opening tip-off for three days. Now he cranked himself into a crouch, waited for Nick Hatcher to pull the string and start the game. Silky was ready . . . except Hatcher was nowhere to be seen. Instead of the game beginning, the PA system roared through metallic sinuses:

"LADIES AND GENTLEMEN. WE HAVE A SPE-CIAL GUEST WITH US TONIGHT TO THROW UP THE FIRST BALL OF THE SERIES. THE FORUM IS PROUD TO PRESENT . . . FIVE-YEAR-OLD PEGGY SUE SMITH . . . MISS MARCH OF DIMES!"

When the celebration was finished and Nick Hatcher had finally twitched the ball high in the air, Silky exploded in its wake. . . . But Jabbar was already there and gone, and the Lakers controlled the opening tip.

Doug Collins clutched the ball, then brought it across the center line slowly, and frugally.

"Four-X-Twenty-two-Norma!" Collins shouted.

The Lakers ran through a couple of brush picks and easy circles, then George McGinnis tossed a pass to Kareem. The big man dribbled with stork-grace, and his body quivered with suggestions. His pumping breaths whistled through the slits and slashes in his mask. He locked an elbow under Jack's armpit, slid unimpeded across the middle. Ardell left his man and came across from the weak side to help out, while Dave raced to the base line to try to deal with McGinnis. But Jabbar already had the basket in his sights: his skyhook shivered the strings and blew the hoop open.

Dave accepted an elbow-nudge from the 245-pound McGinnis and was knocked to the floor.

185

"Play ball," Hatcher said. "No harm, no foul."

Silky Sims always played well against the Lakers—
with the slender John Drew guarding him Silky never
had to take a beating. By common consent, both John
and Silky played in wide circles around Bartholomew and
McGinnis respectively.

Now Silky was high in the left corner with the field
laid out on his right hand. His curved feet did a quick
rocker step, then he snapped three dribbles to his right.
Drew had to lean to catch up, and Silky reversed his direction by slinging the ball behind his back. Silky had to
double-clutch the shot to avoid Jabbar's fingernails, but
he jack-hammered it in off the backboard.

Throughout the game the scoreboard screamed at
large in swiftly moving flashes of light:

NY     LA
7      12

... AN OPEN-HEARTED FORUM WELCOME TO
THE SAN MAZUMA FIRE DEPARTMENT ... TO
LOCAL 268 OF THE ARTICHOKE PICKERS UNION
...

Dave was on the wing of a fast break. He caught
Reed's pass and rose up strong to the basket, but McGinnis crashed into his side and the shot was missed. Hatcher
stood frozen with wide eyes and a still whistle while
Kareem nabbed the rebound.

"Nick!" Dave yelled. "He killed me!"

The teams raced upcourt.

186

"I'm sorry," Hatcher said. "I blew the call. I thought you'd make the shot."

Dave's man scored the fast-break basket on the other end, and Wayne immediately sent Tyrone into the game.

NY    LA
17    26

... SAN CLAMATO LITTLE LEAGUE CHAMPS ... WELCOME TO SENATOR HOWARD COSELL ... TO THE SAN FAULTERINO HIGH SCHOOL STATE CHAMPIONSHIP CHESS TEAM ...

Tyrone played softly and carefully. The slight pain in his wrist was quick to condition his reflexes and trim his instincts, but nothing hurt when Tyrone shot.

Jack followed his coach's instructions and tested the officials on every play. He beat on Kareem whenever he could and was rewarded with three fouls in the first quarter. Wayne kept Jack in the game.

Jabbar hung one out from the base line and Jack banged his hip, the shot falling short without a call.

Silky raced to a free spot in the corner and drilled home another basket. Silky and Tyrone were shooting it out for control of the team.

NY    LA
35    46

... TO THE PONTIAC DEALERS OF SANTA VENTURA ... TO LOCAL ONE TWO EIGHT OF THE HELL'S ANGELS ... TO BROWNIE PACK ...

Phil Chenier tripped over Reed and fell to the floor. Foul was called on New York. Reed raced past the prone body of Chenier to heckle the official, but Ardell reached down an iron hand and pulled Chenier off the deck.

"Brother," Chenier said.

"Brother."

Kevin Harmon reported in when Jack picked up his fourth foul, and Kareem proceded to miss his next three shots as Kevin clumsied all over him. Kevin in fact was so strong, so inexperienced and so willing that Kareem couldn't anticipate, and while he adjusted his game, Tyrone hit four jumpers in a row.

Kareem managed to close out the half by facing the basket and beating Kevin to the hoop with three straight stuffs.

NY    LA

56    69

... A REMINDER THAT THE REFRESHMENT STANDS ARE NOW OPEN AND THAT THE HALFTIME SHOW FEATURES ONE OF THE FORUM FAVORITES ... BERTHA THE SINGING PIG ...

Jeremy Johnson was the most talented big man in the collegiate ranks when he performed at the University of Detroit. He was green, he was frail, but he was the quickest seven footer anybody had ever seen. After J.J. led the Titans to an NCAA title in his junior year he was signed as a hardship case by the Phoenix Suns. The contract ran for two years and was worth $550,000.

The Suns were coached by feisty old Armand "Doc"

Sylvana, the last living member of the original Celtics. At seventy-five, Sylvana was still an alert and knowledgeable basketball man. He coached by creaking, barking, demonstration and by osmosis. But Sylvana was also a basketball shaman who tried to grip and manipulate the personalities of his players, telling them what to wear, where to live and what to drive.

Jeremy was a three-year starter at Phoenix, and even though he was still exploring the pro game he averaged sixteen points and twelve rebounds a game. J.J. was naturally closemouthed and never openly challenged Sylvana; he just bent like a sapling under the old man's powers. When Jeremy's option year was spent, he jumped for a three-year, $700,000 offer from New York.

At first Jeremy was thrilled to be away from Phoenix: out from under Sylvana's controlling hand, away from a land of dry wrinkled senior citizens who never sweated. But New York turned into another frustration. Mathias and Harmon representing Wayne's personal choices in the 1979 college draft, Wayne was committed to giving his two rookie centers the bulk of the playing time. Jeremy finished his only year with the Stars averaging nine minutes, four points and three rebounds a contest. At a mere 201 pounds Jeremy was simply too light to assert himself in the middle. He was snaky and quick, but his body was invisible.

Jeremy Johnson, however, had a secret talent: he was born to play Kareem Abdul-Jabbar. J.J. had forty-three-inch sleeves and tap-dancing feet. He was too insubstantial for Jabbar to push, bully or elbow. Sheer bulk could destroy Jeremy, but not Kareem's fencing for angles and leverage. Kareem would usually get his normal numbers against J.J., but the big man had to fight and scratch and suffer the occasional humiliation of munching a skyhook.

From 1957 to 1966 a flabby ex-Globetrotter named Woody Sauldsberry made a career out of eating Elgin Baylor's lunch: likewise did Jeremy Johnson have a mind-fix on Kareem.

Wayne, of course, knew all about J.J.'s unusual capabilities. He had seen it demonstrated countless times on film, but he was still reluctant to believe it.

At halftime Jack had four fouls, Kevin had three and Kareem had already amassed twenty-seven points. Jeremy knew that his time was coming. He tuned out Wayne's halftime spiel and tried to get ready.

Dave collared Wayne as the Stars headed back out for the second half. "What's going on, Wayne? I read Klurman's column."

Wayne smiled blandly. "I don't know much about it. All I know is that he quoted me correctly. You saw what I said. Why don't you speak to him? Or forget about it. Okay?"

"Maybe," Dave said. "Anyway ... I want to thank you for letting me start the game...."

"Faith," Wayne said dryly. "You gotta keep the faith. Isn't that what they say?"

The second half was delayed when a short man wearing a soiled white robe, head shaved clean and "Jesus Saves" tattooed on his forehead, ran out onto the court. Spectators buzzed, laughed, cheered, and several ran after him to kiss the hem of his garment until two husky blond ushers captured him on the run and spirited him away. California special.

With Dave benched, Tyrone started in the backcourt beside Reed. Reed had played in a total of 389 games in the NBA without ever once fouling out. He played de-

190

fense by perpetrating a multitude of half-fouls and almost-fouls. . . . As now when Doug Collins came twisting and whirling down the left side, with Reed hanging on to his jersey. Collins lost Reed just inside the foul line, so Reed contented himself with swiping at Collins from behind, yelling, "Comin' through," then turning tail and sprinting into the backcourt, looking for a breakaway pass off the rebound.

Jack Mathias used his forearms to break Jabbar's set and try to move him farther away from the basket. It was a maneuver Jack had been allowed all game long, but this time Hatcher called a foul, Jack's fifth, and Wayne convulsed with outrage. . . . "Hatcher, you fucken homer bastard," and so forth.

Wayne also stormed over to scream into the official's face, but suddenly Dave had stepped into his path.

"Take it easy, coach," Dave said. "You know there's no talking to him." Dave rested his arm lightly on Wayne's shoulder. "All you'll do is get a tee."

Wayne nodded ferociously and launched Kevin back into the game to replace Jack.

John Drew drove down the lane, and Kevin moved to challenge him. When Drew went behind his back and the ball popped loose, Kevin was on it like a hungry bear after a crippled salmon, swiping at the errant shot and deflecting it into the basket.

|  NY | LA |
| --- | --- |
|  70 | 86 |

. . . NEXT WEEK AT THE FAB FORUM, THE OS-MOND FAMILY COUNTRY JAMBOREE . . . WITH

ROY ROGERS, DALE EVANS AND THE CHUCK MANSON JUGULAR BAND ... TICKETS AT TIC-KETRON ...

Kareem took a breather late in the third quarter, and during the recess his teammates developed brain fever: little men went into the pivot, big men brought the ball upcourt ... George McGinnis knocked down three men as he tipped in a missed shot.

Quinton was in for Reed and working his base line bustle. Now he raised his eyebrows and faked faking, the non-move sending Chenier sailing and Quinton converted a three-point play.

Tyrone and Silky back-to-backed baskets and the Stars only trailed by ten. Rubin Ruebens, the Lakers coach, immediately sent John Havlicek into the game.

Hondo was forty years old and still stretching his body into unheard-of dimensions. Havlicek could play with his old inexhaustible verve for brief stretches, but he could only manage one appearance a game. During it, though, he spurted around the court like a fly in a glass box, moving the ball and sustaining the Lakers offense until Jabbar got his rest. Hondo doing it. Still.

| NY | LA |
|----|-----|
| 85 | 103 |

... JOHN HAVLICEK HAS JUST ADDED TO HIS OWN ALL-TIME CAREER PLAYOFF RECORDS ... MOST PLAY-OFF GAMES PLAYED, 173 ... MOST MINUTES PLAYED, 7614 ... MOST FG ATTEMP-TED, 3492 ... MOST FG MADE, 1698 ... MOST TOTAL POINTS, 4473 ... MOST ...

Kareem checked back into the game and immediately raised everybody's consciousness by a foot, including Kevin's, who dribbled the ball off his foot and out of bounds and was promptly replaced by Jeremy.

"Jay!" Kareem said, and the two men touched hands.

Jeremy sat underneath Jabbar without touching him, and they moved as though they were dancing. Kareem wheeled to the basket and committed a charge on J.J.'s chest. The next time, J.J. shot out a lank arm and beat Kareem to a pass. J.J. hustled downcourt on the resulting five-on-four break and consummated the play with a dunker.

Dave entered the game for the fifth separate time, and his body was slow to kick over. But Dave did hit on a twenty-foot spot-shot. After that he worried Chenier into a palming violation.

| NY | LA |
|-----|-----|
| 102 | 113 |

... MOST PLAYOFF SERIES, 17 ... MOST PAGES IN NBA RECORD BOOK, 7 ...

Also: Most Lungs, 3 ...

Down the stretch, Jeremy continually forced Kareem into difficult angles and awkward motions: but Kareem shot the lights out.

| NY | LA |
|-----|-----|
| 112 | 129 |

... THE HI SCORERS ... AB-J, 51 ... MAC, 27 ... SIMS, 25 ... WHITE, 21 ... COLLINS, 20 ... CAR-

SON, 17 ... DREW, 17 ... THE PAID ATTENDANCE
TONIGHT WAS !&&(& ... THE FF WOULD LIKE TO
THANK YOU FOR COMING ... CAREFULLY DRIVE
AND SAFELY HOME ARRIVE ...

# CHAPTER NINETEEN

DAVE USUALLY required a long, cauterizing shower after a ball game, but against the Lakers his fractured playing time amounted to only twenty-three minutes and he knew from his days as a scrub that the crush of hot water could never temper his galvanized warrior's soul. He towelled his body dry, packed his gear and dressed in a rush.

Dave traveled across the Forum through a basement tunnel that flared into a tiny alcove before he reached the exit. The chamber was lit by a single flophouse fixture, a pair of wooden chairs were near the door and a bridge table supported a telephone and radio. Lounging up against the wall was a carry-out bag bursting with the remains of a franchised chicken dinner. Two uniformed guards filled the chairs, casually picking their teeth and bending their full attention to the radio:

"Is this Phoebus Phoster? Is this—"

"Yes, it's me, turn off your radio and speak loudly."

"Phoebus . . . ? This is R.G. from Encino. And what I want to ask you is who do you think would of been the best rebounder, King Kong or Godzilla?"

"Well . . . that's a toughie, but I think I have to go with the Kong. Mainly because of his desire. You also have to remember that the Big Z has real bad hands. . . ."

Both sentries stiffened as Dave entered their territory, and one of them rose to push open the door. Dave shifted his Adidas satchel to the other shoulder and peeked through the widening crack, where a hot, vibrant crowd had already gathered. He stepped back inside and lifted the bag of garbage.

"You guys through with this?"

Several teenage girls came running up to Dave. At a signal from their leader the girls unbuttoned their identical red blouses and exposed their right breasts. In their free hands they brandished indelible laundry pens.

"Dave. Sign, Dave. Sign me. Dave. I love you, Dave. I'll never wash it off. Dave, I promise."

"Sorry," Dave said, swallowing hard. He jiggled his double-handed burden, and a drumstick clattered its diversion to the sidewalk. The crowd now sagged back and Dave was able to filter his way through to West Manchester Boulevard.

Dave traversed the parking lot and crossed to the opposite side of the street. Then he paused and looked above him to try and find the night. But the dull, gasping sky lay exhausted around his feet. He sucked in the warm, murky air; it was like breathing through a dirty sock. He tossed the chicken bones into a trash can and walked briskly toward the hotel.

Whenever Dave was still high after a ball game a long walk was usually sufficient to shake him down, but this time had he been wearing sneakers instead of sandals he would have sprinted down the pavement.

After several blocks the Forum's overflow was dispersed into cars and vans, and the sidewalks were deserted. The streets bore the only visible life forms: flashing filaments of sequined lights and squinting chrome ... signaling, honking, flashing, darting, lane-humping.

Turning down a residential side street that was striped with citrine lawns and ashen driveways, Dave quickly shed his sandals and ran lightly down the entire length of the block. He danced through a scattered field of traffic on the corner, and kept running. He ran until his pores ruptured into a graceful, animal sweat. He ran until the ball game slid off his skin, until his soul vacated his body and crested for a moment on a silver pulse. For only a moment, that died like a Phoenix. The same thrilling moment was possible inside the lines and limitations of the arena, he knew, but it was equally fragile. There had been more and more moments, with their crashing aftermath, as the season became more and more impacted. The team would coast together and live in each other's bodies ... until one of them cranked up his mind because he didn't know the play, or because his man had just scored a basket, or because he thought the moment lived in him. Then there would be a forced shot, a careless turnover and the fabric of the future-imperative would be torn to shreds.

Playing against Kareem made the situation even more difficult to maintain. The big man was too distracting. He made some players overly conscious of their own bodies, their own actions. He incited others into futile attempts to cast flapping nets over his horns and jaws. Kareem was also capable of eating the bones of a foolish player's personality.

The tree-lined avenue soon emptied back into the main boulevard. The stores were closed, their neon fires snuffed for the evening, but the belly of the sky was still infused with a chemical incandescence. The stars remained a secret between man and God. It was nearly midnight and the traffic was thinning out. Most of the cars on the road were willfully bent on making time, but there were some that cruised the streets with sharp elbows and sharp eyes hanging from the shotgun windows. Among them Dave noted a bright yellow Cadillac convertible driven by a pigtailed Chinese in a yellow tuxedo. He slowed to a walk and nodded a greeting to a trio of UCLA windbreakers.

At the end of the next block Dave realized someone was following him, a flick of peripheral vision registering a clean-shaven man walking three paces behind his left shoulder. He tried walking faster, then slower; the man likewise adjusted his pace. Dave cut through a gas station onto Wilshire Boulevard; the man followed. Finally Dave executed a neat double-fake and jumped into perfect step at the side of his erstwhile pursuer.

"Hi," Dave said, "out for a walk? Nice night for it."

"Yeah," the man said shyly. He was wearing a baseball cap. For a while the two men matched strides in silence.

"You walk like this every night?" Dave asked.

"Mostly."

"What else do you do? For a living, I mean."

"By day I'm a shrink. But I suffer from chronic insomnia."

"That's awful. Do you ever get to sleep?"

"Yeah. I do. Maybe an hour a night. Sometimes two. But you're walking real fast so I'll probably be very tired. How far are you going?"

"To the Esquire House. What'll you do when we get there?"

"Pick up somebody else. I'm like a hitchhiker. If there's nobody going out, then I'll stroll around the lobby. Sometimes I can even fall asleep in hotel lobbies."

Southern California, Dave thought to himself, and suppressed a smile.

The sky was rotting and Dave was beginning to feel tired as they turned a corner. The hotel's sign was a beacon in the distance.

"What if somebody gets into a car or a cab? And there's nobody else around. What do you do then?"

"I'm usually very careful. I've got a sixth sense about it. It's uncanny. Someday I'm going to write up a scientific paper. . . . But there was this one time when I followed some guy, and he went home. You know, into a regular house. He sure surprised me. I had him pegged for a real long hike. Anyway, I curled up under a bush in his backyard and slept until the sun woke me up. Come to think of it, that was the best sleep I've had in years."

Outside the hotel, Dave's arm was clutched by one of a stumbling pair of teenagers.

"You're Dave Brooks? Ainchu?"

"Yeah. How are you?"

While Dave shook the speaker's hand he noticed that the other boy had pinwheeling microdots instead of eyeballs.

"Looks like your friend needs some air," Dave said.

"I guess so. Both of us were at this party and we got pretty stoned out. You know?"

"Why don't you both take yourselves on a long walk downtown? I'll bet that'll settle you out."

"That's what we're gonna do. We're headed to Pinky's for some chili-dogs."

"Sounds great," Dave said. "Would you mind giving a lift to a friend of mine?"

199

# CHAPTER TWENTY

KAREEM ABDUL-JABBAR pried open the warm-ups with a sensational three hundred and sixty degree turnaround-and-dunk. The capacity crowd, however, endorsed his effort with only a flabby Forum cheer. The houselights were still burning and there was a full complement of celebrities at hand. The Mighty Art Players filled courtside rows, as did O. J. Simpson, Jim Brown and the rest of the ex-jocko-turned-matinee-idols. A host of starlets was also in attendance, wiggling their wares and preening their rhinestone breasts.

Jesse Jeeter was there too, a rickety seventy-eight-year-old ex-vaudeville hoofer who sold peanuts at the Lakers home games. Jesse's white vendor's uniform was topped with a straw hat, which he waved gaily to the crowd as he mounted the apron of the hardwood court, then swung his bones into a creaking soft shoe as the fans cheered and some of the ringsiders threw crumpled dollar bills.

While the crowd dug itself, the Lakers fanned out for shooting practice. Inside the privacy of their own heads the players tossed up quick-draw jumpers and enacted chimeric games of one-on-none. But each player was compelled to trail his own shots to the basket to fetch another one. The metabolic white uniform tuning its free throws received the only courtesy.

The Stars were arranged like a choir around the other basket. Occasionally either Silky or Jeremy moved in to stuff a rebound or rehearse a few hopeful tip-ins. But a continuous spray of basketballs was pumped around the semi-circle as Dave, Ardell and Quinton casually rotated under the hoop.

Wayne sat alone on the bench, his cigarette breath pinching his nostrils, his eyes red with confusion. There seemed to be no cause but Jabbar, no effect but disaster and no apparent remedy for the Stars' meager chances. The game films made several vague promises but absolutely no sense. For the first time in his life, Wayne was forced to accept the power of helplessness.

He smacked a rolled program against his thigh and altered New York's starting lineup: Silky and Ardell remained at the forward positions, Tyrone and Reed played the backcourt, and Jeremy was in the middle.

Dave and Jack rode the bench.

The very first time he handled the ball Kareem went directly for Jeremy's throat. He faked, wheeled and used a neck-high elbow to clear his way across the middle. Jeremy jumped back to protect himself, then had to move again to avoid getting brained when Jabber blasted the ball through the hoop.

| | | NY | LA | |
|---|---|---|---|---|
| 11:42 | JABBAR, dunk | 0 | 2 | +2 |
| 11:25 | SIMS, jumper 20 ft | 2 | 2 | TIE |
| 11:02 | Off. foul, WHITE | | | |
| 10:41 | JABBAR, skyhook | 2 | 4 | +2 |
| | Foul, JOHNSON | | | |
| | JABBAR, 1 of 1 | 2 | 5 | +3 |
| 10:25 | McGINNIS, jumper 25 ft | 2 | 7 | +5 |
| 10:02 | Foul, JOHNSON | | | |
| | JABBAR, 1 of 2 | 2 | 8 | +6 |
| 9:53 | SIMS, jumper 20 ft | 4 | 8 | +4 |
| 9:27 | SIMS, lay-in | 6 | 8 | +2 |

Each shot Silky took tripped the shutter and snapped perfect pictures of jumping strings. Silky also snuffed a lay-up attempt by John Drew, then dribbled the length of the court to drive one down. Silky's hands were twice the size of the basketball and covered with nothing but magic. Silky was hungry.

| | | | | |
|---|---|---|---|---|
| 5:50 | COLLINS, jumper, 10 ft | 12 | 17 | +5 |
| 5:18 | Foul, BARTHOLOMEW | | | |
| 5:13 | JABBAR, skyhook | 12 | 19 | +7 |

Reed held the ball in the corner, looked through Silky's eyes as if they weren't there, then forced up a moonball that plopped on the front rim and crawled through. He smiled with the secret knowledge of his own just desserts. Reed then strangled the next few minutes in a vain attempt to redirect the pulse of the ball game.

| | | | | |
|---|---|---|---|---|
| 2:15 | DREW, off. reb. | 20 | 28 | +8 |
| 1:57 | JABBAR, jumper, 10 ft | 20 | 30 | +10 |
| 1:37 | CARSON, jumper, 15 ft | 22 | 30 | +8 |
| 1:42 | COLLINS, lay-in | 22 | 32 | +10 |

| | | | | |
|---|---|---|---|---|
| 1:06 | CARSON, lay-in | 24 | 32 | +8 |
| | Foul, COLLINS | | | |
| | CARSON, 1 of 1 | 25 | 32 | +7 |
| :38 | BARTHOLOMEW, off. reb. | 27 | 32 | +5 |
| :30 | JABBAR, skyhook | 27 | 34 | +7 |
| | Foul, JOHNSON | | | |
| | SUB: HARMON for JOHNSON | | | |
| | JABBAR, 1 of 1 | 27 | 35 | +8 |
| :03 | JABBAR, dunk | 27 | 37 | +10 |
| | Foul, HARMON | | | |
| | JABBAR, 0 of 1 | 27 | 37 | +10 |

The ache in Tyrone's wrist was slowly squeezing out his concentration. His tentative shot had to be carefully loaded before he dared fire it. Tyrone told no one of his relapse. Pain didn't exist in championship games. He was also hardpressed to remember how to play defense with only his feet and his body.

Colgate Brothers was Kareem's career caddy. Colgate was a seven-foot mulatto with red hair and liver spots on his face. His entrance into the game turned it into a free-for-all. Doug Collins staked a strong claim in this atmosphere by beating Reed twice on easy base line moves.

| | | | | |
|---|---|---|---|---|
| 10:02 | COLLINS, lay-in | 31 | 42 | +11 |
| 9:46 | Foul, CHENIER | | | |
| 9:37 | WHITE, lay-in | 33 | 42 | +9 |
| 9:17 | COLLINS, lay-in | 33 | 44 | +11 |
| | SUB: BROOKS for CARSON | | | |
| 9:02 | Foul, HARMON | | | |
| | BROTHERS, 1 for 2 | 33 | 45 | +12 |
| 8:49 | SIMS, jumper, 10 ft | 35 | 45 | +10 |
| 8:45 | BROOKS, lay-in | 37 | 45 | +8 |
| | SUB: JABBAR for BROTHERS | | | |
| 8:28 | JABBAR, skyhook | 37 | 47 | +10 |
| | Foul, HARMON | | | |

Silky snatched a pass from Dave, turned his back to the basket, then Silky shrugged off Drew's scanty pressure and drilled home a fall-away jumper.

"Inside your eye!" Silky said.

"Jive shit!" said Drew.

| 5:56 | CHENIER, jumper, 20 ft | 44 | 53 | +9 |
| 5:17 | SIMS, dunk | 46 | 53 | +7 |
| | TIME OUT, LA | | | |

A corporate executive, dressed in a gorilla suit, jumped from his seat and commenced screaming and beating his chest. Several hundred fans followed his lead. After doing an imbecile dance and twiddling his fingers to hex the Stars, the famous "Dancing Hairy" sat back down.

| 3:44 | McGINNIS, jumper, 30 ft | 49 | 56 | +7 |
| 3:21 | MATHIAS, jumper, 25 ft | 51 | 56 | +5 |

Silky threw his eyebrows at the rim and Drew tripped forward. The fake opened up Silky's angle and he drove to the basket. Drew was on his back as the ball fell into the net. Silky caught the shot before it bounced and handed it to Drew.

"Here, chump," Silky said. "Here's lunch."

| :47 | JABBAR, skyhook | 56 | 62 | +6 |
| | Foul, MATHIAS | | | |
| | JABBAR, 1 for 1 | 56 | 63 | +7 |
| :32 | SIMS, jumper, 20 ft | 58 | 63 | +5 |
| :07 | WHITE, jumper, 20 ft | 60 | 63 | +3 |
| :02 | JABBAR, skyhook | 60 | 65 | +5 |
| | Foul, MATHIAS | | | |
| | JABBAR, 1 for 2 | 60 | 66 | +6 |
| :00 | BROOKS, 40 ft desperado! | 62 | 66 | +4 |

LEADING SCORERS: Jabbar 21, Sims 20
REBOUNDERS: Jabbar 12, Bartholomew 9
ASSISTS: Jabbar 4, White 3, Brooks 3

Inside the locker room Wayne's lips were moving, but Ardell was hearing only the voice of Jesus. It came naturally to Ardell. . . .

Ardell's father, Gavin, was a fundamentalist Southern Baptist preacher. The family lived in Coxahatchie, Alabama, and included five children who were raised with the Bible and the strap. Ardell was the eldest child and forever the most rebellious. His father's fire-and-brimstone leather belt laced Ardell's butt with scars.

Ardell was a strapping six-foot-six as an eighth-grader, but his father refused him permission to compete in any varsity sports. "They're all worthless games," the pepper-haired old man used to say. "They are traps and snares which Satan has set to catch unwary sinners." And then Gavin would light the fire behind his preacher's eyes and quote from the Bible: "Behold, the Lord will carry thee away with a mighty captivity, and will surely cover thee. He will surely violently turn and toss thee like a ball into a large country: there shalt thou die, and there the chariots of thy glory shall be the shame of thy Lord's house."

Ardell swelled to six-feet-eight as a high school

freshman, but Gavin remained intractable. Then one winter, when Ardell was almost seventeen, the old man caught a chill and died of pneumonia. Ardell lapsed into a month-long paralysis of grief, guilt and relief. The high school basketball coach was moved to suggest that Ardell try out for the varsity. "Basketball has a lot to offer a young man in your position," the coach said. Ardell, a crude, rawboned wonder, soon developed into the star of the team.

With Gavin dead, the family survived on hard summertime labor, child-minding chores, and free vegetable casseroles and hand-me-downs from charitable neighbors. Ardell's mother also earned a weekly pittance as the church organist. Ardell resented the endless pity and the insulting philanthropy of the townspeople. His youthful passions transformed his father into the memory of an iron spike being driven squarely into the earth. He led the high school team to the state championship in his junior year, but the bitterness remained to haunt his dreams. The onus for every missed shot, for every poor grade, for every meal of grits, suet and fried bread was traced to the bosom of his dead father.

Ardell broke his ankle midway through his senior year—an injury that cost him a scholarship to a fancy college. He cursed his fate and enrolled at nearby Alabama Southern for tuition, laundry, room and board. There he drove himself beyond the limits of his reckless, wild talents and became a starting player near the end of his sophomore year. His improvement was slow but irresistible. In Ardell's senior year he earned All-American Honorable Mention and powered Alabama Southern into the final game of the NCAA Small College Championships. The contest, played in Memphis, was nationally televised. Alabama Southern upset previously unbeaten Kentucky Wesleyan in overtime by 65 to 63; Ardell scored only nine points on four for twenty-one from the field, though he did pick off twenty-seven rebounds. Both the announcers and the sportswriters panned his performance. One pro scout said that Ardell was "strictly hamburger."

The Atlanta Hawks drafted Ardell in the seventh round and signed him to a one-year contract worth fifty thousand dollars, contingent on his making the team. The Hawks paid his expenses to training camp, where Ardell reported at six feet, eleven inches, 220 pounds with his sneakers, his jock and a set of clean underwear stuffed into a laundry bag. Still painfully raw as a floor burn, he made the squad on hustle and a bodyful of un-resolved talent.

When he cashed his first big league paycheck Ardell went out and bought a modest house for his mother and an adjacent eight-acre homesite for himself. He also staked his brothers and sisters to a thousand dollars each.

In his rookie season Ardell played more minutes than he was supposed to. He was invisible on offense, earnest on defense, but he played transition basketball as well as anybody in the NBA. He also fed on his undi-minished sense of hatred and betrayal, which caused him often to beat the janitor to practice sessions.

It took Ardell a long time to learn the pro game, but silently, doggedly, painfully Ardell mastered the pressure points, the leverages and the shortcuts. He became a start-er in his fourth season with Atlanta and finished with a solid eleven points, nine rebounds per game. He seemed well on his way to an unpretentious, journeyman's career. Except that the Hawks' brain-trust needed more spectacular possibilities to present to its season ticket holders, and so they dealt Ardell to Chicago for Rashid Hawkins and Skeeter Swift.

Living and playing in a northern metropolis proved devastating to Ardell's sensibilities. He turned sour and lonesome, and his first year with the Bulls was a calamity. Ardell not only became a pussyhound but he rode point. He had trouble working hard in practice sessions and was grateful when the season was over.

The following season, Ardell's sixth on the NBA merry-go-round, saw his effectiveness as a player take a quantum leap forward. He averaged fourteen points and twelve boards; he also led the league in personal fouls. Once again the Bulls missed the play-offs, so Ardell's summer vacation started in late April.

Ardell spent all of his off seasons living with his mother and building at his own place next door. On a searing July afternoon he was laying the floor in his skeletal living room, hammering hot nails and staining the virgin lumber with his copious perspiration. He thought of pausing to douse his head with a cupful of water and turned to look at the well house. Abruptly he dropped his hammer and jerked to his feet. Standing not ten feet from him, clad in his familiar Sunday preaching suit, stood the image of his father.

Gavin's lips never moved, but his voice traced the words of Christ Jesus on the worn pathways inside Ardell's soul: "I am the true vine and my Father the husbandman. Every branch in me that beareth not fruit he taketh away: and every branch that beareth fruit, he purgeth it, that it may bring forth more fruit. Now ye are clean through the word which I have spoken to you. Abide in me, and I in you. As the branch cannot bear fruit of itself, except it abide in the vine: no more can ye except ye abide in me."

The vision of his father vanished, Ardell capitulated, collapsed to his knees and came to Jesus. Ardell heard Him, loved Him, and was Saved. Revenge became love.

Two days before training camp was set to open, Chicago consummated a deal which sent Ardell and assorted draft choices to New York for Walt Frazier and his $400,000 annual wage. New York offered Ardell a one-year no cut for $85,000, and Ardell accepted. His salary was the lowest of any starting player in the league.

Several of the Stars veterans were well acquainted with Ardell and welcomed him to the team with sly winks and glad hands. But Ardell bore witness and proclaimed to them his new faith. He spoke lovingly of the memory of his father.

"Sounds great," said Tyrone. "See you later."

"Who you boolshittin'?" asked Quinton.

"Terrific," said Reed. "Lots of luck."

"Another Jesus freak," Murray Klurman said when he heard the news. "Just what the world needs. Why don't they cut that faggot down and let him die in peace?"

Wayne sat on the trainer's table and rubbed his hands in the warmth of his words.

"So this is what let's try to do in the second half. Everybody listen up. Ardell. Come back to us. Okay? We're only down by six and each of our big men has three fouls. That's where we're at. Okay? So J. J. will start at center and stay there until he picks up number four. Kevin? You'll come in and play until you get your fourth too. Then it's Jack's turn. And then back around again to

J. J. Okay? This way everybody plays, and Jabbar has to keep his game moving. Let's just see what happens. We'll go with the same lineup that started the game. Okay!"

Wayne paused to light a cigarette. "Let's go out there and sock it to 'em!" He began to cough.

The start of the second half was delayed so that a special presentation could be made to Kareem Abdul-Jabbar. A Chicano youth stepped proudly up to midcourt and accepted a hand mike from a maintenance man. The young man shaded his eyes with a strange looking trophy and looked straight up at Kareem.

"Holy smokes!" the young man said, "I didn't never stand next to you so close before. How's the weather up there?"

The crowd laughed but only threw coins, so the young man cleared his throat and recited his speech.

"Kareem? My name is José Morales. Pleased to meet chu. I'm here to say that the Pepper Pickers Union of Santa Rujo have chosen you as the most popular Laker basketballer of the year. We all like to see you play and especially to shoot the skyhook. Speaking for the field-workers, the pitters and the union officials . . . I would like to take the honor to present you Kareem with this gold-plated mimento of the occasion."

Silky came out flying like a silver-footed shooting star. He hit four straight shots and laughed in Drew's face.

|  | NY | LA |  |
|---|---|---|---|
| 8:17  SIMS, long jumper | 78 | 81 | +3 |

Ardell got an unexpected rest in the middle of the

third quarter, and watched with awe as George McGinnis flipped in an acrobatic thirty-footer on the run.

"Fuck!" Wayne screamed.

"Nice one, George!" Ardell said.

4:27   JABBAR, skyhook        88   90   +2

Doug Collins scored on two short pops and Dave replaced Reed, who took a seat, looping a towel around his neck. The ball game still absorbed his full attention, and he absently blew his nose into the towel.

1:58   WHITE, lay-in        93   96   +3

Kareem was showing visible signs of wear. He had to follow Jack's jump shot outside and also labor against Kevin's bulk and J. J.'s speed. Kareem had the additional obligation of scoring at least forty-five points.

:00   Foul, HARMON
JABBAR, 0 of 3        99   +1   98

Fourth quarter: Dave filched Chenier's dribble out from under him and was turning upcourt when the whistle killed the play. The foul was Dave's third.

"Nick," said Dave, "I don't think I touched him."

9:49   Foul, BROOKS
TIME OUT, NY

"Yes, you did," Hatcher said. "With the body."

211

But the Forum's ten million dollar scoreboard ran a slow-motion rerun of the play.

"You missed it," Dave stated from the edge of the huddle. "I never touched him. Look at it, Nick."

"I know what happened. I know what I called. You hit him underneath. With the body."

6:56   SIMS, short jumper            110  +2  108
        SUB: HAVLICEK for COLLINS

Reed grabbed a stray towel from the floor and wiped his face with nose jelly. "Damn." he said. "Gahd damn!"

3:53   HAVLICEK, off reb      114  116  +2

Silky wondered how many points he had. He'd lost track somewhere around twenty-five. Then he speculated on how many he might have for the entire game. He'd once, he recalled, scored fifty-eight in college.

2:13   HAVLICEK, lay-in         117  121  +4
        SUB:  BROOKS for BROWN
               COLLINS for HAVLICEK
        TIME OUT, NY

Nick Hatcher stood impassively near the scorer's table. He saw a man wearing a business suit, a black mask and a white ten gallon hat step up to the side of the empty playing floor. The man began to rage at the Stars and fire his cap pistol at their huddle. Nick blotted his face with a neatly folded handkerchief and nodded for a guard to shoo the man away.

Nick smiled with the satisfaction of a job done superbly. He'd been carrying his junior partner Phil Keller all game long, but everything was well under control—there hadn't been a single fight or technical foul. Now out of the corner of his eye, Nick thought he saw a red light flash on. He peeked expectantly up at the scoreboard, to see an instant replay of Phil Keller dramatically mopping his brow with a garish red bandana. Nick smiled.

1:42   BROOKS, lay-in          120    121    +1

Tyrone, wheezing, blinking and appearing to stifle a yawn, retreated sluggishly as Chenier ferried the ball across the line. Chenier looked past him to see where Jabbar was setting up, and Tyrone suddenly slashed forward and knocked the ball loose. Tyrone then scooted downcourt but veered off to his left when he felt the floorboards tremble. The pain in his wrist flashed through his whole body as George McGinnis came roaring by.

Tyrone treaded water, waited until several players from both teams caught up with the play. It was Silky who came sailing down the middle, untouched in George's big wake, and Tyrone tossed a perfect alley-oop pass to Silky, who busted the ball through the basket.

:56   SIMS, dunk          124    +1    123

Jabbar backed in on Kevin Harmon and lost him with a nifty fake, but Kevin stumbled into Kareem and they both crunched to the floor.

:35   Foul, HARMON
SUB: JOHNSON for HARMON
JABBAR, 2 of 3          124    125    +1

Dave hustling the ball into play caught Kareem lag-

213

ging. He also discovered Jeremy alone at the foul line and threw him a pass, but the ball attracted Doug Collins and John Drew. J. J. had no shot, but Dave cut to the basket and Jeremy found him with a crisp bounce pass. Big George was occupying the middle, so Dave scooped the ball to Silky.

Only George McGinnis' incredible agility and quickness prevented the right side of Dave's body from being totalled as George pirouetted in midair and made a vain attempt to pressure Silky's shot.

> :35  SIMS, shot jumper                 126  +1  125
> 20 SEC INJURY TIME OUT, NY

The blow electrocuted Dave's bones and numbed his mouth, although he wasn't bleeding and his head was clear. Indeed, aside from a swelling lip there didn't seem to be serious damage. Buddy ran over and tried to shove smelling salts under his nose, but Dave waved him off.

"I'm all right," Dave said.

"What day is it outside?" Buddy demanded.

"Thursday, April 21, 1981."

"Where are you?"

"I'm perfectly sane, Buddy. There's thirty-five seconds left and we're up by one."

"Yeah." Buddy stuck his cigar back between his teeth. "It's your tooth that's what's broke."

Dave's tongue immediately searched the empty space. "It doesn't hurt," he said. "Let me stay in."

"Naw. Not a chance. It'll hurt you plenty later on."

Dave realized he couldn't smell Buddy's cigar.


SUB: CARSON for BROOKS

The Lakers worked the ball with affirmative deliberation: there was no question that Kareem had to take the last shot. McGinnis lurked near the boards, shadowboxing with Ardell. Collins dawdled near the foul line, making his jumper an available option.

But Jabbar didn't need any help. He rode Jeremy along the base line and took a fifteen-foot skyhook. Unfazed by Jeremy's challenge, the shot dropped cleanly through the net.

:11  JABBAR, skyhook        126  127  +1

Wayne pulled the team tightly around him. "Remember that play we used against Seattle?" he stuttered. "Silky? Remember that play? You came out high . . . ?"

"Yeah, yeah. I remember it."

"Does everybody remember it? Where's my fucken board? Do *any* of you remember it?"

Ardell recalled setting a pick for somebody near the foul line and then going to war under the boards.

"Sure," Ardell said. "Yeah, I remember it."

Tyrone figured if Ardell knew the play, then so did he. It soon developed that everybody nodded they had a nodding recollection of the play.

"Okay," said Wayne. "Then let's run it again."

Tyrone took the ball out of bounds while his teammates straddled the foul line. He then clapped the side of the ball and everybody started moving. The Lakers cooperated by putting poor pressure on the inbound pass, and Tyrone easily whipped the ball to Silky.

"Ten," Buddy shouted. "Ninemissipieightmissipi . . ."

Silky put a sloppy fake on Drew and jumped over him. Drew's shoulder bumped Silky's arm just as the ball

215

was released. The shot went spinning off to the basket like a buzz bomb. It missed.

The ball hit the rim and bounded high above the backboard. Jabbar timed it perfectly, but as he leaped for the rebound the ball kicked off the rim on its way down. Jeremy, jumping as Kareem landed, tipped the ball in just underneath the final buzzer.

:01  JOHNSON, tip in          FINAL SCORE:
                              NY - 128
                              LA - 127

LEADING SCORERS:   Jabbar 53, Sims 42, McGinnis 20, White 19
REBOUNDERS:   Jabbar 21, Bartholomew 19, McGinnis 12
ASSISTS:   Jabbar 7, White 5, Brooks 5

# CHAPTER TWENTY-ONE

THE STARS spilled into their chartered jet promptly at ten o'clock the following morning. Quinton occupied his customary spot near the bulkhead, and Silky sat beside him. Playing in a championship series brought a sportive glimmer into Quinton's eyes . . . he expected that winning the NBA title would somehow vindicate his entire life . . . but Quinton had also flown over three hundred thousand miles in his career and as the seat belt signs blinked on Quinton's travelling habits grabbed him like a bear trap. Shaking off his shoes, leaning back, he was fast asleep by the time the plane was aloft. The seats were a little tight, and Quinton's leg slowly slid out into the aisle. A stewardess emerged from the service area, wheeling her pushcart over Quinton's outstretched toes.

"Whazz zat?" Quinton said.

"Sorry, sir. Would you care for a drink? A candy bar?"

"Nothin'," said Silky. "Just a stew."

Quinton carefully scratched the crust from the corners of his eyes. "The redhead?"

"Yeah," said Silky. "I've been clockin' her too."

"Sheyit," Quinton squealed, "better dead than red in the head." Quinton ran a licked pinkie around the inside rims of his nostrils, then burrowed back into his coast-to-coast nap.

Silky stared out the window for several long minutes. He had already read the sports sections of all four L.A. dailies, especially the three separate articles just about him. The entire experience was frantic and delicious, but it was also unreal. For Silky, winning the NBA championship meant blowing smoke in the likes of John Drew's face.

"Quinton," Silky finally said. "You up? I need some advice."

"Hunh?"

"Some personal advice."

Quinton jerked upright and his eyes turned into ears. "Sure," he said sagely, "go 'head. Ax me anythin' you want."

"When you first signed . . ."

"With the Pistons. Back in '69."

"Yeah. But what I wanna know is how long did your money last?"

Quinton squinted with suspicion. "Not too long."

"No, no." Silky opened his hands to demonstrate the purity of his motive. "I ain't askin' you what you got. Just how long it lasted."

"Un hunh," said Quinton. "What you been gettin' into, rookie? Some more trouble?"

Silky choked on a bubble of resentment. "No, man. I been partyin' and gettin' it on . . . not botherin' nobody."

"Sounds fine, brother. Have yourself a nice time." Quinton sniffed out a pressure change in the cabin, then closed his eyes.

Silky immediately yielded. "I've been spendin' money I ain't got yet," he said ruefully. "I'v been borrowin' from Kersh, my agent. For my new apartment. For my digs, man."

"Oh, oh," Quinton said. "You're in trouble. Them dudes can fuck you up bad. I know. I was through the same riff myself. When I signed, man, I didn't fool with no deferred payments or nothin'. Un unh! This nigger wanted his bread right now, you dig? It wasn't till later that I got wise to lawyer's fees, agents' fees, percentages of the gross, taxes. And peeling five dollars outta my pocket every time I moved. I was cleaned out by the start of my second year. The Pistons didn't want to hear about no advance, so I did the same as you. Loaned some bread from my agent. But I mean to tell you, man. That honky cat cheated me up, down and sideways. Whew! I didn't get straight with him until I signed up with Clyde's people. Man, you got to be careful with them agents. They'll cut into your heart if you let them."

"I'm hip," Silky moaned. He flicked his head trying to shake out some other words. "I'm hip."

"What kind of contract you got with your man?"

"Personal. Ironclad. No way out." Silky was pouting. "The sucker can't even get me a jive soda commercial."

"What you got going with the Stars?"

"Two more years after this one."

"Silky, my man," Quinton announced as he faded back into his seat, "can't give you nothin' but advice. Just sit tight until your option runs out. Then you settle up with the cat and then you dumps the motherfucker. It won't make no difference how much you owe him. 'Cause by then you'll be a stone millionaire."

"I'm hip," Silky said as he slapped Quinton's lodestone palms. "But I need some bucks yesterday."

219

"That's different," said Quinton. "That's a whole other thing, man. There's still plenty of ways a dude in your shoes can turn some extra bread. Lots of ways."

"Like what?"

"Legal or illegal?"

Silky pondered his predicament for a few more moments. "Let's hear the legal part first."

"It's easy, Silky. All you gotta do is get your back up."

In deference to his discomfort, from the aftermath of the McGinnis hit, Dave was allowed a double seat all to himself. He sat immobile and silent throughout the flight, feeling the pain pills eating up his senses. Off in the distance, his mouth was numb and sore.

Dave dreamed of silver bullets plunging into dead bodies: of pedestrians wearing stainless steel goalie's masks. He also conjured the image of Nancy moving buoyantly through the last heavy weeks of her pregnancy; of Nancy budding into the rose of another soul.

# CHAPTER TWENTY-TWO

NEW YORK, Monday, June 11 (UNI)—The surprising New York Stars shocked the basketball experts again by beating the Los Angeles Lakers 114-113 at Madison Square Garden last night. Not even a record-setting 64-point effort by the Lakers' Kareem Abdul-Jabbar could stem the tide in the closing minutes of the fast-paced contest. The dramatic win gives New York a 2-1 edge in the National Basketball Association's championship series.

Los Angeles built a 14-point lead early in the second quarter on the back of some sensational shooting by Abdul-Jabbar. The Stars were down by 11 at the half. Their cause seemed hopeless. But New York opened the second half with a fullcourt press that harassed the Lakers into multiple turnovers, and the Stars finally caught the Lakers at 86 late in the third quarter. There were 14 lead changes in all

## Swiftly Intercepts

The key play in the stretch was made by Dave Brooks, New York's playmaking guard from Ohio State. With only 23 seconds left in the game the Stars were up by one, but LA had the ball. It looked like curtains for New York as George McGinnis loosed the pass to Jabbar in the pivot. But Brooks sprang into action, intercepted the pass and dribbled the length of the court to score a bucket making it 114-111 with 19 seconds remaining. Abdul-Jabbar hit on a sweeping skyhook at the buzzer to make the final score 114-113.

## Secret Surgery

Dave Brooks was not expected to play in the game. He'd spent several hours the morning of the contest undergoing dental surgery on a tooth broken in Game #2 of the series. The news remained a secret to the capacity Madison Square Garden crowd. Because of the painful operation, Brooks did not enter the game until Reed Carson fouled out with 3:14 left.

## Big Play, Big Thrill

The stage was set for Brooks' clutch play when Silky Sims (35 points and another good floor game) hit a bomb to put New York ahead 112-111 with 37 seconds left in the see-saw contest.

"I was overplaying everything," said Brooks. "It's one of the Lakers favorite plays. They like George (McGinnis) to draw a crowd and dish it off to Jabbar. We've gone over the play a thousand times in practice."

Brooks agreed that his clutch play was perhaps the most important and satisfying of his tour-year pro career.

### Big Mac Shuns Horns

George McGinnis was undisturbed about wearing the goat horns for game number 3. McGinnis shot a miserable 2-11 for only seven points after having a brilliant series to date.

"It was a good pass," said McGinnis. "It wasn't even a pass I'd like to have back. Brooksie just made a hell of a play. He slid off the pick and was there."

### Coach Has No Questions

"There's no question that Dave's play was the pivotal one," said NY coach Wayne Smalley. "It was certainly the straw that broke the Lakers back. Now it's up to us to press our advantage."

### Jabbar Issues "Personal Challenge"

Kareem Abdul-Jabbar scored his record-breaking 64 points on 23-34 from the field and 18-22 from the charity stripe. (The previous single game play-off high was Elgin Baylor's 61 point performance against the Boston Celtics on April 14, 1962.) Abdul-Jabbar, recently voted the NBA's Most Valuable Player also garnered 19 rebounds and 5 assists.

In the last 2 minutes and 17 seconds of the ball game, Abdul-Jabbar took only one shot—his meaningless basket at the buzzer.

"You can't shoot without the ball," said a grim Abdul-Jabbar after the game. "I think the Stars might have caught us by surprise. We beat them 4 for 4 during the regular season, maybe we took them a little too lightly. But that's over with. We learned a lesson tonight. We realize now it's really going to take something to win the championship. Personally, I enjoy the challenge."

The series is scheduled to resume in New York on Wednesday.

| LAKERS | | | | STARS | | |
|---|---|---|---|---|---|---|
| | FG | FT | TP | | FG | FT | TP |
| Ab-Jabbar | 23 | 18-22 | 64 | Sims | 15 | 5-7 | 35 |
| McGinnis | 2 | 3-5 | 7 | Bartholomew | 4 | 2-4 | 10 |
| Collins | 5 | 4-4 | 14 | Johnson | 3 | 1-3 | 7 |
| Chenier | 5 | 1-1 | 11 | Carson | 6 | 3-3 | 15 |
| Drew | 3 | 2-2 | 8 | White | 8 | 1-1 | 17 |
| Havlicek | 3 | 1-1 | 7 | Mathias | 4 | 0-0 | 8 |
| Brothers | 0 | 0-1 | 0 | Harmon | 1 | 0-2 | 2 |
| Brimley | --------DNP-------- | | | Brown | 0 | 6-6 | 6 |
| Jarrelle | --------DNP-------- | | | Brooks | 2 | 0-0 | 4 |
| Batson | --------DNP-------- | | | Graham | --------DNP-------- | | |
| | 41 | 29-38 | 113 | | 43 | 18-26 | 114 |

| | | | | | |
|---|---|---|---|---|---|
| Lakers | 30 | 29 | 25 | 29 - 113 |
| Stars | 23 | 25 | 31 | 35 - 114 |

*KLURMAN'S KORNER–Nobody Asked Me,*
*But Remember Where You Hoid It, Bub*

Way back in 1901 nobody knew a guard from a forward from a center. The best basketball team around was the Buffalo Germans, winners of that year's Pan-American Exposition Basketball Tournament. The championship game was played on Buffalo's home court, a 40' x 60' patch of grass, and the Germans won 134 to 0. One of a handful of spectators at that historic game was a nearsighted cattleman who thought he was watching a livestock exhibition of German buffaloes. After the contest the myopic cattleman approached the Buffalo coach.

"I'll give you two bits for each of the

little ones," the cattleman said. "But that big one in the middle is a fifty center for sure."

And the big ones have been called "centers" ever since! You better believe it!

—Remember where you hoid it, bub.

Even way back in 1901 Kareem Abdul-Jabbar would have been worth his weight in 50-cent pieces. At least. A-J's 7' 4" frame not only makes him the biggest player on any court, but also the niftiest center the game has ever seen. Not even the legendary "Wilt the Stilt" Chamberlain ever matched the phenomenal season A-J just completed. A-J led the NBA in seven different categories including scoring, rebounding and assist-making! A-J's achievements in the play-offs have been even more unbelievable. In case you were stranded in the boondocks, A-J scored a record-shattering 64 points in a dramatic loss to the Stars yesterday at the Garden. That'll teach you to be stranded in the boondocks!

With A-J scoring at will and hooking them in from never-never land—what I want to know is, how the hell is New York up two games to one for the World's Championship of professional basketball?

June 12 is a memorable date for New York sports fans. Exactly one year ago today Silky Sims was arrested for crawling across the main lobby of the Americana at four o'clock in the AYEM! Today, Silky's face is only seen on the sports pages and he has become a superstar of the highest magnitude, scoring 34 points per against a tough Laker defense.

But Silky Sims is only one reason for New York's turnabout.

Something else happened a short year ago today—Red Holzman announced his

225

retirement. Stars fans were doubly shocked when the news was announced during halftime of one of the Celtics-Suns play-off games. (This year, Stars fans get all the news they want from the scoreboard.)

From this humble Korner, it looks like the main wheel turning the Stars new fortunes has to be its talented young mentor, Wayne Smalley, the early line favorite for Coach of the Year garlands. Already known for his clever tactics and ready sense of humor, Smalley has outdone himself in the championship round. To combat the fearsome A-J, Wayne has devised a rotating system of substitution: Jeremy Johnson, Kevin Harmon and Jack Mathias alternate in the middle. And it works!

A-J was so worn down he couldn't get his skyhook up for the crucial stretch run of game number 3. Matter of fact, in the last 2:17 the best A-J could manage was a meaningless bucket at the buzzer.

—Remember where you hoid it, bub.

It hasn't been an easy season for Wayne Smalley. Several of New York's veteran players balked at his rigorous training methods. They were too used to Red's velvet glove and loose rein. Wayne had to fight for the respect of the team before the ball club could hope to get it together. He also had to contend with certain prima donnas, religious fanatics and, recently, a clubhouse lawyer (to say nothing of key injuries to Tyrone White and Kevin Harmon!).

—Remember where you hoid it, bub.

A-J has scored 168 points so far in the series, while the three New York centers have tallied a *combined* total of only 48 points! It may sound strange, but according to Wayne Smalley, these very figures tell the tale of the Stars' success.

Wayne is dead serious these days. World titles are nothing to joke about. "The center position is an artificial one," Wayne said via telephone from his home in Bayside. "The concept of a high scoring pivot man interferes with the real movement and natural rhythm of the game. All I'm trying to do is get back to basics. The statistics bear me out. Ten teams qualified for this year's NBA play-offs. The Lakers were the only one with a center who averaged more than 20 points a ball game!"

? ? ? ? ? ? ? ? ? ? ? ? ? ? ? ? ? ?

Could it be that the Stars biggest "big man" is only 5' 9½" and never plays a minute? Could Wayne Smalley be the best coach in the NBA? Could it be true that the great Silky Sims is only 22 years old? Are the Stars headed for the championship? Would you believe a dynasty?

—Remember where you hoid it, bub.


## NY BEATS LA

NEW YORK, June 13 (AP)—Tyrone White scored the last 7 points of the ball game in leading the New York Stars to a 109-102 win over the Los Angeles Lakers in the NBA's championship series. NY leads in games 3-1 and hopes to wrap up the title when the series resumes Friday night in LA.


### Lakers (102)

Abdul-Jabbar 15 11-14 41, McGinnis 6 3-3 15, Drew 9 3-5 21, Collins 3 4-4 10,

Chenier 2 3-3 7, Havlicek 3 2-2 8, Brothers 0 0-0 0, Brimley 0 0-0 0. Totals 38 26-31 102.

## Stars (109)

Bartholomew 7 3-6 17, Sims 3 3-4 9, Johnson 5 2-2 12, White 10 5-5 25, Carson 6 2-2 14, Brooks 4 2-2 10, Brown 2 4-4 8, Graham 1 0-0 2, Harmon 1 2-3 4, Mathias 4 0-0 8. Totals 43 23-28 109.

| | | | | |
|---|---|---|---|---|
| LA | 24 | 25 | 28 | 25 - 102 |
| NY | 28 | 29 | 22 | 30 - 109 |

Fouled out: Harmon, Mathias, Sims, Chenier. Technical foul: Sims. Total fouls: LA 23; NY 34. A: 20,146.

# CHAPTER TWENTY-THREE

IT WAS nearly midnight when Silky hobbled from the living room out onto the terrace: Silky always affected a limp after a bad ball game. His half-brother Lamar was out gallivanting, so Silky was alone in the apartment. Outside, the air was still and pungent with the expectation of an early summer shower. Silky paused to lock the sliding glass doors behind him, then hunched up his bathrobe and hooded a fresh towel around his head.

Lamar was getting on his nerves. . . .

Lamar Jamieson Sims was seven years Silky's senior. Except for their mother, Lamar was the sole survivor of the family's only legitimate marriage. When the two boys were growing up in Trenton, Lamar would pummel Silky regularly in the name of "educating and toughening" him. The almost daily beatings stopped only when Lamar ran away from home at the age of sixteen. Lamar was never much of an athlete but he was always quick on his feet. He headed for New York and soon developed a successful panhandling technique. One of Lamar's specialties was haunting fancy restaurants in odorous, tattered clothing and demanding money from people either just after or just before they'd eaten. On rainy days Lamar walked the A-train wearing shades and shaking a blindman's cup. Sometimes he slept in cheap hotels, sometimes in flophouses, and sometimes he bedded down on cardboard mattresses shoved under deserted tenement stairwells. Eventually a street-crawling friend introduced Lamar to the financial rewards of setting insurance fires. A few months after his eighteenth birthday Lamar had enough money to move into a two-room flat in West Harlem. Then one year later Lamar was busted in conjunction with the torching of a warehouse in the garment district. The judge gave him the choice of three years in the army or 366 days in jail.

Lamar, opting to serve the U.S. of A., shipped out to Vietnam as a member of an all black platoon. Within weeks sixty-five per cent of them were junkies—including Lamar. Heroin was cheap, relatively pure, absolutely available and an easily preferable alternative to death and carnage. After serving sixteen months on the front line and ten more in the stockade, Lamar was granted a dishonorable discharge.

Over the course of the next eight years Lamar waited tables in San Diego, dug ditches in Waco, washed dishes in Houston, shined shoes in Dallas, sold dope to sixth graders in Cleveland, drove a cab in New York, creeped the strung-out streets of St. Louis and lived in drug rehabilitation centers in Boston, Dee Cee and Baltimore. He was drying out in Lexington when Silky signed with the Stars.

Dressed in his ripest suit of rags, Lamar appeared one night at Madison Square Garden and tearfully offered his services as aide-de-camp and flunky to his long lost brother.

Over the year and a half since then, Silky and Lamar had numerous bitter arguments, but Silky still bought his brother fifty-dollar shirts and two hundred-dollar suits. The simple fact was that Silky loved to have his big bad brother who'd once knocked him around now toady around, chauffeur after his car, like that. . . .

Beneath the gathering weather the city sparkled with a riot of prismatic colors, and Silky squinted his eyes until the crystalline fires danced and flared at his bidding.

Then on a sudden impulse Silky spun around, to see Lamar pulling back the curtains and tapping on the glass door.

"Dufus," Silky murmured to himself as Lamar beckoned him inside. "What's that fool want now?"

Silky unlatched the door and ducked back into the living room as Lamar immediately attacked his hand and called his name in a loud, hoarse whisper: "Silky, my man. Silkee! I didn't know where you was, man. I thought you was kidnapped or somethin'. I jus' want you to meet that little firecracker bitch I tol' you about."

Lamar poked his head in invitation to the far corner of the room where an attractive black woman sat in fetching pose on a mink-covered aqua couch. Silky carelessly rubbed a wizard's eye against her shapely body. It was part of the brothers' agreement that Silky had first crack at all the foxes Lamar brought up to the apartment.

"Vanetta," said Lamar, "this here is the famous Silky Sims, 'zactly like I tol' you. My own little brother."

Silky grimaced and rubbed at a bruise on his thigh, but he was definitely interested in the lady's legs. "How you doin', mama?"

"I saw y'all play this afternoon," Vanetta said. "And you were looking sweet as sugar, baby. Like always. Just some bad luck, sugar daddy. I been waiting to meet you

231

for a long time. I didn't even believe him when he said you was his brother."

"Can't help who your relatives are." Silky seized her with a smile. He knew she loved him forever. "Why don't you sit it right down here, mama, and I'll show you a couple other things you won't believe."

Vanetta giggled and started to slide across the room but Lamar intercepted her by the fireplace.

"That's right," Lamar said as he escorted her the rest of the way. "Don't you worry about a thing, my man. Lamar's here and on the case. I'll have breakfess all done up and waitin' at seven oh clock sharp so's you won't be missin' you flight. Leave it to Lamar. Three eggs sunnyside and oncst over lightly, wif some bacon and four pieces of toast on the side. Ain' nothin' to worry, my man. You in good hands. Only played thirty minutes tonight so's you can party late as you want."

*. . . Drew 9 3-5 21 . . . Sims 3 3-4 9 . . . Technical foul: SIMS . . . Fouled out: Harmon, Mathias, SIMS SIMS . . . Drew 9 3-5 21 . . . SIMS 9999999999999999 . . .*

Silky angrily grabbed at Vanetta's crotch. "I gotta early plane," he said, his mind still trying to shake loose of the vile stats. "But, hey girl, why don't you bring those legs around here after I gets back from the coast?"

While Silky slept in the master bedroom, Lamar tried to romance Vanetta. He clasped her, grasped her and licked her, but every time he got serious she shook him off and wandered out of reach to inspect the furnishings. The walls of the living room were lined with an off-white moiré silk, the ceiling with tanned aromatic leathers.

232

Vanetta pressed her body against the cool marbled fireplace.

"Come on, baby," Lamar said petulantly from the couch. "Get over here. Let's get it goin'."

Ignoring him, Vanetta flopped down onto the bearskin rug, closed her eyes and luxuriated in its texture. Lamar was on her in a flash, rubbing his hot groin slowly into hers.

"Let's go inside," he said precipitously. "Into my room."

Vanetta wiggled out from under him. "Easy, brother," she said. "I ain't finished with this one yet."

It took Silky some time to settle into the darkness but once he got there, he was at the bottom of a well. He was barely disturbed when Lamar came tumbling into the room two hours later.

"Hey, Silky," Lamar said. "Hey, my man. Waken up, man. C'mon, brother." Lamar nudged Silky's shoulder.

"Nein," Silky muttered. "Nein, nein . . ."

"Aw, man. Wake up, man. It's me, Lamar. It's important, Silky. A matter of life or death. Wake up, brother. Sylvester! C'mon. Shit, sucker! Wake up. Aw, man."

"Jacccarr," Silky spittled. "Gabbaarree."

"Yeah. It's Lamar. Your brother. Yeah. Wake up man. It's the chick, man. She don't wanna give me no pussy, man. She say she wants to fuck wif you first. I tol' her you was sleepin' but she ain' listenin'. She's a nice piece, man. Got some mumbo-jumbo thunder in her thighs. Do her, man. I'll bring her on in. Won't take but a minute."

"Freww," said Silky. His right arm twitched after a slumberous jump shot. "Freww."

233

"Here she is, Silky. Do her, man. It'll be good for your game, man. Yeah. Straighten up your entire game."

Vanetta snuggled her nude body up between Silky's legs and coaxed his soft penis into her mouth.

"Glompff," said Silky.

Vanetta grabbed the quivering fingers of Silky's right hand and held them fast against her clitoris, then moaned and slobbered until Silky's body began to shudder.

As Silky came, he crafted the falling rain into a shower of golden snowflakes. And some of his semen dribbled from the corner of Vanetta's mouth and onto her chin.

"GwumpfffFFF!" Silky said in his dream. "In your face, sucker!"

# CHAPTER TWENTY-FOUR

ALL THROUGHOUT her pregnancy, Nancy cried herself to sleep whenever Dave was on the road. She wasn't apprehensive about having a natural childbirth. Nor was she afraid to be alone in the city. Weeping at night was simply one of the prerogatives of a pregnant woman. Nonetheless, Nancy found her proud tears poor consolation for not being able to see her toes, or for rising from her rest like a camel on roller skates, or for her husband's being "away."

On the threshold of her ninth month, Nancy had never felt uglier. . . .

Dave snapped off the bedside lamp and let Nancy snuggle her head into the crook of his arm. He trickled a hand down Nancy's shoulder, across the latticed front of her nightgown and down onto her rotund womb.

"You look great," he said. "Have you been thinking it over about the names?"

"Sure. And it's still coming out the same. I like Laura if it's a girl."

Dave kissed her temple. Tomorrow night he would

be sleeping in a transient's bed somewhere in Los Angeles. "Laura Brooks," he said. "That's a pretty name."

"Laura Lee Brooks," Nancy reminded. "After my mother."

"Yeah. Laura Lee. It's been sounding better and better to me too. Laura Lee Brooks."

Nancy wiggled her cold toes between Dave's calves. "And if it's a boy?" she asked. Nancy was carrying low and slung on her right hip; she felt certain the little six-shooter was a male child.

"I don't know," said Dave. "What do you think?"

"Oh, I don't know," Nancy said coyly. "I think maybe John Benjamin Brooks, Junior, sounds distinguished enough for me."

"You," Dave said, and he hugged her for his joy. "You're the most beautiful, most radiant woman I've ever seen—"

Nancy poked her hip into his, which sudden movement caused the baby to step on her bladder.

"Not to mention the sexiest," Dave added.

Nancy laughed defensively, but Dave dug into her neck and tattooed her with a playfully ferocious hickey.

"Just what are you trying to pull, buster?" Nancy mugged.

"Who, me? Nothing. Not a thing. I never get indiscriminately involved with pregnant ladies."

"Well," Nancy said, "all I know is that the doctor said it's all right until four weeks before due date. That gives us three days to be as discriminate as we want."

They kissed, and prudently embraced. Their tongues tripped each other shyly. They turned, and they whispered, and they sighed, and they became one flesh.

The airport was filled with echoing, empty noises;

people were standing and screaming at their wristwatches . . . but the ballplayers were already travel zombies, walking unseeing in the same dead time. They spoke to one another in coded cadences, followed each other blindly through the terminal and into an X-ray machine.

As Dave mounted the portable boarding ramp, he glanced up at the suicide sky. It looked as though the entire airport was indoors.

Dave ducked into the plane, and a man in a purple uniform seemed to jump in front of him. "There he is," the man cocked a finger, "that's who you're looking for. I told you I could recognize him. Hi, Dave, my name's Gordy Roberts, I'm the copilot on flight 235 here and I'd like to personally welcome you—"

"Dave Brooks?" A pretty stewardess stuck a tapioca smile into Dave's chest. "Mr. Brooks? There's a message for you on Trans-Continental Airways courtesy hotline. Follow me, pleeese."

"See you later, Dave. Nice to have you aboard."

The stewardess led Dave into a cramped vestibule just behind the cockpit, pointed to a red telephone hanging on the wall and left him alone in the room.

Dave knelt into a midget's chair. "Hello?"

"Mr. Dave Brooks?"

"Yes?"

"Is this Mr. Dave Brooks?"

"Yes it is, operator."

"One moment, pleeese." . . .

"Dave?"

"Yes . . . ? Nancy!"

"Honey, it's me! Everything's happening so fast! It's been crazy time."

"What happened? Are you all right?"

"I'm fine! I'm scared! I'm happy! I'm going nuts! My water broke right after you left. Would you believe that? Max got a cab and took me to the doctor's office. The doctor said it looks like this is it. He said sometimes very large babies are premature. He said he wasn't surprised and there's nothing to worry about. He said the nurses in Riverdale General are all trained in the Lamaze method. I'm packing my things right now and Deidre is picking me up and driving me . . . whoop! . . . I think that was my first official contraction. I've got to write down the time. Dave?"

"Yeah, honey, I'm here, it's okay . . ."

"It's been going like this since you left . . . there's Deidre at the door, I have to get moving. I love you, Dave. *I love you more than anything.*"

"I love you too, Nan, I'll meet you at the hospital . . ."

Outside the vestibule Wayne was buzzing with the copilot but broke off the conversation when Dave emerged from the room.

"Coach? Could I speak with you?"

Wayne shook his head and pointed to the copilot. "Not now. Are you kidding? We're going to take off."

"That's right, Mr. Brooks," said the copilot. "We'll get involved with different traffic patterns and variant weather situations if we're unduly delayed."

Wayne put a confidential arm around Dave's shoulder. "Let's go sit down and buckle in. Okay? I've been wanting to have a heart-to-heart with you anyway."

"I've got to talk to you, coach. Right now. It's *important.*"

"Stand back everybody," Wayne said merrily. "It sounds like a shoot-out."

"Right now, Wayne. In private. No theater."

238

Dave turned to shake hands with the copilot. "What about a few extra minutes, Gordy? Can you manage it?"

"Sure, Dave. No trouble. I've always been one of your biggest fans. . . ."

Wayne followed Dave out the door onto the top of the boarding platform. He immediately lit up, tiny knots of hostility holding up the edges of his mouth.

"Okay," he said, "what's this all about?"

"Coach, I just got a phone call from Nancy. She's having a baby."

"That's terrific. Congratulations. I promise not to tell anybody. Or to tell everybody. You name it. Let's go."

"No," Dave said. He nudged a stiff-arm at Wayne's shoulder.

"Hey," Wayne said, "what the fuck are you doing?"

"She's having the baby right now, Wayne. I've got to be there."

"Where? What are you talking about?"

"I can't play tonight, Wayne. I'm not going to L.A. with the rest of the team. Nancy's having a baby, I have to be there at the hospital with her. It's nothing personal, Wayne. It has nothing to do with you—"

"Okay," Wayne said hastily. "Okay. I understand. I'm surprisingly calm. But I don't understand why you can't play. I never heard of such a thing. Be reasonable, we're playing for the championship of the world. It's the ultimate basketball experience. How many players even get a chance? . . . Would die for a chance? I mean, Dave! What the fuck are you saying? What are you trying to do to me? What the fuck do you mean you can't fucken play? What are you? Crazy?"

"It's all right, Wayne. You'll win anyway and it won't make any difference. I'll play in game six. . . ."

". . . *if necessary!*" Wayne screamed. "*If necessary, you*

239

bastard! You know what, Brooks? You're not a winning ballplayer! How the fuck do you like that? You're nothing but a fucken quitter—"

The copilot rapped sharply on the door.

"I've got to go," Dave said. "Wayne, listen to me, it has nothing to do with you but you have to do me a favor. I've never asked you for anything, Wayne. Never once. Just please speak to Joe Cunningham before you do anything. That's all you have to do and we'll be straight. Look, we've both got to go. Good luck tonight. Don't worry, you'll be a winner anyway. Okay?"

"Yeah!" Wayne slapped away Dave's open empty palm. "Fuck you, Brooks. . . . Fuck you *and* your whole fucken family. . . ."

He said it to Dave's back.

# CHAPTER TWENTY-FIVE

MUNICIPAL HOSPITALS don't like publicity, so Nancy was registered as "Theresa Gonzalez." When Dave arrived he was taken to the maternity wing via a back elevator, a stealthy staircase and the heart attack ward—past yawning rows of garbled memories and private evenfalls, where a last few prayers and anxious lies pleaded for mercy in beep-tones.

Nancy didn't go into hard labor until Thursday evening. But she blew out her numbered hisses and measured puffs, trying to tumble her mind off the pedestal of her own agony. Early on Friday morning the doctor suggested a minor sedation.

"You don't need any more pain, Mrs. Brooks. We're almost there."

"I can make it," Nancy said. But her eyes were soft with fear, and forgiveness. "I promise I won't hurt myself. I promise."

Nancy was finally wheeled into the delivery room on Friday evening. It took another hour of pushing and endeavoring before her womb convulsed and sloughed out a slick, filmy, bloody monkey of a blue baby boy. The doctor slapped him pink, and the tin chamber was splashed with crowded laughter.

"A healthy baby boy," the doctor said.

The protesting infant was swabbed, washed, weighed, tested and tagged before his mother could cuddle him and soothe his rage. Nancy kissed his fingers and toes as she secretly counted them. "Look at him, Dave," she said. "He has his daddy's big nose."

The telephone rang unanswered for several minutes.

"Who's this?" the old man finally gruffed.

"It's me, pop. Dave. You're a grandfather again. It's a boy."

"Hot damn!" old John said. "I knew you'd amount to something! What's the varmint's name and when the hell can I see him?"

Dave called the rest of his kin and friends with the good news. He even left a message at the Garden for Wayne. Then he strolled undetected out the main entrance to buy a dozen long-stemmed roses from a florist across the street, he rode back upstairs in the visitors' elevator, sharing bashful, fragrant smiles with an elderly woman and two young nurses. He found a quiet seat in the corner of the maternity lounge, and waited to be summoned.

A half hour later Nancy's obstetrician poked his ominous head into the room.

"Too bad, Dave," the doctor said. "It's hard to believe."

"What?!" Dave jumped to his feet. "What happened?"

The doctor's professional decorum broke into the

hint of a malignant smile. "We had all of it pumped into the OR. The Lakers won by thirty-six points. The Stars got killed. I was embarrassed just listening to it. . . . Oh, Dave, if you want to, you can go inside and see your wife."

---

*LAKERS COME BACK FIGHTING*

LOS ANGELES, June 15 (AP)— Kareem-Abdul-Jabbar scored 53 points in leading the Los Angeles Lakers to a 138-102 drubbing of the New York Stars. The Lakers now trail 3 games to 2 in the National Basketball Association's championship series.

Los Angeles scored the first 14 points of the contest and were never headed. The margin at halftime was 72-41, and the home team led by as much as 42 points as early as the third quarter.

Kareem Abdul-Jabbar continued his record-smashing pace, hitting a game high of 53 points. The 7′ 4″ center out of UCLA now has a total of 263 points for the five games played so far. The previous mark for championship series was 237 points scored by Norman Bailiff against the Celtics in 1962.

Silky Sims led New York with 32 points, 25 of them coming in the second half. The Stars offense was frayed by 38 turnovers.

Dave Brooks was a late scratch from the New York lineup. A team spokesman said an illness in the family prevented Brooks from making the trip. There were no further details.

The series resumes Sunday afternoon in New York.

## NEW YORK STARS (102)

| | MIN | FG | FT | RB | A | PF | TP |
|---|---|---|---|---|---|---|---|
| Bartholomew | 34 | 3-5 | 0-1 | 10 | 3 | 3 | 6 |
| Sims | 42 | 12-28 | 8-10 | 6 | 1 | 4 | 32 |
| Johnson | 17 | 3-7 | 1-1 | 5 | 1 | 5 | 7 |
| Carson | 31 | 4-9 | 2-2 | 1 | 1 | 3 | 10 |
| White | 37 | 10-23 | 3-3 | 3 | 2 | 2 | 23 |
| Brown | 28 | 3-5 | 7-8 | 0 | 2 | 2 | 13 |
| Graham | 20 | 1-6 | 0-1 | 7 | 0 | 2 | 2 |
| Harmon | 21 | 1-5 | 1-3 | 8 | 0 | 6 | 3 |
| Mathias | 20 | 3-5 | 0-0 | 4 | 2 | 6 | 6 |

## LOS ANGELES LAKERS (138)

| | MIN | FG | FT | RB | A | PF | TP |
|---|---|---|---|---|---|---|---|
| Ab-Jabbar | 41 | 22-39 | 9-16 | 24 | 5 | 3 | 53 |
| McGinnis | 37 | 8-18 | 4-7 | 13 | 3 | 4 | 20 |
| Collins | 32 | 6-11 | 2-3 | 3 | 3 | 2 | 14 |
| Chenier | 36 | 7-16 | 4-5 | 4 | 2 | 3 | 18 |
| Drew | 35 | 5-12 | 2-4 | 7 | 1 | 2 | 12 |
| Batson | 18 | 1-2 | 0-1 | 1 | 2 | 2 | 2 |
| Brimley | 17 | 2-4 | 1-2 | 5 | 1 | 3 | 5 |
| Brothers | 7 | 2-2 | 0-1 | 3 | 0 | 3 | 4 |
| Havlicek | 5 | 3-4 | 1-1 | 2 | 2 | 1 | 7 |
| Jarrelle | 10 | 0-3 | 3-3 | 0 | 1 | 0 | 3 |

| | | | | | |
|---|---|---|---|---|---|
| Stars | 19 | 22 | 28 | 33 - 102 |
| Lakers | 37 | 35 | 34 | 32 - 138 |

A: 17, 505

244

# CHAPTER TWENTY-SIX

AFTER THE game Wayne presented his team with the shortest locker room harangue of his coaching career.

"Okay. This is it, it's time to have it out. You guys were unadulterated shit out there. It was the most humiliating event I've ever been connected with. You made fools of yourself on national television. But what we've got to do to win this thing is to forget it. Put the game right out of our heads. Make believe it never happened . . . Silky. Don't you be laughing, Silky. That was the worst thirty-four point all-garbage performance I've ever seen. Drew made you look like a clown when it counted. I hope all your people were watching. I got nothing more to say to any of you. Practice and films tomorrow afternoon. Be prepared to stay late."

Wayne then turned and left the room before the players could react: before Silky could curse him, before Quinton could laugh, before Tyrone untied his sneakers. Before even Ardell could pray the pall from off his soul.

Ardell padded to the shower, the scars on his buttocks wiggling like incestuous white snakes, then paused in front of the bathroom and tried to stutter out a word of hope and consolation to his teammates. He wound up throwing a towel across the room at Quinton.

"Ardell, baby!" Quinton laughed impudently into the gloom. "I always wanted to ask you what them marks on you ass are. Looks like stretch marks when dudes lose a lot of weight, or after ladies have babies. I'm tellin' you, brother, you musta had some kinda big ass when you was a kid down in the 'Sipp. Hey, Ardell. Fess up! You ever do some of that farm boy boogie?"

A few players smirked out loud. "Don't listen to him," Ardell said, but he grinned.

"Hey, J.J.," Quinton piped, "I seen your latest."

"Yeah," Jeremy said warily.

"Yeah. I think you already a long ways too late, brother."

"Aw, man. Don't be jivin' me, Quinton."

The room shivered with laughter, but loud voices could now be heard in the corridor and the ballplayers settled back into themselves.

"Shit!" Jeremy crowed. "Quinton! You old fuck! You got hardenin' of the arteries of the *eyeballs!* You couldn't never sniff up close enough to that bitch to *feel* how good she looks."

Quinton broke into a laid-back, gamboling smile. "Righteous, brother," he said. "Old cats like me got to depend on that Braille method."

The team laughed and remembered they were still up a game and headed home. . . .

"I'll kill that motherfucker," Silky murmured to himself.

Wayne had always hated airport bars. They were, he assured himself, phony sanctuaries for boring people.

246

For the Boys. Shooting the shit. Sipping beer. Hoping for a woman so they wouldn't have to look at each other. Downing shots. Trying to impress the bartender.

"Hey, Fred," Wayne said. "Another beer."

Wayne still hated airport bars, but the ball game had crumpled his composure. He couldn't understand anything. Where did those turnovers come from? Carelessness? How come Reed only got nine shots? Selfishness? Silky selfishness? Showboat Silky . . . What happened in the fourteen-to-nothing blitzkrieg? He vaguely remembered a fullcourt press. Until he scrutinized the films he'd have nothing to say to the press.

"Some more peanuts, Fred. Okay?"

Before he'd found Silky one of Wayne's SSU teams was beaten 140-74 by a Bible school from Georgia. He had reeled in all his outstanding favors to keep the score off the wire services. Not this time.

"Fred. Let's have a J and B."

A gleaming black hearse came wheeling up the departures ramp. It screeched its whitewalls against the curb and came to a bouncing stop. A liveried driver got out and stepped elegantly around to the back of the vehicle. A small crowd gathered. The chauffeur rapped three times on the doors. There was a noisy scrabbling from within and something banged on the wall. Then the back doors slowly creaked apart and a crouching black man in a spiffy leather outfit leaped out onto the sidewalk.

It was Silky.

Fixing his tie and his fly. Smiling at his public and straightening his haberdashery.

The crowd squealed in appreciation, followed by a smattering of applause. Next a slender ebony arm reached out of the limousine's quilted darkness and handed Silky his Adidas bag. Another slinky limb stretched out to tuck a telephone number into Silky's pants pocket. The crowd dug it. When a third arm handed Silky his shades, the crowd began to move in on him but Silky danced through it like a child running through rain.

Buddy Patella was waiting for Silky near the information counter. "Yizza late," Buddy said. "Smalley's peed. He wants to see you in the bar."

"YOUR ATTENTION PLEASE. TRANS-CONTINENTAL AIRWAYS CHARTER FLIGHT NINE FIVE SEVEN-A LEAVING FROM GATE EIGHT TO NEW YORK WILL BE READY FOR BOARDING IN TWENTY MINUTES. TRANS-CONTINENTAL REGRETS THE DELAY AND REMINDS ITS PASSENGERS THAT COM-PLIMENTARY COFFEE IS BEING SERVED IN THE LOUNGE. THANK YOU."

Wayne drained his third Scotch and saw Silky survey-ing him through the bottom of the glass.

"You're late," Wayne said.

"I was visiting a sick friend." Silky took a seat. "That last announcement . . . nine something to New York de-layed, wasn't it? That was us, right?"

"Doesn't make any difference," Wayne snapped. "I hope your sick friend is feeling better. Your visit just cost you two hundred dollars."

Silky spoke as deliberately as he could. "But the plane ain't even loaded yet. You know that ain't right, Wayne."

"It's not when the plane leaves. It's when I say to be

248

here. I can fine you, Silky. Two hundred dollars for being late. That's all she wrote."

Silky looked at him as his anger gargled up into the roof of his throat. He slammed his hand to the hardwood bar.

"I ain't doin' no more talkin' to you, motherfucker," he said.

Then he stormed to his feet and strode out of the bar. Wayne fumbled with his wallet and hustled fast after Silky's heels. Silky stooped through a side door and into a maintenance area he had already inspected. The spot looked enough like an alley for Silky to conduct the business at hand.

"Hold on, man," Wayne said. His bleached out smile showed his willingness to negotiate. "There's no call for anything heavy. Okay? . . . It's nothing personal . . . rules is just rules. They either have to be for everybody or for nobody. Okay? Last week Quinton showed up late for a flight and I fined him. Right? See what I mean?"

Silky slapped the cigarette out of Wayne's mouth. "All I know, faggot," Silky said, "is I'm about tired of listenin' to all your boolshit."

"You ungrateful son of a bitch," Wayne said. "I found you playing in a fucken schoolyard in your fucken underwear with a fucken rag around your fucken head. Don't tell me about who's bullshitting who. Okay?"

Silky clenched his fists and Wayne's blighted eyes turned into sirens.

"C'mon," Wayne dared. "C'mon. Throw a punch. You always wanted to do it. Come on. I'll kick your ass, nigger."

"I'll kill you, motherfucker," Silky growled. He bent over and whipped a razor from a scabbard taped to his calf. "I'm gonna cut your eyes in a million pieces. I'm gonna make you a pizza face."

Wayne bounded into an exaggerated karate pose. "C'mon, you punk. Just touch me once. You're finished, Silky. You're done. This time you went too far. No matter what happens here, you're ruined."

"What?" Silky said. "you must be crazy!"

"You're finished, Silky." Wayne threw a sloppy left-hand lead that Silky easily dodged. "You're through. You got no heart, Silky. You got no heart without me."

Silky stepped back. He pulled up his blade and started laughing, slowly. Then his laughter started to run down hill, taking Silky with it. He laughed until there was drool swinging from his chin.

Wayne aimed another misguided swipe. "Your career is over, nigger. Come on and hit me." And Silky laughed until his aching lungs felt like empty paper bags.

"You pattycake, pussyass, jive motherfucker," Silky exclaimed. He flung the razor at Wayne's head. "Here, asshole. Go cut your own throat."

*"Good morning. Kersh Enterprises."*

*"Operator? I have a person-to-person collect call for Mr. Seymour Kersh from a Mr. Silk E. Sims in Los Angeles."*

*"Thank you, operator. One moment, pleeese."*

*"One moment, pleeese."*

*"Mr. Kersh will accept the charges. Go ahead, please . . ."*

"Kersh?"

"Silky. Sure, it's me. What's the matter?"

"Kersh. Get me an appointment tomorrow afternoon with a doctor."

"A doctor? What for? You get hurt? I don't remember seeing nothing."

"No, no," Silky said. "Not a real doctor. One of them Jewish skylark doctors who chase ambulances. One of the ones who used to keep all the white dudes out of the army. Out of the draft. A back specialist."

"Schneider," Kersh said. "Dr. Hyman Schneider."

# CHAPTER TWENTY-SEVEN

### LAKERS EVEN SERIES

NEW YORK, June 17(AP)—Kareem Abdul-Jabbar broke open a tight ball game with 24 4th-quarter points, boosting the Los Angeles Lakers to a 118-104 win over the New York Stars and knotting the NBA's championship series 3-3. Abdul-Jabbar's total of 59 points was high for both teams.

Silky Sims, New York's outstanding young forward, sat out the game with a back injury. Sims is also expected to miss the final game in Los Angeles on Tuesday night.

### Lakers (118)

Abdul-Jabbar 22 15-23 59, McGinnis 6 5-7 17, Drew 8 2-3 18, Collins 4 3-3 11, Chenier 9 2-2 20, Havlicek 0 3-3 3, Brothers 0 0-0 0, Jarrelle 0 0-1 0. Totals 49 30-41 118.

### Stars (104)

Bartholomew 7 4-7 18, Graham 1 0-0 2,

Johnson 5 2-4 12, White 9 7-7 25, Carson 3 1-1 7, Brooks 11 4-5 26, Brown 2 5-6 9, Harmon 1 1-1 3, Mathias 1 0-0 2. Totals 40 24-32 104.

| | | | | | |
|---|---|---|---|---|---|
| LA | 29 | 27 | 34 | 28 | - 118 |
| NY | 27 | 25 | 29 | 23 | - 104 |

Fouled out; Harmon, Johnson, Chenier. Technical Fouls: NY coach Smalley, Graham 2, Drew. Total fouls: LA 24; NY 36. A: 20,146.

*KLURMAN'S KORNER—Some Rags and
Rumors from a Beggar's Purse*

. . . . Without Silky Sims the Stars don't have a glimmer of a chance in Tuesday night's L.A. showdown. Silky sez he felt a "twinge" in his back on Saturday morning. Silky immediately took a cab to see his personal physician, Dr. Herman Snider. The verdict was "an osteopathic lumbar stress situation" which is "probably" chronic. Dr. Snider sez "playing Tuesday night could endanger Silky's entire career."

. . . . Dr. Panawanta Fijimotto, the Stars' official sawbones, sez "back complaints are hard to diagnose." You pays your money, you gets your choice.

. . . . As if Coach Wayne Smalley doesn't have enough troubles these days, one of his veteran players is about to get involved in a noisy paternity suit with a Puerto Rican welfare mother.

. . . . Does anybody out there know whatever became of Davey Budd?

. . . . A spokesman for the police department is claiming that the Stars 118-104 disaster might have been what triggered off Sunday nite's garbage burning riot in Bed-Stuy.

253

. . . . Is it true that at a recent White House fiesta commemorating the golden wedding anniversary of Mr. and Mrs. Abe Beame, the mayor got up and recited his bar mitzvah speech?

. . . . Dave Brooks deserves a kudo for his 26 points, 10 rebounds and 8 assists in Tuesday nite's loss at the Garden. Let's hope Dave hasn't gotten his game together too late to do the Stars any good.

. . . . Isn't it a shame and a disgrace the way today's pampered play-for-play athletes use the slightest pretext to desert their responsibilities to their teammates and their fans?

. . . . The early line on last Sunday's 36-point shocker was LA with 4½ points. The spread jumped to 10½ several hours before it was publicly announced that Dave Brooks was still in New York. Maybe it's something for the NBA's security staff to look into.

. . . . The fans at MSG are rightly acclaimed as basketball's most knowledgeable and most sophisticated. Yet many out-of-towners often ask why Kareem Abdul-Jabbar, a native NYer, is always booed here and called "Lewie". So I took an informal mini-poll in Section 335 the other night-

. . . . Louis Fisher, Queens: "He's too big." . . . Harold Witt, Brooklyn: "He shoulda stayed home and gone to Columbia, NYU or Brooklyn College and made them the best in the country." . . . Marie DeSantis, Brooklyn: "It's easy for him. All he has to do is reach up and stick it in." . . . John Dawson, Manhasset: "He's a freak."

. . . . The wonderful way NYers treated each other during the recent water strike tells me we're still the world's greatest people. Hail, Big Apple!

254

# CHAPTER TWENTY-EIGHT

GENERAL MANAGER Joe Cunningham made a point of sitting next to Dave as the Stars chartered jet blasted off for Los Angeles.

"Cheez," Joe said, "all this time and I'm still not used to a takeoff." The passing years had seasoned Joe's blarney hornpipes into a reedy baritone, but his face retained the same lean, potato look it had when he was one of the NBA's premier set-shooting guards. "My heart always goes gulpity-gulp and I still get rust-stains in my drawers. If you ask me, man was never meant to fly."

"I know what you mean," Dave agreed. "But I'm sure it must have been worse in the old days. What kind of crates did you fly around in back then?"

"The old days?" Joe chirped. "Nobody flew in the *old* days. The old days was when I was playing with my father on a team called McGinn's Iron Bellys. When the courts were set up inside big wire cages. Not too many points, not too many rules, and everything stayed inbounds. That was the old days."

"That's just a little before my time," Dave said. "I was thinking more about when you were in the NBA."

"Yeah," Joe said. "Sometimes we flew in the pros. I remember the last season I played was for the Fort Wayne Pistons in 1951. Freddie Schaus. Larry Foust. Ever hear of them?"

"No, I don't think so," Dave said.

"The old Fort Wayne Pistons," said Joe. "A businessman name of Fred Zollner owned the ball club. Zollner owned this rickety single-engine job we used to travel in. It took four stops and seven hours to get from Minneapolis to Boston. But none of us knew any better so we always had a good time. . . . Cheez . . . Ken Murray. Ralph Johnson. Jack Kerris. Duane Klueh. A fella named Murray Mendenhall was our coach. . . . Cheez . . . what a crew. Yeah, sometimes we used to fly . . ."

A stewardess dropped by, offering earphones for the movie. Joe waved her away.

"How's Nancy doing? And the baby?"

"Real fine," Dave said. "We're thankful for the flowers and the kind words.."

"My pleasure." Joe beamed. "I know what it's like to start a family. Would you believe it? I already have four grandchildren. God bless 'em. If you ask me, a newborn baby is the greatest miracle God ever wrought—"

Their conversation was interrupted when Seymour Kersh suddenly nodded his bland face at Dave and clinked his porcelain smile into Joe's ear.

"Howdy, folks," Kersh said. "Um . . . Joe. I've got to . . . um . . . Silky says he wants to see you. Right away."

Joe pulled a handkerchief from his pocket and loudly honked his nose. Joe Cunningham had been the Stars general manager for the past twenty-three years, and things at this point were definitely not looking up.

"Tell Silky to sit tight and I'll be with him in a couple of minutes. Tell him none of us is leaving for a while. Tell him five minutes."

Joe sank back into his seat with a sigh. "We used to love to play ball," he said. "That's all we thought about. We couldn't believe we were actually getting paid. George Mikan made twenty-five thousand dollars in his best year. We were invisible. But what a crazy monster basketball has become. It's nuts. And I don't even remember how it happened."

Joe unlocked his seat belt and turned to face Dave. "I'm sorry, son. But we've got to do something about you."

"Don't worry about it," Dave said, knowing all along what was coming. "I understand."

"They decided they want to fine you a thousand bucks for missing the game. A thousand. Yeah. I know. It hurts you more than it hurts me. But they promised not to announce it publicly until after the season's over. And they said, if you want, they would deduct the money from your play-off check. . . Hey, you had yourself quite a game, boy. Keep it going. . . ."

Joe walked wearily down the aisle and crumpled into the vacant seat on Silky's right hand. Kersh clambered into the empty row behind them.

"Take a walk," Silky said to his agent. "Me and my man got some personal business to transact before we start dealin' in dollar signs. I'll come get you later. Go on." Silky's waving hand pushed Kersh into the second class cabin.

"Solid," Silky said. "Y'all 'scuze me, while I get this heatin' pad settled on the right spot. Here we are. Now we cookin'. What's on your mind, Joe?"

"Your back."

"Yeah," Silky said. "My back. Ain't it somethin'? I guess I just been totin' a heavy load, brother. Dig it. Here's where it's all at. Take your pick. Me or that motherfucker Smalley. You get us another coach. Even for next year. And I got a feelin' my back's gonna get the magic overnight cure."

"Can't do it, Silky. The Stars are committed to Wayne."

"Dig yourself, Joe. I'll run it by you one more time. It's either me or him."

"It's him."

"Solid," Silky said, masking his surprise. "That's solid. Now we know where the both of us stand."

A waitress came around to plump their pillows and serve them soft drinks. Silky dug a tinfoil packet from his wallet and emptied it into his Coca-Cola.

"Ginseng powder," he explained. "If you eat right, you live right."

Joe downed his ginger ale and began munching on the ice cubes. "If you want," Joe said, "we could trade you to Cleveland. They already offered us Jim Chones and Campy Russell for you. We have to let them know before the college draft. Make it easy for us. Just say the word and you can spend next winter in Cleveland."

"Or I can spend it inside my livin' room."

"Sure," Joe said. "And who's going to pay your rent? Look, Silky. What are you? Broke or something? You should have come to us. Things like that happen. It's nothing to be ashamed of. If you want, we can negotiate another contract. Anytime you say. Rip up the old one and make a new one. Anytime."

"How about right now?"

"Fine," said Joe. "You want to go get Kersh?"

258

"He'll find out later. From the newspapers."

"That's your business," Joe said quickly. "How about three years for one million and you waive your option rights."

"No way," Silky said.

"What about five years for one and a half million and you waive your option rights?"

"You crazy, man. I ain't signin' away my future."

"Silky. We want to make you happy here."

"Then keep talkin' and see if I smile."

"All right," Joe said. "But this is as far as we can go. Eight years for two and a half million. No option clause. One million dollars in cash when you sign."

"A million dollars?" Silk's eyes turned into bugles. "A million?"

"In your hand. The second you put down the pen."

"Smokin'!" Silky said. "Now all you 'gotta do is get me rid of Kersh."

"Hold your horses," Joe said. "I don't even know what kind of agreement you have with the man. How can I say anything about it? It's not ethical."

"Kersh goes or I sit Tuesday night. That's where it's at."

"All right. Kersh goes."

"And I'll trade you my option rights for a no-trade guarantee."

"You got it."

"Outasight! Just one more item and we got ourselves a deal. No jive. No bullshit."

"Let's hear."

"Get me a soda commercial."

"Bullets and deuces cooks your gooses!" Quinton shouted. "Heh. Like playin' with children. Like stealin'."

259

Quinton's periodic celebrations were rubbed out by the roar and rumm of the jet engines. Nobody heard him but the other cardplayers. A world apart . . .

A matron slippered her way through the length of the plane, unfolding a network of viewing screens from the ceiling, followed by a rich, diaphragmatic voice crackling from the mechanical twilight: "Welcome aboard, ladies and gentlemen. This is Cap'n Morris speaking. We're cruising at an altitude of thirty-six thousand feet and at a ground speed of seven hundred ten miles an hour. Faster than the speed of sound. There's a little turbulence along our primary route so we're swinging a bit south. This may cause a slight delay, but if you look out of the starboard windows you can see Lincoln, Nebraska. I'd also like to remind you that our movie this afternoon is *Hawaiian High,* starring Gloria Chambers. Headphone sets can be rented from the matron for five dollars. I hope you enjoy both the movie, the rest of the flight, and the gourmand buffet which your lovely hostesses will be preparing during the show. It's ten-four time, ladies and gentlemen. So this is Cap'n Morris saying thanks for being with us. And ten-four. . . . Wel—"

"Lookie here!" Quinton yelped. "A surprise feature! 'NBA Play-off Action. Semi-final rounds. Presenting L.A., Boston, Seattle, and' . . . the mighty us! . . . Dealer takes fi . . ."

The screens sizzled to life in thirty-second intervals. There were staggered sequences of the Lakers castrating the Celtics in four straight. Four-inch figures. Domino dunk shots. Next came scenes from the Sonics-Stars series. An unreal continuum of dazzling plays and impossible bull's eyes. Then a dramatic sweep of a frenzied Madison Square Garden crowd. Another flurry of disconnected plays. A lingering flash of the scoreboard—

Spencer Haywood takes Silky home again from the base line. A two second time out. Tyrone's pass to Silky. The quick dribble. The leap. The shot. . . .

"YOOOWEEE!" Silky screamed. He grasshoppered out of his seat and began to boogie in the aisle. "One more time, for a million bucks!"

Silky shook it over to the next screen. "B'DOOOM!" he yelled as his shot was good again. "One more time!!"

After three replays Silky dashed through a curtain and into the rear section of the plane. The curtain had barely stopped shivering when an outraged, vindicated Murray Klurman came bursting through it from the other side.

"What the hell goes on here?" Murray shouted. "Wayne? Where the hell is Wayne? Joe? Where the fuck is everybody?"

"Over here," Joe said. "Sit down and I'll tell you the whole story."

"Joe! Silky's in there screaming like a banshee and jumping around like a lunatic! What's with this bad back bullshit?"

"I was just preparing a press release," Joe said. "But I thought I'd wait until after the movie. I suppose you might as well hear it first."

"You're goddamn right I hear it first!"

"Everything's fine," Joe said. "Silky's back is all better. He's going to play Friday night."

Murray's eyebrows banged against the edge of his hair piece. "I thought so. The guy's a cripple one day and he's playing the next. I tell you there's something smells to heaven here, Joe. I don't believe in miracles."

"It's all on the level," Joe said, with open, guileless hands. "Whether you believe it or not is up to you."

261

"What does Fijimotto say about all this?"

"Fijimotto," Joe said. "Fijimotto's your man, Murray. He'll explain better than I can." Joe laughed through a porthole into a cloud. "Fijimotto was the one who's responsible—"

Murray slapped his forehead. Suddenly a believer. "Acupuncture! Of course. . . ."

# CHAPTER TWENTY-NINE

ON THE morning of the game the Los Angeles Police Department received an anonymous telephone message. "Off the pigs," the caller said. "Fuck the Forum."

The bomb squad was immediately alerted and the Forum was evacuated while they conducted a secret search of the premises. . . .

"WON'T ALL OF YOU AT HOME PLEASE JOIN ALL OF US HERE AT THE FORUM IN THE SINGING OF 'THE STAR SPANGLED BANNER'? IT'S YOUR SONG, AMERICA."

A monkey dressed in an Uncle Sam costume waved a tiny flag while an organ grinder played the national anthem. The 17,505 lucky ticket holders applauded themselves. Then everybody sat down and cleared their throats.

Silky was the first player out on the court. He waited for Kareem at the center jump circle. He looked up into Kareem's eye-holes and they both laughed.

"This is Vince Kelly at courtside, fans. Well, the seventh and deciding game is about ready to begin. The Lakers open up with A-J at center, Drew and McGinnis at forward, and Collins and Chenier playing the backcourt. For New York . . . Sims and Bartholomew man the corners with Johnson starting at center. White is at one of the guard spots and we see where Coach Wayne Smalley is trying to shake up his ball club. Dave Brooks is at the other guard replacing Reed Carson. . . . Referee Nick Hatcher bounces the ball. . . . Hatcher steps on the El Ropo sign. . . . El Ropo, that fine cigar. . . . The Lakers control the tip. . . ."

Kareem hit three baskets before New York could get off a shot. Tyrone turned the ball over twice and Silky committed a charging foul. When the score reached 9-0, Tyrone yielded and let Dave handle the ball. Dave immediately aimed the Stars offense at Silky until the game settled down and he could read what was happening.

"This is incredible, fans. A-J and Silky Sims are the only players to score so far! The count is A-J sixteen and Sims twelve! Nobody else on either team has a point. This game is beginning to look like a shoot-out at the OK Corral."

L.A.'s offense was dynamically predictable but its defense was unusually itchy. Both Drew and McGinnis were listing and yearning for the break.

Silky remained the focus of New York's attack, but Dave's hands now saw his other teammates open at the foul line, cutting underneath and standing juiced in the corners. Tyrone played honest defense and scored his points when no one was looking. Ardell went after missed shots like a missionary accosting lost souls. J.J., Kevin and Jack were fodder for Kareem.

FIRST QUARTER STATISTICS ... NY 30 ... LA 28 ... POINTS ... SIMS 18 ... A-J 15 ... REBOUNDS ... BARTHOLOMEW 8 ... A-J 6 ... ASSISTS ... BROOKS 3 ... MCG 2 ...

The Lakers tried McGinnis on Silky, but George couldn't catch him. Silky spurted and scurried all over the court, meeting the ball only in the empty spaces in L.A.'s two-three zone defense.

"Brooks dribbles across the line in a hurry. The Stars are moving the ball better than I've ever seen them. Brooks pulls up. He passes to Sims. Now the jumper's in the air. . . . It's good! Like Nedicks! Where your mouth scores a basket every time. New York leads forty-two to thirty-eight."

Silky's level of concentration even precluded trading insults with John Drew. And if Silky learned anything in the streets and in the schoolyards, it was never to sound a cat who was wearing a mask.

Dave snuck under the boards and tipped in a rebound to put the Stars up by six. The Lakers called time-out and Dave saw Kareem having a few quiet words with Chenier.

The next time Dave ventured near the boards, Chenier elbowed him in the side of the neck.

"Ten seconds left in the half. Here comes McGinnis. It's been another quiet game for Big George so far. Over to Chenier twenty feet out on the left side. Here's the

265

pass inside to A-J. Now the skyhook. . . . Swisheroo! And the Lakers trail by only three. At the buzzer."

The bomb squad found a whoopee cushion hidden under Murray Klurman's seat at the press table. They also discovered that all of the toilets in the lower level ladies' bathrooms were filled with Jell-o. And way down in the sub-basement, in a plywood shack near the main fuse box, the night watchman's bed had been Frenched.

Phil Chenier carried his dribble a little too high, and as he changed direction Dave reached over his shoulder and sniped the ball away. But a whistle shot Dave in the back of the neck and killed the play.

"Never touched him, Nick. Not this time."

"No, no. I had the angle. You got him with the body."

"The call was late. You missed it. Admit it, Nick. Just admit it."

"With the body," Hatcher insisted. "You guys never see that, right? You guys never feel nothing, right? Bullshit! The case is closed. From here on, it's a hundred dollars every time I hear your voice. Play ball."

The Stars did, and with an insensible brilliance. Their lives were welded to an identical perception of the passing, leaping, celebrating moment.

A-J 19 ... BARTHOLOMEW 18 ... ASSISTS ... BROOKS
6 ... A-J 3 ... CARSON 3 ...

"In case you tuned in late, fans, it's been seesaw all
the way. There've been twenty-eight lead changes in the
game. Thirteen in the fourth quarter. . . . And here we
go now into the last pressure-packed minute of the play.
The score is tied at one hundred eighteen. The Stars
have the ball, fifty-five seconds left. . . . Brooks brings it
over under some loose pressure from Chenier. Brooks
over to White. . . . Sixteen on the twenty-four-second
clock. . . . White back to Brooks. Looks like they're trying
to set up something for Silky Sims. Brooks on the move.
Comes back around. Here's a pass. . . . INSIDE TO
SIMS! HE'S ALL ALONE UNDERNEATH AND HE
STUFFS IT! A BEAYOU-TIFLE PLAY BY NEW
YORK! Sims went without the ball and Brooks threaded
the needle. New York leads one hundred twenty to one
hundred eighteen. That's fifty-five points for Sims. What
a game he's had. A-J has fifty-two. Both teams are out of
time-outs so Collins brings it up quickly. Stars lead by
two. Clock ticking down. Everybody in the building
knows where the ball's going. Johnson climbing all over
A-J's back. A lot of contact but no call made. Here's the
pass inside. Here's Bartholomew over to double-team the
ball. Kareem turns. McGinnis is wide open but A-J can't
see him! HERE'S A JUMPER BY JABBAR . . . ! AND A
WHISTLE! IT'S GOOD! AND IT COUNTS! Score the
clutch bucket for Kareem Abdul-Jabbar to tie the game.
That gives A-J fifty-four for the game. Johnson's foul is
his sixth, he's out of the game. His season is over. Mathias
checks in for him. And A-J can be a hero. He can put
New York into a pressure cooker. Twenty-two seconds

267

left. We're knotted at one hundred twenty and A-J stands at the foul line. Special K takes a deep breath and readies himself for the most crucial shot of his career. He bounces it once. Twice. He one-hands it up . . . AND IN! THE LAKERS LEAD BY A POINT! New York immediately signals for a time-out. . . . Hold on, fans. According to our unofficial tally the Stars have no more time-outs to take. Yes! We're right! Referee Hatcher is calling a technical foul on New York for an illegal time-out. The Lakers get a free throw. But I think the Stars retain possession. Doug Collins will shoot the technical. Collins is an eighty-five per cent shooter from the charity stripe. The Stars are clustered around their coach. I can see Smalley diagramming a play. But here comes Hatcher to break up the huddle. He's right, fans. It's not an official time-out! Now Smalley and Hatcher are screaming at each other . . . ! AND COLLINS BLOWS THE SHOT! The ball dinked off the front rim! Collins is holding his head. He can't believe it! . . . So, here we are! The Stars will in-bound the ball trailing one twenty-one to one twenty with twenty-two left to go. Plenty of time . . . now Brooks comes up quickly. He drives to the middle. Nothing doing. He pulls back out. Still dribbling the ball. Now Brooks spins at the top of the key. He collides with Drew! And here's a pass out to Sims! THE JUMPER FROM TWENTY-FEET . . . ! It's . . . NO GOOD! NO GOOD! Bartholomew . . . MISSES the rebound! SIMS ON A FOLLOW . . . ! HE misses. And JABBAR comes down with the rebound! The Lakers have the ball! Fifteen seconds left. They can kill the clock. Jabbar swings his elbows to protect the ball. Sims is knocked to the floor! Sent sprawling! But there's no whistle. Both coaches are off the benches screaming! Jabbar throws ahead to Collins. Now Collins is double-teamed in the backcourt! Triple-teamed! L.A. has four seconds to get it across! Nine in the game! A pass to McGinn— INTER-CEPTED! BROOKS AHEAD TO SIMS! IT'S SIMS AND JABBAR ONE-ON-ONE . . . !"

The foul line marked the end of the known universe as Silky blindly jumped. There was a dragon between him and the sun. Silky threw the basketball into the eye of the light and it caromed hard off the backboard. Silky's left hand reached around the dragon and claimed the wild rebound.

On his way down, Silky drove the sun like a comet through the hoop.

# CHAPTER THIRTY

BY WEDNESDAY afternoon Silky was a national sensation. Two different publishing companies had commissioned competing quickie bios; Dorothy Evans had started preparing a documentary on him for prime-time fall viewing; and the State Department wanted Silky to head an NBA players' tour of China.

On Thursday night, Silky hosted a private team bash at his apartment. . . .

The bathtub off the guest room was a cornucopia of ice cubes, beer, soda, wine and champagne. There were steaming buckets of fried chicken, fried shrimp, barbequed spare ribs, egg rolls and Lobster Cantonese in the kitchen.

"Lamar," said Silky. "You did it *right* one time, brother."

"Yeah," Lamar said. "Just yeah."

The first guests to arrive were Quinton and a matched set of gorgeous black women. Behind them came Larry Graham and his fiancée, Renee. Silky whisked them all straight into the master bedroom while Lamar answered the door and tended to the soul-disco beat.

> *Keep on pushin'*
> *Sugar, day and night*
> *Keep on pushin'*
> *Till you do it right*

Quinton sliced, diced and powdered the cocaine with a single-edge razor blade. Larry produced a joint.

"I want to see me the bathroom," said one of Quinton's ladies.

"You'll see all you need later on," Quinton said. "Got to get funky first."

"Have to see that bathroom, sugar," pouted Quinton's other lady. "Just to take a peek."

> *Keep on pushin'*
> *Got to keep on movin'*
> *Keep on pushin', mama*
> *Got to keep on groovin'*

The bathroom suite opened into a seven by seven by seven-foot shower room. The floor was covered with plush rugging. Ceramic showerheads were placed strategically all along the ceiling and the walls. The stall also featured red, blue and green lighting and concealed quadraphonic speakers. A low redwood bunk lined the far wall.

> *Got you by my side*
> *Where you want to be*
> *Let's get crackin' babe*
> *You ain't foolin' me*

271

Lamar turned the music up a touch, and the sound of an energetic gathering slipped under the bedroom door.

"Quinton, baby. Let's go inside."

"Yeah, sugar. I feel like dancin'."

"You two go on," Quinton said. "I'll be right in with you. Got somethin' to discuss with my man."

"Hey, Q," Silky said when they were alone. "You okay?"

"It's that lousy airplane food," Quinton whispered. "I had the shits all week. I'll meet you inside. . . ."

The apartment was suddenly teeming with beautiful people, most of them strangers.

"Oh, really?"

"Is that him?"

"Isn't that nice?"

"Who's he?"

"Did you know that Sweden has more people per capita than any other country in the world?"

"Silky! What's *happenin'*?"

"Silky! How ya *doing'* . . . ?"

Jack Mathias hugged a wall and slowly sipped on a glass of red wine. He smiled with satisfaction and casually reconnoitered the passing ladies.

"Here's Silky Sims himself," Jack said deliciously. "The Million Dollar Man! The Billion Dollar Baby!"

"Black Jack." Silky grinned. They salved each other's hands. "You got what you require, brother? A chick? Some blow? Some reefer?"

"Yeah," said Jack. "You know, I think I would appreciate some smoke. I've been straight since training camp."

Silky snapped his fingers. "Lamar. Take charge of my man and set him into some of them tie sticks."

"Outasight, brother," Jack said.
"Catch you later."

*Move on up*
    *Want to sock it to ya*
      *Won't you move on up?*
        *Gonna whoopdeedoo ya*

Jeremy danced with a statuesque blonde. His right hand steered her left breast while his other hand ruddered her tail.

"Hey, honey," Jeremy said. "You want to take a gold-plated shower with J.J.?"

"Shower?" the blonde said. "I ain't dirty."

"You mean you ain't never heard of Silky Sims famous bathroom fuck-o-rama?"

"Bathroom?" the blonde said. "I don't gotta go . . ."

Reed and Deidre Carson floated on the water couch drinking champagne and staring moodily at the goings on.

"I don't want to go back to Dallas," she told her husband.

"Leave me alone," said Reed. "This is a party. . . ."

Kevin hung like a vulture over the spareribs. His hands and face were thick with sauce and grease. A lanky movie star in a string bikini came into the kitchen to peruse the food.

"Hi," Kevin spluttered. "I'm Kevin Harmon of the World Champion New York Stars." He wiped his right hand clean on his pants.

"Pleased to meet you," the actress said brightly. "Don't I know you from someplace. . . ?"

Ardell and his wife Sondra leaned back onto the windowsill in the dining room.

273

"Ardell," Silky said. "You're the best cat I ever met. That ain' no lie. And we did it, brother. We beat 'em. We conquered Mount Jabbar."

The two men laughed and squeezed one another in a roughhouse, macho embrace.

"Love you like a brother," Ardell said. "Like a brother."

> *She got flash, she got style*
> *She acts very cool*
> *She gets close to her lover*
> *She obeys his rule*

Tyrone wasn't expected. No one had seen him since the hurried meeting at the baggage counter to split the play-off pot. Nor would anybody see Tyrone until the first day of training camp.

Dave said he'd probably be late.

He was entitled.

Nancy nursed the baby on the living room couch while Dave packed a last few things. The walls of the apartment were stripped and both the tv and the stereo were disconnected.

The baby's mouth slid off the nipple and framed a resounding belch. Nancy laughed with delight.

"Well, excuse me, little mister."

But the nipple was gone and the baby screamed up an instant frenzy.

"He gets his second wind real quick," Dave said as he crossed the room carrying a bulging suitcase.

Nancy shifted position and quieted the baby. "Dave?" Her voice was urgent.

Dave resigned his burden to the floor and cozied beside her on the couch. "What's up?"

"You still look tired," Nancy said. "We could stay another day if we had to."

"No, no," Dave said quickly. "We're almost ready. There's just some stuff I left out for tonight and tomorrow morning. I want to get out of here as soon as possible. There's no reason to stay."

"Don't you want to stop over at the party? Everybody'll be there. I know you want to see them."

"I'm fine," Dave insisted. "We said all the goodbyes we needed at the airport. I'd rather be here." But he stood up and hovered above the suitcase. "Maybe you're right, maybe I should at least call Silky . . . and Wayne."

"Does Wayne know?"

"About the play-off shares? No. I was supposed to tell him but I still don't feel good about it. I know, honey, after what he did, the fine and all. . . . And there's nothing to tell us how to divide the money, it's strictly the players' decision. And I'd bet the Garden will make it up to him, but it's a real bad insult, humiliating . . . from his own players. It was Silky's idea. First Silky, then Quinton and J.J. Then almost everybody. All it took was a minute. Well, at least the play-off split is always kept secret. Nobody else will ever find out."

The fear of which, of course, would be over Wayne's head for the rest of his life.

> *She got class*
> *She got power*
> *She's as tall*
> *As the Eiffel Tower*

Quinton gazed out the window at the morose remains of New York City. He thought of all the money due to him. Each of the Stars' shares came to $25,233, including Wayne's unvoted eleventh share that would have cost Quinton $2,393,33. Quinton rubbed his knee-ache. He understood at last that the thrill was only in the doing, that feelings could never be recalled. Whenever he tried to remember his life, all that Quinton remembered were his sins.

And where would Quinton live out his days? What would he do? What did he have to shake? Who would he be? How fast could he run? What would he do tomorrow morning?

Quinton turned on the shower and went inside to fetch his women. . . .

"Reed. I want to go home."

"Keep still. We're staying. It ain't polite. You want another drink?"

"No. And neither do you. . . ."

Silky was oiling an astonishingly beautiful Oriental fashion model with loose talk of his forthcoming tv special when Lamar pushed against his elbow. "Telephone, Silky. For you."

"I tol' you, Lamar, I ain' talkin' on no phone to no more reporters."

Lamar shrugged. "It's Dave Brooks. He say he wants to talk to you."

"Dave. My man."

> *Keep on pushin'*
> > *Got to keep on groovin'*
> > *Keep on pushin'*
> > > *Got to keep on moovin'*

"Silky? My name is . . ."

"Silky? I'd like you to meet . . ."

"What's happenin', baby? What's happenin'?"

Ten minutes later Silky picked up the extension in the master bedroom. "Dave. Where are you, man? How come you ain' here?"

"How's the party?"

"Just takin' off, man. Everybody's askin' for you. When you gettin' here?"

"I'm up in Riverdale, Silky. Sorry, man. I can't make it downtown tonight. We want to leave early tomorrow."

"Leave? Where you leavin' to? Hey, hey, brother. You uptight or somethin'? You sound fucked up. The kid okay? Your ol' lady okay?"

"Everybody's good, Silky. We're going back home, to Michigan. I went down to the Garden the day before yesterday to take care of the paper work—"

"What paper work? What kinda paper work?"

"I'm retiring, Silky. I'm taking my family back home. It's hard to explain. Once is enough for me. More than I deserve."

"You are fucked up," Silky said. "Fucked up in your head."

"Don't worry, Silky. It's cool. I mean, I know what I'm doing."

"You must be crazy! It's the NBA, man. It's heaven in the streets! And dig it . . . we can't win shit without you."

"Sure you can," Dave said. "You're the man, Silky. The next time it'll be different, that's all."

"But wait a second, man. Did you tell Wayne about the play-off bread?"

"Not yet," Dave said. "I guess Quinton'll have to tell him. Or else you can, Silky. Sure. You're the man now."

"Yeah." Silky drew it out, testing. "How about if I tell

277

him like this . . . Mr. WaynoExBossManMotherfucker? You ain' gettin' shit! You flibberlip faggityass chump! *Not a fucken penny!* Tha's from all of us, most especially me, to *you . . ."*

"Take it easy on him, Silky. He can't touch you anymore."

"He can't touch you either. That's for sure."

Lamar was there annoying Silky's sleeve again. Silky disguised the receiver with his hand.

"What you want, Lamar?"

"I thought you'd want to know . . . Wayne and that writer dude just blew in. . . ."

"Dave," Silky pleaded. "Dave, mannh. What you doin'?"

But Dave had hung up.

> *I'll make you feel good baby*
> *Make you feel fine*
> *Make you feel so good, baby*
> *Make you feel mine*

The celebrities bred and multiplied like wire hangers in a closet. Through it all Larry Graham held fast to his fiancée's hand and continued his vigil at Silky's trophy table. He actually trembled and moaned as he glimmered over Silky's latest award: The Championship Series MVP loving cup.

"What's that, honey?"

"Nothin'," Larry said softly. "Nothin' yet."

> *She got clothes, she got class*
> *She got sophistication*
> *She got thrills, she got chills*
> *She got a love vocation*

Quinton and his two playmates tossed and tumbled in the shower. Quinton's naked body was covered with water, with tears and with erotic drippings. He couldn't tell if he was laughing, sobbing, coming or having a heart attack. . . .

"Silky!" Wayne said merrily. "I was in the neighborhood and I thought I'd come around to thank you in person. I knew you wouldn't mind if I brought Murray."

"Wayne," Silky said. Something soft, in spite of himself, stirred in Silky's heart and his mouth ran away and smiled.

"Guess who's the Coach of the Year?" Wayne said grandly. "And Joe Cunningham just offered me a two-year deal. Silky. Do you know what this means? Silky. I owe it all to you. . . ."

"That's wonderful," Silky said. They shook hands warmly. "All the hassle. All the jive. I guess that's what you have to do. I guess it's all been worth it after all. . . ."

Wayne's puffy jowls glowed with a flash fever. "You bet it is," he said. "You bet your mother's sweet black ass it is. *Anything's* worth it. . . . Yeah, Silky. I owe it all to you."

Silky bled tears behind his eyes. "Hey," he said weakly, "there's food, champagne. Help yourself."

> *Wanna hear some*
> *Sweet soul music*
> *Gonna show you*
> *How to use it*

Wayne and Murray stood in a corner of the kitchen drinking champagne from separate bottles.

"You read the Voluntarily Retired List lately?" Wayne asked.

"Yeah," said Murray. "I also heard about the thousand-dollar fine."

"I'll tell you something," Wayne said. "Off the record. I won't miss him. He's a cheeky bastard. Arrogant too."

Murray nodded vehemently in agreement. "Except for that one game in the Garden he didn't do diddly-shit. What he get in the seventh game? Four points? That's easy to replace. Fuck him. Good riddance. Move Reed back where he belongs. You got Silky. You don't need any troublemakers."

"I know," Wayne said thoughtfully. "Jesus! I hope we can talk Quinton into playing another year."

"You're sitting on a dynasty!" Murray said. "A dynasty!"

They clinked bottles.

"Red Holzman?" Wayne said. "Red who?"

The children were asleep and Joan Smalley was lying on the couch munching Darvons. The phone startled her and for an ugly, angry moment she hoped that Wayne was in a car accident. Maybe he'd be crippled—in a wheelchair—needing her. She sobbed until the drug made her laugh. Then she prayed that the call was a wrong number.

"Hello," Joan said numbly.

"Hello? Is Wayne there? This is Dave Brooks."

"No," said Joan. "He's out."

"Umm . . . when is he expected back?"

"I don't know," Joan said. "I don't know where he is either."

"Do you think I could leave a message for him?"

"No," Joan said. "You can't." And she hung up.

*Keep on pushin'*
   *Got to keep on learnin'*
     *Keep on pushin'*
       *Got to keep on burnin'*

When Wayne finally made it into the shower with two leftover chicks, Murray decided it was overtime for him to leave.

But Silky intercepted Murray at the front door. "Glad you stopped by," Silky said.

"My pleasure, big fella. Thanks for the hospitality."

"Hey, Murray," Silky said with a wink. "My man. Before you split. Dig it. Make sure you call me tomorrow afternoon. You hear?"

It was easy, much easier than Silky thought it would be. Garbage points, right? He swallowed his tears.

"Yeah," Silky said. "My main man. Have I got a story for you."

For you and fucking yours.

## ROSTER OF THE 1980–81 NEW YORK STARS

### Coach - Wayne Smalley

| NO. | PQS | NAME | HGT | WGT | PRO EXP | COLLEGE |
|-----|-----|------|-----|-----|---------|---------|
| 25 | F | Ardell Bartholomew | 6-11 | 235 | 7 | Mississippi Southern |
| 8 | G | Dave Brooks | 6-6 | 215 | 3 | Michigan |
| 10 | G | Quinton Brown | 6-5 | 210 | 12 | Southwestern State |
| 12 | G | Reed Carson | 6-3 | 205 | 4 | Houston |
| 34 | F | Larry Graham | 6-9 | 220 | 1 | Colorado |
| 17 | C | Kevin Harmon | 6-9 | 245 | 0 | St. Bonaventure |
| 14 | C | Jeremy Johnson | 7-0 | 211 | 3 | Detroit |
| 20 | C-F | Jack Mathias | 6-10 | 228 | 0 | USC |
| 7 | F | Sylvester Sims | 6-7½ | 205 | 1 | Savannah State |
| 16 | G | Tyrone White | 6-4 | 185 | 10 | UCLA |

### Trainer - Buddy Patella